GAME ON

BY JANET EVANOVICH

THE STEPHANIE PLUM NOVELS

One for the Money

Two for the Dough

Three to Get Deadly

Four to Score

High Five

Hot Six

Seven Up

Hard Eight

To the Nines

Ten Big Ones

Eleven on Top

Twelve Sharp

Lean Mean Thirteen

Fearless Fourteen

Finger Lickin' Fifteen

Sizzling Sixteen

Smokin' Seventeen

Explosive Eighteen

Notorious Nineteen

Takedown Twenty

Top Secret Twenty-One

Tricky Twenty-Two

Turbo Twenty-Three

Hardcore Twenty-Four

Look Alive Twenty-Five

Twisted Twenty-Six

Fortune and Glory (Tantalizing Twenty-Seven)

Game On (Tempting Twenty-Eight)

GAME ON

A STEPHANIE PLUM NOVEL

JANET EVANOVICH

**SIMON &
SCHUSTER**

London · New York · Sydney · Toronto · New Delhi

First published in the United States by Atria Books,
an imprint of Simon & Schuster, Inc., 2021

First published in Great Britain by Simon & Schuster UK Ltd, 2021

1 3 5 7 9 10 8 6 4 2

Simon & Schuster UK Ltd
1st Floor
222 Gray's Inn Road
London WC1X 8HB

Simon & Schuster Australia, Sydney
Simon & Schuster India, New Delhi

www.simonandschuster.co.uk
www.simonandschuster.com.au
www.simonandschuster.co.in

A CIP catalogue record for this book
is available from the British Library

Hardback ISBN: 978-1-3985-1012-8
Trade Paperback ISBN: 978-1-3985-1013-5
eBook ISBN: 978-1-3985-1014-2
Audio ISBN: 978-1-3985-1029-6

Printed and bound in Great Britain by
CPI Group (UK) Ltd, Croydon, CR0 4YY

MIX
Paper from
responsible sources
FSC
www.fsc.org   FSC® C020471

The clock on my bedside table said it was 2:00 a.m. Lights were off in my small apartment and my bedroom was totally dark. Something pulled me out of sleep and now I was in bed, awake and terrified. I was listening to someone moving around in my living room. My gun was in the brown bear cookie jar in the kitchen. My cell phone was charging in the bathroom. I kept a two-pound Maglite next to my clock, and at the moment it was the closest I could come to a weapon.

My name is Stephanie Plum and I'm a bail bonds enforcement agent. It's the sort of job that might require self-defense skills like kung fu and eye gouging, but I'm not proficient in either. I coerced my cousin Vinnie into hiring me during a time of desperate unemployment and to date I haven't migrated on to a better job.

I heard the intruder walk into my bedroom and drop something heavy onto the floor. I fought through the panic, clicked my flashlight on, and pinned the beam to a face. I recognized the man and went breathless for several beats before getting my heart under control.

"Diesel?"

"Yeah. You want to drop the beam a little, so I don't go blind."

Diesel is over six feet of hard muscle and bad attitude. He has sun-bleached hair that's thick and unruly, talents that are difficult to explain, and a job that's similar to mine but on an international level. Hell, for all I knew he worked at an intergalactic level.

"You scared the beejeezus out of me," I said. "What are you doing here?"

"I got dropped off here. I've got a job in Trenton. Lucky me. That's sarcasm in case you didn't figure it out. I'm beat. It was a long trip."

"Where did you come from?"

He kicked his shoes off. "Bangkok." He stripped off his T-shirt and dropped his jeans.

I sat up in bed. "What are you doing?"

"I'm going to bed. Move over."

"No. No, no, no, no. You aren't sleeping here."

"I always sleep here when I'm in town."

"Twice. Three times, tops, and I didn't want you in my bed then, either. And I haven't heard from you in what . . . two years?"

"Has it been that long?"

"I have a boyfriend. He doesn't like when I have other men in my bed."

"It isn't still the cop, is it? Bordatello?"

"Joe Morelli."

"I was close."

He dropped his briefs, and I snapped the flashlight off. "Would it be asking too much for you to at least leave some clothes on?"

"Yeah, it would be asking too much."

"Sleep on the couch."

"I don't fit on the couch."

"Terrific. *I'll* sleep on the couch."

I got out of bed, grabbed my pillow, and ripped the quilt off the bed.

"Your loss," Diesel said. "And you need to do something about the cranky attitude."

I slammed the bedroom door shut and carried my stuff to the couch. "One night and you're out of here!" I yelled back at him.

I have a long relationship with my current boyfriend, Joe Morelli. And I have an unconventional relationship with a security expert named Ranger. My relationship with Diesel defies description. I suppose it's more of an occasional friendship of convenience than a relationship. Kind of like a stray cat that shows up every two years, invites himself into your home, eats your food, and stays just long enough for you to get used to him. Truth is, I know shockingly little about Diesel.

———

Diesel sauntered out of the bedroom into the kitchen, squinting against the early morning sunlight. He was dressed for the day in jeans, scuffed brown leather boots, and an untucked gray T-shirt advertising tequila. He tapped on the glass aquarium that was home to my hamster, Rex, received no response, and moved to the coffeemaker.

"Is there anything alive in the cage?" he asked.

"Rex," I said. "He's sleeping in his soup can den."

Diesel took a mug from the over-the-counter cupboard and filled it with coffee. "I'm looking for a loser named Oswald Wednesday, also known as O.W. I don't suppose you know him."

"I absolutely know him. Vinnie posted a bail bond for Oswald, and he didn't show up for his court appearance. I've been looking for him for two weeks now and I have nothing."

"What's the charge on Oswald?"

"He broke into a townhouse that was rented to a cop and he came out on the losing end of a wrestling match. Oswald said it was mistaken identity, but he was charged with breaking and entering and assault with a deadly weapon. He was armed with a gun and a knife. He got released on a high bond. Why are you looking for him?"

"He's hacking into a system that's supposed to be secure. I work for one of the involved parties."

"How do you know it's him?"

"The IT people found his digital footprint. Now it's my job to physically find him."

"Are the police involved?"

"No. This is a private problem."

"Who is your employer?"

Diesel smiled. "I'd tell you but then I'd have to kill you."

It was a clichéd line, but I got the point.

"What do you know about Oswald?" Diesel asked me.

"He's fifty-two years old, five foot nine inches, black hair pulled into a ponytail, medium build, gave us an address of a short-term rental on Dugan Street. He hasn't been seen in the neighborhood since he was arrested. I wouldn't be happy if you snatched him up and whisked him away before I could collect my recovery money."

"Understood. Maybe you should rethink letting me live here."

"I don't need the recovery money that bad."

Diesel grinned. "That's brutal. What's wrong with me?"

"You don't know how to *share* an apartment. You take it over. You have no sense of personal space or privacy. You always have to get your own way and you have a problem understanding the concept of *no*."

"That's it?"

"That's the tip of the iceberg. You can't stay here. It'll be uncomfortably crowded in my bed when Morelli sleeps over."

"I'll concede that one."

I poured coffee into a to-go mug and grabbed my messenger bag and a sweatshirt.

"I have to go," I said. "Things to do. Make sure the door is locked when you leave."

I live in a one-bedroom apartment on the second floor of a three-story apartment building. It sits on the edge of Trenton proper, making it a twenty-minute drive to the bail bonds office, my parents' house, my boyfriend's house, and my favorite bakery. I took the stairs instead of waiting for the elevator, exited through the back door, and crossed the parking lot to my previously owned, slightly dented Ford Focus.

I wasn't entirely comfortable leaving Diesel alone in my apartment but I was a working girl and I needed to check in at the office.

CHAPTER TWO

Vincent Plum Bail Bonds is located on Hamilton Avenue, on the edge of my parents' neighborhood. I parked in front of the small storefront-type office and marched in. Connie Rosolli, the office manager, was at her desk and my coworker, Lula, was pacing back and forth across the room.

It's hard to say exactly what Lula's job entails, but she mostly hangs with me. She's a former professional erectile engineer who after years of practice has perfected the art of successfully squeezing her size 16 body into size 7 dresses.

"I've got a problem," Lula said when I walked into the office. "My hairstylist is moving out of Trenton. Can you believe it? Why would someone want to do that? And what am I supposed to do? Where am I going to find someone to replace her? She's a hair genius."

I have curly shoulder-length brown hair and Lula has hair du jour. At the moment it was a huge puff ball of midnight blue enhanced with silver pixie dust.

"It's not like I can have any kind of hair," Lula said. "I need hair that can hold its own with my big, voluptuous body. Most hairdos get overwhelmed with the rest of me. You see what I'm saying? And if that isn't problem enough, Connie didn't get doughnuts this morning. She got bagels."

I went to the box of bagels on Connie's desk and selected a sesame seed.

"I thought I'd change things around," Connie said. "Especially since the bakery got shot up last night, and I couldn't get past the crime scene tape this morning."

"Say what?" Lula said. "I didn't hear about that. Who would shoot up a bakery? That's just wrong."

"Was anyone hurt?" I asked Connie.

"No. It was after hours," Connie said. "It was empty except for the lunatic who broke in, went gonzo, and emptied a couple clips into the display case with the éclairs and cannoli."

"That's sick," Lula said. "What the heck's wrong with people these days. You just don't go around shooting éclairs and cannoli. If you gotta shoot something, you want to at least shoot something undesirable, like something with no gluten in it."

"Did they catch the shooter?" I asked Connie.

Connie spread cream cheese on an onion bagel. "The police responded to the alarm and caught the shooter leaving the bakery. Vinnie already bonded her out. Mary Jane Merkle."

"We went to school with her," I said to Connie. "She was a cheerleader. She was prom queen."

Lula took the file from Connie and paged through it. "Here's her booking picture," Lula said. "She looks like she stuck her finger in an electric socket."

I glanced at the photo. Mary Jane had fright night hair. It looked like she'd lacquered it with hair spray in the middle of a cat 4 hurricane. Her eyes were wide open and crazed. Her face was streaked with mascara. Note to self: If you're going to go gonzo and get arrested, use waterproof mascara in case you cry.

"You never know about people," Lula said. "One minute they're prom queen and then next thing they're whackadoodle."

"We had two new FTAs come in this morning," Connie said, handing me the paperwork. "Nothing big. A homeless guy who keeps killing and stick-roasting the ducks in the park, and an indecent exposure."

FTA stands for Failure to Appear. If you get arrested and don't want to hang around in jail waiting for your court date, you put up some money and you're released. If you haven't got the money, you can pay a bail bonds agent, like my cousin Vinnie, to essentially loan you the money. If you fail to appear for your court date or violate the rules of your release, Vinnie's money is forfeited. This makes him unhappy, and he sends me out to find you. If I bring you back in a timely manner, Vinnie can recoup his money.

"You need to find Oswald Wednesday," Connie said to me. "It's a high-money bond and Vinnie's bottom line isn't going to look good this month if Oswald is in the wind."

"Diesel dropped in last night," I said. "He's also looking for Oswald."

"Is that going to be a problem?" Connie asked.

"Possibly."

"That's a problem I wouldn't mind having," Lula said. "Diesel's that big, sexy, scruffy blond guy, right?"

"Right," I said. "You left out *annoying*."

"It's just I got priorities," Lula said. "Big, sexy, scruffy, and blond are high on my list compared to annoying."

I stuffed the two new FTA files into my messenger bag. "Run a credit check on Oswald one more time," I said to Connie. "It would help if a new address popped up."

Lula followed me out and stopped at my car. "Someone spray painted '*wash me*' on your car in pink paint," Lula said.

"It's been like that for a couple weeks."

"I never noticed."

"It partially got absorbed into the top layer of dirt, but it rained last night and washed some of the dirt off."

"Goes to show you there could be benefits to dirt," Lula said, wrenching the door open. "Where are we going?"

"Dugan Street. I want to see Oswald's apartment."

"Inside?"

"Yes."

"I'm all about it."

Dugan Street's glory faded fifty years ago. At one time the large homes housed large, wealthy families, but times have changed. The grand old houses are now in disrepair and the interiors have been carved up into low-income apartments.

I took Hamilton Avenue to Chambers Street, turned at Greenwood Avenue, and after several blocks I left-turned onto Dugan. I parked across the street from Oswald's house and Lula and I watched the house for a couple of minutes.

"Doesn't seem like anything's happening here," Lula said. "There's some cars parked on the street but nobody's moving around."

"Let's look inside."

Oswald's apartment was one of three on the second floor of the two-story house. The front door wasn't locked, so we let ourselves in, climbed the stairs, and I knocked on Oswald's door. No answer. I knocked again and tried the doorknob.

"It's unlocked," I said to Lula.

"Seems like they don't lock anything here," Lula said. "It looks to me like this neighborhood might be sketchy and if it was me, I wouldn't be so trusting."

I opened the door, stepped inside, and yelled "bond enforcement."

Still no answer. We were standing in a small living room with a couch, a club chair, and a television. There were no personal items lying around. We moved into the kitchen. Nothing in the fridge. Minimal pots and pans, silverware, plates, and bowls.

"This is what you would find in a rental unit with no one living in it," Lula said, walking into the bathroom. "There isn't even a toothbrush here."

The bedroom also seemed untouched.

"Only one thing here doesn't make sense," Lula said, standing by the perfectly made bed. "There's a stepladder under the trapdoor in the ceiling. I think someone's going in and out up there. I bet Oswald might even be living there. Who knows what's in the attic? It could be all fixed up into another apartment. You hold the ladder steady, and I'll look into this."

Lula was wearing five-inch spike-heeled sling-backs, a black spandex skirt that barely covered her ass, and a yellow knit tank top with a scoop neck that was low enough to be in nipple territory. She looked like a giant bumble bee with blue hair.

"Are you sure you want to climb the ladder in those shoes?" I asked her.

"Hell yeah. These are good ladder-climbing shoes. And I'm not necessarily going *into* the attic. I just want to take a peek."

Lula went up the ladder and examined the latch.

"This isn't even locked," she said.

She unlatched the trapdoor and let it swing open. She climbed a couple more steps on the ladder and looked into the attic.

"It's dark in here," she said. "There's no light that I can see." She pushed the flashlight app on her cell phone and flashed the beam of light around. "Hello?" she shouted. "Anybody home up here?"

Chirping and fluttering sounds carried down to me and in seconds a hundred bats rushed out of the trapdoor and into the bedroom.

"Holy hell!" Lula screamed. "What the fork!"

She came down the ladder in a cloud of bats, missed a rung, and broke the heel off one of her shoes. She hit the floor, shrieking and dancing in place. "Eeeeeee!"

I grabbed Lula by the arm and pulled her into the living room. I slammed the door to the bedroom shut, leaving most of the bats behind.

Lula was bug-eyed, waving her arms, still dancing. "I got bat cooties. I can feel them. They're crawling all over me. Lordy, Lordy. And I got the rabies. I can't breathe. I can't swallow. Look at me, I'm drooling. Am I drooling? Am I getting all foamy at the mouth?"

"I don't see any foam and you're only drooling a little. You haven't got rabies. You have to get bitten by an infected bat to get rabies."

"They looked real infected to me," Lula said.

Her hair wasn't a perfect puffball anymore but aside from that she looked okay. "I don't see any bite marks on you," I said.

"Yeah, but I got that kind of skin that would make it hard to see a bat bite mark. It would be just two little fang marks and it could look like enlarged pores. I got some of them."

"I think the bats were mostly trying to get away from you."

I opened the front door to leave and bumped into Diesel.

"You're late for the party," I said to Diesel.

"I had to wait for my fixer to deliver wheels," Diesel said.

"You have a fixer?"

"Doesn't everyone?" He looked around. "What's happening?"

"Lula decided to investigate the attic and had a *Born Free* moment with a swarm of bats."

"It was terrible," Lula said. "They were bumping into me and chirping. I can still hear them. It's like they're in my head and won't go away.

"I can hear the chirping," Diesel said. "It's coming from you." He leaned in and studied Lula's hair. "You've got a bat stuck in there."

"*What?* For real?"

"It's looking at me," Diesel said. "I can see its beady little eyes."

"*Eeeeeeee*," Lula said. "*Get it out. Get it out.*"

She jumped up and down and flapped her hands and the bat flew out.

"Problem solved," Diesel said.

"A lot you know," Lula said. "I got a broken shoe and bat hair. I probably got lice. And the stupid bat could have pooped, and now I've got bat poop in my hair. I gotta go. I need a hair salon. I need a cheeseburger and fries. I haven't got my car here." She looked at me. "You gotta take me back to the office so I can get my car."

I understood her dilemma. I wouldn't want to walk around with bat hair, either, but I didn't want to take off and drive to the office. This was Diesel's first stop. He'd look around, reach the conclusion that Oswald wasn't here, and Diesel would continue tracking. And knowing Diesel, he'd have some success. He had background information on Oswald that I didn't have. The horrible fact of life was that my best shot at catching Oswald was to stick close to Diesel.

I handed my car keys over to Lula. "I'm not done here. Leave my car at the bonds office. I'll catch a ride with Diesel." I looked at Diesel. "That's okay, right?"

"It would come with a price," Diesel said.

I rolled my eyes and grunted.

"There you go, thinking the worst," Diesel said. "You don't even know the price, and you're doing that eye-rolling thing."

"What's the price?" I asked.

He shrugged. "Let's see how the day goes and then we can negotiate."

Good grief.

Diesel did a quick scan of the living room. "I assume you've already been through the apartment," Diesel said. "Or did Lula get bat attacked early in the search?"

"I've been through the apartment. There's nothing to see. I suspect Oswald never lived here. This was just an address to hand over to people like Vinnie."

"Sounds like Oswald," Diesel said. "He's clever. Good at covering his tracks. Money to burn."

"If he has so much money, why is he hacking information?"

"It's the way he makes the money."

"Okay, I get that, but if he has all this money, why would he need Vinnie to bond him out?"

"It was a high bond and I'm sure he never intended to make his court date. Why forfeit your own money when you can stick a bail bondsman with the loss?"

"I'm guessing you've had past experience with him."

"Our paths have crossed. He's not my favorite person."

"How unfavorite is he?" I asked.

"As unfavorite as it can get."

"Do you want to tell me about it?"

"No," Diesel said.

"You'd have to kill me if you told me?"

"No. I'd depress myself if I had to list out all the reasons why I dislike this man."

"Do you have other addresses for Oswald?"

"He keeps a condo in Zurich and a condo in Manhattan. I know he's not in either condo," Diesel said.

"Why is he in Trenton?"

"Good question. I don't know the answer."

"Where do we go from here?"

"We follow his obsessions. Fast cars, beautiful women, religious icons, and the Rolling Stones."

"Anything else?" I asked. "Favorite food? Is he a sport fanatic? Does he have a favorite team?"

"He likes to give and receive pain," Diesel said. "That's his sport."

"Lula might be able to help with that. She has some friends from her former profession who specialize in giving pain."

"I doubt they operate at Oswald's level, but we can ask Lula to look into it. No stone unturned. In the meantime, let's start with fast cars," Diesel said. "He favors Porsche."

I followed Diesel out of the apartment house to a black and red Ducati.

"Nice bike," I said.

He handed me a helmet. "It's a Multistrada 1260 Enduro. It's good on a chase and even better when you're trying to lose someone."

"And when it rains?"

"We get wet."

Lucky us that it was a sunny day in September without much chance of rain. I tucked my hair into the helmet and straddled the bike.

Diesel powered up, returned to Chambers, and minutes later we were on Route One, on our way to a Porsche dealer. I'd like to say it was exhilarating to ride behind Diesel on the 1260, but a better word would be terrifying. Jersey drivers are for the most part fearless and totally lacking patience. Speed limits are taken as mere suggestions. I have to admit that I'm a typical foul-mouthed Jersey driver with rude hand signals and a lead foot when I'm encased in three thousand pounds of steel and fiberglass. Zigzagging through traffic on a crotch rocket is a whole other deal.

Diesel pulled into the dealership and parked in front of the showroom door. We got off the bike and removed our helmets.

"Are you okay?" he asked. "You're whiter than usual."

"You're a maniac driver. I said the rosary for the entire time we were on the highway, and I made promises to God that I couldn't possibly keep."

"Go figure. I thought you were screaming because you were excited."

"I was screaming for you to slow down!"

The grin returned. "It's not the first time I've heard that."

"No doubt. Now what?"

"Now you flash your fake badge around and show everyone Oswald's photo, and hope we get lucky."

"Just because I bought it online doesn't mean it's fake. It says fugitive recovery agent."

"Whatever."

CHAPTER THREE

I cruised through the showroom and spoke to four salesmen. Three couldn't remember seeing Oswald. The fourth said he might have seen him bring a car into service. I left the sales floor and went to the service department. I showed his photo to a woman in the receptionist cubicle.

"He was here last week," she said. "I remember him because he ate all of the complimentary mini doughnuts and then got verbally abusive over his loner car being a base model."

"Can you give me some information on the vehicle he dropped off? Did he leave it for service?"

"It was left overnight," she said, scrolling through the shop history. "Here it is. Oswald Wednesday. He brought in a 911 turbo S for an oil change. It was one year old."

"Color?" I asked.

"Black. 9,432 miles on it."

"Did he give an address? Phone number?"

"He gave a New York address. He declined to leave a phone number."

"Do you have a license plate?" I asked.

"It was a New York plate. I'll print the information out for you. We're always happy to cooperate with the police."

Diesel was standing a couple of feet behind me. "Did he pay with a credit card?" Diesel asked.

"He paid with cash."

I thanked the woman for her help, and we left the building.

I called Connie and asked her to run another check on Oswald Wednesday. "I have an address for a condo in Manhattan. See if that turns up anything new."

"What's Oswald's Trenton connection?" I asked Diesel. "Has he been here before? Does he have friends or relatives here?"

"I couldn't find a Trenton connection. That doesn't mean one doesn't exist."

"Are you fibbing to me?" I asked him.

"Possibly," he said.

It was hard to work up too much anger over this since I didn't feel compelled to be totally honest with him, either.

"I assume you've been through the Manhattan condo," I said.

"I have and it's clean."

"And you left some illegal surveillance devices behind?"

"Yes. No activity."

"Does Oswald do anything besides hack into computers?"

"He has degrees in mechanical engineering and computer

science from MIT. He's never stayed at a job for more than six months. He holds a bunch of patents, mostly on obscure but essential nuts-and-bolts type stuff associated with artificial intelligence."

"Wow."

"He's also a psychopath who feeds on suffering and chaos when his hacking projects get boring. He's been involved in some of the most high-profile hacking incidents in the last few years. Most of those incidents were never revealed to the public for security reasons."

"Wow, again. Does he work alone, or does he have partners?"

"He mostly works alone but he communicates with a loose network of other hackers and artificial intelligence researchers and tool makers. I know where some of them are located, but not all of them. It's believed that two of them have been involved in at least one major ransomware job. They've disappeared."

"None in Trenton?"

"None that I know about. They're spread all around the world. Glasgow, Singapore, Nova Scotia, Boston, Atlanta, Osaka."

"Where are his relatives?"

"His parents are gone. He has no siblings, and he doesn't seem to have a relationship with any relatives or childhood friends. He grew up in LA but no longer has a home there."

"Never married?" I asked.

"He had a wife, but she hasn't been seen in eleven years. They were living in London when she disappeared. Several other female companions have mysteriously disappeared as well."

"Connie has the best search software out there and we didn't uncover any of this."

"He periodically scrubs his history," Diesel said. "My employer has sources not ordinarily available to the public."

"This is the employer who needs to remain anonymous, sends you all over the world doing God-knows-what, and gives you a fixer?"

"Yeah," Diesel said. "That's the one."

I thought the mystery employer was starting to sound almost as scary as Oswald.

———

Connie was alone in the office when Diesel and I walked in.

"Have you heard from Lula?" I asked Connie.

"Not since she swapped out your car for hers," Connie said. "She stopped in long enough to tell me you were with Diesel and to tell me about the bat in her hair and then she took off."

"Did you get anything on Oswald?"

"Nothing new. He didn't list a car on his bond application," Connie said.

"It turns out that he didn't list lots of things we would have found interesting. For instance, the women in his life tend to disappear without a trace, and Diesel is looking for him in connection to a hacking incident."

"As in computer hacking?" Connie asked. "Maybe Melvin Schwartz knows him."

"Who's Melvin Schwartz?"

"Vinnie bailed him out a couple of times," Connie said. "He never skipped so you wouldn't remember him. When he was a senior in high school he hacked into the system and shut all the schools down for two weeks. He had a scholarship to Harvard, but he got kicked out for hacking into the system and adjusting his first semester grades. A couple months ago, he got arrested for replacing the six o'clock evening news with a porn movie."

"Where can I find him?" I asked Connie.

Connie pulled Schwartz's file up on her computer, printed it out, and handed it over to me. "He's probably at home. So far as I know, he doesn't have a job."

"What happened with the evening news arrest?"

"He got a slap on the wrist, just like always. He's never done time. Trenton hasn't got jail cells for pranksters. We're full up with drug dealers and shooters."

Diesel and I left the bail bonds office and stood on the sidewalk.

"I'm driving," I said.

"The Ducati is more fun," Diesel said.

"And you're all about fun?"

"I'm all about taking a nap on a tropical island, in the shade of a palm tree, but that's not going to happen."

"How about if I drive and you close your eyes and pretend about the palm tree?"

Diesel got into my car and buckled up. "This doesn't smell like a tropical island. It doesn't even smell like a car."

I blew out a sigh. "It smells like wet dog. I took Morelli's dog, Bob, to the dog park yesterday and we got caught in the rain." I pulled into traffic. "Where are we going?"

Diesel paged through the file. "Beeker Street."

"That's an odd address. It's off State Street and it's mainly warehouses and auto body shops."

I went south on State Street, turned left onto Beeker, and

stopped in front of Deacon Plumbing Supply. It was a cavernous cement block building with a showroom on the ground floor.

"This is it," I said, pulling into the lot and parking. "If Melvin Schwartz doesn't live here, I can price out a new toilet just for the heck of it."

There were several cars in the parking lot but only one man in the showroom. I approached the man and told him I was looking for Melvin Schwartz.

"Melvin's upstairs," he said. "There's a door by the loading dock on the side of the building."

"Thanks," I said. "I was sure I had the wrong address."

He nodded. "Happens all the time. No one can ever find him. We should have a sign out front."

Diesel and I walked around to the loading dock and rang the buzzer by the side door.

"What?" someone yelled on the intercom.

"Melvin Schwartz?" I asked.

"Maybe."

"I have a computer question. Can I come up?"

"Who's the big Neanderthal with you?"

"That's just Diesel."

The door clicked open, and Diesel and I walked up two flights of stairs to an open loft. There was an unmade bed in a corner and some cardboard packing boxes and a couple of laundry baskets by the bed. From the distance it looked like the boxes and baskets were filled with clothes. Hard to say if they were clean or dirty. Another corner of the loft held a small kitchenette with a table and two kitchen chairs. The rest of the loft was cluttered with workbenches and desks filled with electronic equipment and computers. A lumpy couch faced a massive flat-screen TV. A large wooden coffee table sat in front of the couch. A bunch of fast-food bags, crumpled soda cans, and two laptop computers were on the coffee table.

Melvin Schwartz was standing in the middle of the loft. He was five feet ten inches tall, and he looked like a giant, chubby cherub. He had wispy blond hair, apple cheeks, and a soft Pillsbury Doughboy body. He was wearing gray wool socks and pajamas with dinosaurs on them. According to his file he was twenty-six years old.

"I charge $145 an hour for computer consultation," Melvin said.

"I don't want computer consultation," I said. "I'm looking for Oswald Wednesday."

Melvin's eyes popped wide open. "Oswald Wednesday? For real?"

"We know he's in Trenton, and we thought you might have heard something."

"Oswald Wednesday is my god," Melvin said. "I worship him. He's famous! He's only the best hacker living or dead, ever. He's made millions in ransom. He's shut down pipelines and cruise ships and hacked into satellites. He's fearless and brilliant. I'd give my right thumb to meet Oswald Wednesday. And he's in Trenton? Are you sure? I mean, I knew something big was going down, but I never dreamed O.W. would be operating out of Trenton."

"Tell me about the something big," Diesel said.

"No can do," Melvin said. "That would violate the hacker's code."

"Hackers have a code?"

"It's one of those understood things," he said. "Why are you looking for O.W.?"

"It's personal," Diesel said. "He has something that belongs to my employer and my employer would like it back."

"Who are *you*?" Melvin asked me. "What's your story?"

"I'm Stephanie Plum. I'm looking for Oswald because he missed his court date."

"Stephanie Plum!" Melvin said. "I thought I recognized you. You're the disaster bounty hunter. I saw your picture in the paper a couple of months ago when you jumped out of the hooker hotel. And I remember when you and your grandmother burned down the funeral home."

Diesel looked around the loft. "Why do you live here?" Diesel asked Melvin.

"It's free," Melvin said. "My uncle owns the building, and this space wasn't being used for anything."

"Convenient," Diesel said.

"Yeah," Melvin said. "It's a win-win. I'm an embarrassment to my family. This gets me out of their house. Out of sight. Out of mind. They're happy and I'm happy because I have these cool digs, and I can pursue my calling."

"What's your calling?" I asked him.

"Hacking, of course."

"Are you any good?" Diesel asked.

"I'm brilliant," Melvin said. "Maybe I'm not at O.W.'s level yet, but I'm good enough to hack into O.W.'s network."

"You've hacked into Oswald's computer?" I asked.

Melvin's energy level went up a couple of watts. "Not me, personally. My group, Baked Potato. We were only in his network for a couple seconds, but you have to understand, hacking O.W. is *huge*. O.W. either noticed right away or he had some sort of amazing emergency protocol code that noticed. We're locked out again, but we're working to get back in. It's like a challenge."

"Who else is in Baked Potato?" I asked.

"There are seven of us," Melvin said. "I don't know who any of them are beyond their hacker names. I'm HotWiz."

"If you have the skills to hack into O.W.'s network, why don't you get a real job?" Diesel asked.

"This is my job. My problem is that I haven't totally found my focus yet. I haven't found that big project that really puts you on the map."

"This could be your lucky day," Diesel said. "Help us find Oswald and you'll have your moment of fame."

"You want me to go snitch on O.W.? I'd be the most hated hacker in history. O.W. is revered."

"Fame has its price," Diesel said. "And you're wrong. You wouldn't be hated. Oswald is a black-hat hacker. You'd be a hero if you took him down as a gray-hat hacker. And you'd replace him as the number one hacker."

"Oh man, that would be awesome," Melvin said.

"Tell me about this big thing that's happening," Diesel said.

"I don't know anything about it," Melvin said. "There's just lots of chatter. I'd have to go snooping."

"And the best way to go snooping is by hacking into Oswald's network again," Diesel said.

"I'd have to think about it," Melvin said. "I guess it could be fun."

Diesel took a page off a yellow pad that was on one of the

desks and wrote his email address and cell phone number. "Here's my information," Diesel said. "Get in touch with me if you learn anything."

I gave Melvin my card. "I'm also available," I said.

"One more thing," Diesel said. "Do you have any idea where Oswald might be hiding out while he's in Trenton? Does he have any hacker friends here?"

"Not that I know about," Melvin said.

We left the loft and walked back to my car.

"What's a black-hat and a gray-hat hacker?" I asked Diesel.

"Black-hat hackers are criminals who break into networks with malicious intent. Sometimes for sport, sometimes for personal financial gain, sometimes for cyber espionage. White-hat hackers break into systems with owner permission and perform various services for the owners. A gray-hat hacker doesn't have the owner's permission but wouldn't necessarily be hacking for evil purposes."

"We're asking Melvin to be a gray-hat hacker."

"Yes."

"Where do we go from here?"

"Drive out of the lot and find a place to watch for Melvin. He's going to get dressed and help us find Oswald."

"Do you think he knows where Oswald is hanging?"

"No, but I think he does know one or two of the people in Baked Potato. Probably geek friends, left over from high school. And one of those geeks might be sheltering Oswald. I'm counting on Melvin getting out of his jammies and paying a visit to the number one candidate to have Oswald stashed in his apartment."

CHAPTER FOUR

I drove out of the Deacon Plumbing lot, crossed Beeker Street, and parked at the edge of a driveway leading to several rows of self-storage units. A half hour later, a dented tan Nissan Sentra with Melvin at the wheel turned onto Beeker.

I followed Melvin to a low-income neighborhood of single-story bungalows and row houses. He parked in front of a row house on Kubacky Street and went to the door. Moments later, the door opened, and Melvin disappeared inside.

"Let's be sociable, and go say hello," Diesel said.

I parked behind Melvin's car and followed Diesel to the door. He knocked and no one answered.

"Probably didn't hear me knock," Diesel said. He stepped back and put his boot to the door and the door popped open. He looked at me. "What is it we're supposed to say now?"

"Bail bond enforcement."

"Right," Diesel said. "Bail bond enforcement," he said to Melvin and a guy who looked close to cardiac arrest.

"Sorry about your door," I said. "It sort of opened on its own."

"We're looking for Oswald Wednesday," Diesel said. "Is he here?"

Both men shook their heads, no.

"We haven't met," Diesel said to the man standing next to Melvin.

"Clark Stupin," he said. "I live here."

"And I assume, from all the equipment I'm seeing in your living room, that you're a hacker," Diesel said.

"No, no, no. I'm a computer expert. And I like to play games. Computer games."

"Do you play these games with Melvin?"

"Sometimes."

"How about Oswald? Do you play computer games with Oswald?"

"No! I swear. Oswald doesn't play games with people like me. I don't even know Oswald." He glanced at Melvin. "We don't know O.W., right?"

"Right," Melvin said. "We don't know him, like, personally."

Diesel wandered into the kitchen. He checked out the bathroom and bedroom and returned to the living room.

"Oswald isn't here," Diesel said.

"Why would Oswald be here?" Clark asked.

"They think he's in Trenton," Melvin said.

Clark went bug-eyed. "Get out! Really? Oh, wow."

"We thought he might have dropped in on you guys," Diesel said.

"No way," Clark said. "He doesn't know us. We don't exist to him."

I thought this was a good thing, because from what I now knew about Oswald, I doubted he'd be happy about getting hacked.

"If things change and you bump into him, let us know," Diesel said.

"You bet," Melvin said.

"For sure," Clark said.

We returned to my car and buckled ourselves in.

"What do you think?" I asked Diesel.

"I think they're in over their heads with Oswald."

I drove back to the office and parked.

"Now what?" Diesel asked.

"A couple new FTAs came in this morning. I should try to find them."

"I have some things to catch up on, too. We can get back to Oswald over dinner."

"Not tonight. It's Friday. I always eat dinner with my parents on Friday."

"No problem. Tell them to set another plate."

"Bad idea. Friday is a date night with Morelli. We have dinner with my parents and then Morelli sleeps over."

"Could your life get any more tedious?"

"It's not tedious. It's comfortable and satisfying."

Diesel grinned. "Like an old shoe?"

"Like a cashmere shawl," I said. "All warm and wonderful when you wrap it around you."

"I'm going to gag."

"Not in my car. Get out and gag and we can reconnect tomorrow."

———

Connie was alone in the office. No Lula and no Vinnie.

"Do you think my relationship with Morelli is tedious?" I asked her.

"I can't imagine anything being tedious with Morelli," Connie said. "He gives hot a whole new meaning."

"We might be in too much of a routine. Like, every Friday we have dinner with my parents."

"Lucky you," Connie said. "You don't have to cook and then you get to take a bag of leftovers and Morelli home with you. It sounds good to me."

The front door banged open and Lula marched in.

"Look at this," she said, pointing at her hair. "How am I supposed to live with this?"

"What's wrong with it?" I asked.

"It's brown," Lula said. "Have you ever seen me with brown hair? No. I'm supposed to have fabulous and outrageous hair. This hair is normal. Even the cut is normal. And do you know why I'm looking like this? It's because my regular girl, Shanesha, left the salon and when I went in just now, I had to get my hair done by the new girl, Amy. I just don't think anyone named Amy could understand my hair needs."

"Okay, but the good news is that you don't have a bat in it," I said.

"That's true," Lula said. "You always gotta look at the good news. Do we have any good news besides the bat? How's it going with Oswald Wednesday? Did you find him?"

"No," I said, "but we have some leads. And Diesel said Oswald likes pain. I thought you might know some specialists."

"I can ask around," Lula said. "The S&M trade isn't as profitable as it used to be, being that the world is so depressing most people are self-inflicting these days."

I pulled the two new files out of my messenger bag. "I thought we could look for one of these guys. We've got a duck roaster and an indecent exposure. Pick one."

"I'm up for the indecent exposure," Lula said. "We always have good luck with them."

I paged through the file. "Camden Krick. Self-employed. Lives in an apartment in Hamilton Township. Thirty-six years old. He looks average in his photo."

"What's his story?" Lula asked Connie.

"I don't know," Connie said. "He has no history. Vinnie wrote the bond, and Vinnie is in Miami doing an out-of-state felon pickup."

"Maybe I should go home first and change my clothes," Lula said. "I'm not put together right. My hair is all wrong for my clothes. I need lawyer clothes."

"You're not a lawyer."

"No," Lula said, "but this hair makes me look like a lawyer. And I can feel my brain synapses firing away under this hair. It's like they aren't distracted by fun and fashion."

I hiked my messenger bag up on my shoulder. "I'm going after Camden Krick. Are you coming?"

"I suppose I am," Lula said, "but I feel all discombobulated."

I drove to a garden apartment complex in Hamilton Township and parked in a slot reserved for Krick's apartment. He had a ground floor unit in the middle of a row of apartments.

"This is a nice place," Lula said, "but it doesn't have any personality. All the buildings look the same and there's no landscaping. They should at least let people paint their front doors representative colors. Like, some people would want their door to be sunshine yellow and you'd know right off that you were going to like that person. Or if someone painted their door black and purple, you might not want to knock on that door. Or if you did knock, you would know to bring the occupant some antidepressants. There could be rainbow doors and doors painted to look like hemp. You see what I'm saying? This lawyer hair is making me feel real entrepreneurial. I've got a bunch of insightful ideas."

"No doubt," I said. "Let's see if Krick is home."

We left the car and walked the short distance to Krick's boring front door. I rang the bell and a pleasant-looking man answered.

"Camden Krick?" I asked.

"Yes," he said.

I showed him my identification. "I represent your bail bondsman. You missed your court date, and you need to reschedule."

"I already did that," he said. "I did it online."

"You can't reschedule online."

"Are you sure? I'm almost positive I rescheduled online."

"You have to reschedule in person at the courthouse," I said. "Lula and I can expedite it for you, if you come with us. It'll only take a couple minutes."

This was totally bogus. He would have to post another bond, or they would keep him locked up until his new court date.

"This isn't a good time for me," he said. "You should have called ahead."

"We hear that a lot," Lula said.

I had cuffs in my hand. "We're going to have to take you in, Mr. Krick."

"I told you, this isn't a convenient time. I have a job and I'm already late."

"What kind of job?" Lula asked.

"I'm a professional mooner," he said.

This grabbed Lula's attention. "Seriously?"

"Yeah," he said. "I have no shame. And I have a really cute behind. Do you want to see it?"

"No," I said.

"I wouldn't mind taking a look," Lula said.

Krick dropped his pants and mooned Lula.

"It's a cutie all right," she said.

He pulled his pants up and grinned. "Thanks. I get a lot of compliments."

"Is that how you got the indecent exposure ticket?" Lula asked. "Were you just plying your trade?"

"Someone sent me to moon a cranky old lady who didn't want to be mooned. It's my first arrest. Usually, people think it's funny. I get a lot of ladies' luncheons. Birthday parties and baby showers. Lately I've been doing baby reveals. That's where people find out if it's a boy or a girl. I write the baby's gender on my butt cheek."

"That's clever," Lula said. "Entrepreneurial. And I'm all about that. How's the pay?"

"I'm doing okay."

"I could drop my pants," Lula said. "I'd be a good mooner."

"There aren't a lot of women in the profession," Krick said. "You could corner the market."

"Getting back to your court appearance," I said.

"Yeah, but he said he had a job," Lula said. "I'm interested in this. Where are you working, honey?"

"It's a birthday luncheon," Krick said. He took a note card out of his shirt pocket. "Mae Horowitz is turning sixty-five today and a bunch of her lady friends are throwing her a lunch party. It's at one of their houses. It's on Jigger Street."

"I know where that is," Lula said. "It's on our way to the courthouse. We could drive him to Mae's party and then after the ladies all get to look at his behind, we could take him to the courthouse."

"I guess that would be okay, as long as he doesn't spend too much time with Mae."

"A couple minutes tops," he said. "That's the good part about mooning as opposed to being a stripper or a clown. No one expects you to stay and entertain. I go in and sing happy birthday, I drop my pants and wiggle my butt, and I leave."

"I'm learning a lot here," Lula said. "I'm taking notes."

I had big plans when I was a kid. I fully expected that Tinker Bell would seek me out, douse me with fairy dust, and I'd be able to fly. When I grew out of my Peter Pan fixation, I had a secret life as a superhero. The superhero phase morphed into more adult aspirations and delusions of grandeur. I toyed with ideas of being a doctor, a supreme court judge, a microbiologist, a fashion designer, a fireman, a marine biologist.

None of those aspirations stuck, and when I graduated from college, I got a job in retail. Retail was an epic fail, and now here I am attempting to capture a professional mooner who probably makes more money than I do. How did this happen? When did my bright future go astray and get lost on the road to the shitter? I'm pretty sure this is all Tinker Bell's fault.

We loaded Krick into my car, and I drove us to Jigger Street. I parked at the curb, behind three other cars.

"These cars must belong to the birthday party ladies," Lula said. "And we know we're at the right place because there's a Happy Birthday balloon attached to the mailbox."

"Give me ten to fifteen minutes," Krick said. "This is an easy gig."

Lula and I watched him walk to the door, ring the bell, and get let in by a smiling sixty-something woman. Fifteen minutes later, we were still waiting.

"I'm going in if he's not out in five minutes," I said to Lula.

"They might have kidnapped him," Lula said. "I understand that these older women can get aggressive. They might not have seen a really nice behind in a while and got carried away."

"I think it's more likely that he skipped out the back door and called Uber to come pick him up."

"That would be disappointing," Lula said.

After four minutes I got out of the car, went to the door, and rang the bell. The same smiling woman answered.

"I'm looking for the mooner," I said.

"He left about ten minutes ago," she said. "He was fun. He's an excellent mooner."

I returned to my car and drove around the block. "Keep your eyes open," I said to Lula.

"I don't see him," she said. "Keep driving."

I turned a corner and Lula leaned forward. "There he is!" she said. "He's standing on the next corner. I bet he's waiting for someone to pick him up. Drive closer and I'll jump out and cuff him."

I stopped directly in front of Krick, Lula jumped out, waving her handcuffs, and Krick took off.

Lula was wearing five-inch spike-heeled pumps and a red spandex dress that barely covered her hoo-ha. She was running flat-out, knees up, and she was screaming out cuss words at Krick. Krick cut between two houses, and I sped around the block, hoping to cut him off. I screeched to a stop, got out of my car, and looked around. No Krick. Lula ran up, gasping for breath.

"What the fork!" Lula said, tugging her dress down over her ass. "Where did he go? I lost him when I had to get over the fence."

We listened for footsteps.

"I only hear traffic," Lula said.

"He's here. He's hiding."

"There are a lot of bushes behind this house," Lula said. "He has to be in the bushes."

Lula and I walked toward the back of the house and pushed through a gate to a fenced-in yard that was bordered with overgrown hedges and shrubs. Lula pointed to a small shed near the back door. There were a couple of trash cans by the shed, plus a clump of ugly bushes, a kid's Big Wheel bike, and a scooter.

Lula advanced to the shed, and when she was four feet away, Krick jumped out and trained a hose on her. Lula freaked out, tripped on the scooter, and went down. I fought my way through the water spray and tackled Krick. We were locked together, rolling around on the ground with water shooting out everywhere. Lula pounced on us and pinned Krick long enough for me to cuff him. I shut the water off and yanked Krick to his feet.

"What the heck were you thinking?" Lula said to Krick.

"I was thinking I didn't want to go to jail," Krick said.

"We would have bonded you out again," Lula said. "And it's not like you even committed a real crime. You aren't going to get sent up the river for ten years because you dropped your drawers. And even if you do get a couple days, it's not a big deal. Martha Stewart did time, and she came out looking real good. Now there's a woman I admire. She knows how to accessorize, and she has excellent advice on home goods. Her laundry basket recommendations are all quality items."

"I guess I panicked," Krick said.

I marched Krick out of the yard to my car and settled him into the backseat. Lula and I were soaking wet and caked with mud.

Lula put her hand to her head. "What about my hair?" she said. "Do I have Sandra Bullock hair?"

"You never had Sandra Bullock hair. You look like someone with brown hair who got drenched and almost drowned."

"That's probably not a good look," Lula said. "I'm thinking I'm done for the day."

"Yep. Me, too. We'll drop Krick off at the cop shop and go back to the office so you can get your car."

CHAPTER FIVE

I didn't see any sign of Diesel when I returned to my apartment. This was turning out to be a good day. I'd made a capture and Diesel had obviously found another place to live. I tossed my wet clothes into my laundry basket. Martha Stewart hadn't personally recommended the basket to me, but it was cheap and plastic, so it met my needs.

I jumped into the shower and by 5:30 PM my hair was dry and brushed into waves as opposed to the usual curls and frizz. I was wearing clean jeans and a scoop-neck fitted T-shirt. My messenger bag was hung on my shoulder, I had a beach towel under my arm in case my car seat was still wet, and my laundry basket was balanced on my hip. Yet another advantage of the weekly visit to my parents' house was the use of their washer and dryer.

My parents live in the Burg, a small community of modest houses and mostly hardworking Americans that's stuck onto the larger city of Trenton. While many parts of the country are struggling with changing ideologies, the Burg continues to march to the beat of its own drum, thumbing its nose at political correctness. The Burg is awash in immigrant origins and Jersey attitude. The inhabitants are God-fearing busybodies who settle arguments with neighbors the old-fashioned way—with a bag of flaming dog poop on the offender's front porch.

My grandma Mazur was at the front door when I drove up and parked. Grandma moved in with my mom and dad when Grandpa went upstairs to live with Jesus. She's still alive because we took my father's gun away from him and he's too squeamish to butcher Grandma with the carving knife.

Grandma and Lula use the miracle of spandex to good advantage. Lula uses it to contain an abundance of flesh and Grandma uses it to shore up body parts that have begun to sag. In Grandma's case, that's almost *all* body parts. She was wearing a zebra-striped spandex top, black spandex Pilates pants, and white sneakers. Her hair was cut short and had returned to its natural shade of gray, after a trial period of red.

She held the door open for me so I could squeeze through with my laundry basket. "Don't you look nice," Grandma said. "I like the ponytail but it's good to see your hair down and wavy like this. You have such pretty hair. It comes from our Hungarian side of the family. That and a good metabolism. All the women on our side keep a good figure to old age."

Okay, to be honest, Grandma has a body like a plucked soup

chicken, but she isn't fat, and she makes the best of what she has. I mean, at the end of the day, isn't that what we all strive for in life?

My dad is retired from the post office and now drives a cab part-time. He was currently in his chair in the living room watching television with his eyes closed. We tiptoed past him and took the laundry into the kitchen.

"Look who's here!" Grandma said to my mom.

Grandma said this like it was something extraordinary. I'd been coming home for dinner almost every Friday night since I graduated from college and moved out of the house, but to Grandma it was special. And this made it special to me. It was nice to be wanted somewhere after a day of chasing down losers who dreaded seeing me at their door. Even though I'd brought my family countless hours of embarrassment and disappointment, they still loved me. Amazing, right?

My mom was at the counter, mashing potatoes. Tonight's dinner would be pot roast and gravy, mashed potatoes, red cabbage, and green beans. Only the vegetable varied on Friday nights. Sometimes the green beans were changed out for cooked carrots or peas. Because Morelli was present, dessert would be his favorite chocolate cake.

"Set the basket in the corner," my mom said to me. "I'll get to the laundry tomorrow. How was your day?"

"It was good," I said. "I brought an FTA in."

"Was it a big one?" Grandma asked. "Was it a murderer or a drug dealer?"

"No," I said. "It was a mooner."

My mom stopped mashing. "A mooner?"

"He's a professional," I said. "He takes jobs mooning people at birthday parties and baby showers."

"What's his name?" Grandma asked. "Was it Camden Krick?"

"Yes," I said. "Do you know him?"

"He's the best. I've been to a couple of his moonings. He mooned at Mary Kulicki's seventy-fifth birthday party last year. Why was he arrested?"

"He mooned someone who didn't want to be mooned and he got charged with indecent exposure."

"That's a shame," Grandma said. "Personally, I think they should legalize mooning. I even thought about going into it. I have a pretty good behind for a woman my age and I could use some extra income."

"Lula had the same thought," I said to Grandma. "Maybe you should team up."

My mother made the sign of the cross and cut a glance at the cabinet where she kept her liquor. "This is why I drink," she said to no one in particular.

At six o'clock my father opened his eyes and took his place at the dining room table. Two minutes later Morelli walked in.

I've known Joe Morelli all my life. All through grade school he was the problem child of the neighborhood, and from ninth grade on, he was the heartthrob of half the women in the greater Trenton area. He enlisted in the navy out of high school, eventually got a college degree, and decided he wanted to be a cop. He's now working plainclothes in crimes against persons, and he's good at his job. He's good at other things, too, which is why I'm wearing pretty undies.

He's six foot tall with a lean, muscular build, lots of wavy black hair, and classic Italian movie star features. He has a big orange dog named Bob and a small house he inherited from his aunt Rose. A lot of people think Morelli and I should get married. Morelli doesn't seem to be one of them. That's okay with me. I tried being married and it was a disaster.

The food made its way around the table and the bottle of wine followed.

"Stephanie caught a mooner today," Grandma said to Morelli.

Morelli draped his arm across the back of my chair and smiled at me. "A mooner?"

"Camden Krick," I said. "Professional mooner."

"I know about Camden," Morelli said. "He's famous. He's my mother's favorite mooner."

"Mine, too," Grandma said. "He has the best butt, and he's a good wiggler."

My father was working his way through the mound of food on his plate, oblivious to the conversation.

"There's something different about the pot roast," he said.

"It's chuck roast," my mother said. "They didn't have any rump roast."

"How could they not have rump roast?" my father said. "Benny knows we have rump roast every Friday."

"Benny sold his butcher shop six months ago," my mother said. "The new owner made it into a tattoo parlor. I get my meat at the supermarket now."

My father shook his head. "This country's going to heck in a handbasket."

"I remember when Stephanie almost married a butcher," Grandma said.

"I didn't almost marry him," I said. "I didn't even *nearly* marry him."

"Well, he was sweet on you, and we got some good pork roasts out of it," Grandma said.

"I can't compete with that," Morelli said. "The best I can do is quash a parking ticket."

"Gravy," my father said. "Somebody pass the gravy, for crying out loud."

Grandma passed the gravy and turned to Morelli. "How was your day?"

"Average," he said. "I got caught up on paperwork this morning and spent the afternoon watching an autopsy."

"Anyone we know?" Grandma asked.

Morelli shook his head. "An out-of-towner. We had information that he was carrying drugs, but he got knifed in an alley before we could get to him."

"Did you find the drugs?" Grandma wanted to know.

Morelli helped himself to the wine. "Yep. Three balloons in his colon. The guy with the knife only looked in the victim's stomach."

"Amateur," Grandma said. "I would have gone for the colon."

"The chuck roast isn't bad," my father said. "It just needs more gravy than the rump roast."

Everyone stopped eating and looked at my father.

"What?" he said. "Did I miss something?"

My dad has figured out how to get through the day and stay sane. He's developed selective hearing. He tunes out whatever annoys him or doesn't interest him. More to the point, he tunes out Grandma entirely. My mother manages with the help of whiskey straight up.

"I wouldn't mind seeing an autopsy," Grandma said. "Especially if it was someone who had balloons in their colon. Do you think mules need colonoscopies or do the balloons scrub off the polyps? That could be a real advantage to smuggling drugs."

"How are you doing?" I asked Morelli. "Can you stick it out for another hour?"

"I'm doing great," Morelli said. "I'm counting on chocolate cake for dessert."

My family doesn't even register on the dysfunctional family meter compared to Morelli's. His father was an abusive drunk and a womanizer. His brother has been married three times to the same woman. And his Sicilian grandmother skulks around, dressed in black, giving people the evil eye.

Morelli's phone buzzed and I did a mental groan. He was done for the day, but he was on call. He read the text message and he pushed back from the table.

"I have to go," Morelli said. "There's a problem on Kubacky Street."

That got my attention. "I was on Kubacky Street this morning," I said. "What's the house number?"

"315 Kubacky," Morelli said.

My heart did a flip and missed a beat. "Crap," I said on a whisper. "That's Clark Stupin's address."

"Is it a murder?" Grandma asked Morelli. "Kubacky Street can be dicey."

"I need to go with you," I said to Morelli. "I'll talk to you in the car."

"There's chocolate cake," my mother said.

Five minutes later I was in the car with Morelli and half a

chocolate cake. Morelli was behind the wheel and the cake was in a small cooler in the backseat.

"Talk to me," Morelli said.

"I'm looking for Oswald Wednesday. He broke into a rental unit and was taken down by a cop who was living there."

"I remember," Morelli said.

"Two weeks ago, he went FTA. I got a tip that he's a hacker, so I paid a visit on Melvin Schwartz today, and Schwartz led me to Clark Stupin."

"There's more?"

"Maybe. Schwartz and Stupin knew Oswald Wednesday. They didn't know him personally. He was kind of their hero. Apparently, he's famous as a super hacker. Supposedly Schwartz and Stupin's hacker group momentarily hacked into Oswald's private network. Stupin sounded nervous about Oswald being in Trenton. There's some sort of online chatter about Oswald having something big about to go down."

"Do you think Oswald would kill over someone knowing about this big thing or leaking information?"

I shrugged. "It seems extreme, but he could have some personality problems."

"Such as?"

"He likes to give and receive pain, and over the years, several of his female companions have disappeared. More recently two of his hacker partners disappeared."

Morelli stopped for a light and looked over at me. "How do you know all this?"

"I have a source."

"I don't suppose you want to reveal that source?"

"I'd rather not."

"Tell me anyway," Morelli said.

I blew out a sigh. "It's Diesel."

"You're kidding."

"Nope. It's Diesel. He's looking for Oswald."

"Since when?"

"Since yesterday," I said. "He showed up last night. He said Oswald hacked his employer and might have some sensitive information."

"So, he got in touch with you?"

"He was looking for a place to stay."

"And?"

"And he's staying someplace else."

"I'm surprised Diesel is employed. I thought he just hung out around the world, looking for a good hammock and the perfect wave."

"He's always more or less employed," I said. "The employer is a big secret."

Morelli drove down Kubacky Street and parked behind an EMT truck. Several uniforms were standing, talking on the sidewalk. The front door to Clark's house was open. I followed Morelli out of the car and into the house. The front room was filled with two more uniforms, a couple of EMTs with their bags, and a stretcher. Clark was on the floor, on his side. His hands were bound behind his back. There was some blood around his head.

Morelli took it in and looked back at me.

"Clark Stupin," I said.

The medical examiner walked in with a forensic photographer.

Everyone went to work, collecting evidence, recording the obvious.
I went outside to get some air and let Morelli do his thing.

I didn't see so much of this type of thing that I was hardened
to it. Or maybe you never got hardened to it. Morelli was able to
wade through it, but I'm sure it took a toll on him. He managed
because he believed in the job and justice. And because he had a
need to solve the crime.

I was standing off to the side, by myself, and Diesel ambled
over.

"What's up?" he asked.

"It looks like someone killed Clark Stupin."

"Bummer."

"What are you doing here?" I asked.

"My office heard the call go out for this address."

"You have an office?"

"I have a guy who does whatever."

"Is this guy in Jersey?"

"Zurich. I don't think he sleeps. What are the details here?"

"I don't know. I came with Morelli. He's in there with the ME."

"Cause of death?"

"Not sure. Stupin was on the floor with his hands bound.
There was some blood. The two uniforms looked nauseous."

"Had the room been tossed?"

"Didn't look like it."

"No messages written in blood on the walls or floor?"

"Didn't see any."

"We should check on Melvin," Diesel said.

"Do you think Oswald did this?"

Diesel shrugged.

I went back inside to tell Morelli I was leaving. He was standing a couple of feet away from Stupin, watching the ME work.

"Diesel is here," I said. "We're going to check on Melvin Schwartz." I glanced down at the body. "What's on the floor by Stupin?"

"His tongue," Morelli said. "The killer cut off Stupin's tongue."

There was a loud clanging in my head, and everything went black except for tiny flashing dots.

Morelli grabbed me, sat me in a chair, and bent me over so my head was between my legs. A paramedic came over with an ice pack.

"What the fork," I said.

Morelli had the ice pack against the back of my neck. "Are you okay?"

"I wasn't ready for the . . . you know."

"Tongue," Morelli said.

"Yes. The t-t-tongue."

"If it's any consolation, I had a moment of horror, too, and one of the uniforms threw up."

I sucked in some air. "Okay, I'm feeling better."

Morelli walked me out to Diesel.

"Long time no see," he said to Diesel.

Diesel nodded. "I've been busy."

"Steph said you're going to check on Melvin Schwartz," Morelli said. "Keep me in the loop."

"Absolutely," Diesel said.

Morelli turned to me. "I'll be over later with Bob."

Diesel watched Morelli walk away. "Who's Bob?"

"His dog."

"The big orange one that eats furniture?"

"He's better now. He hardly ever eats furniture."

It was dark when we rode down Beeker Street. No streetlights and no lights on in Deacon Plumbing. Diesel parked the Ducati by the door to Melvin's apartment, and we got off the bike. He rang the bell twice and no one answered.

"No lights on. No cars in the lot. No one home," I said.

Diesel twisted the doorknob and opened the door. "Let's make sure."

"How did you do that?" I asked. "I tried to open it and it was locked."

"Just one of my many talents."

We went up the stairs, Diesel flipped the light switch, and we took a moment to scan the room.

"I don't see any dead bodies sprawled on the floor," Diesel said.

"And no signs of struggle. It looks like Melvin is just out on the town."

We snooped through file drawers and desktop scribblings, but we didn't turn up anything that might lead us to Oswald.

"Melvin's laptop is missing," I said to Diesel. "He was working on a ThinkPad laptop with a Spider-Man decal on it when we were here this morning."

We walked around one more time, looking for the laptop.

"It's not here," Diesel said. "He probably took it with him in case he suddenly feels an urge to hack into a bank or a small country."

We left Melvin's apartment and Diesel drove me to my parents' house so I could retrieve my car. I waved him off and went inside to say good night to my parents and Grandma. My father was asleep in his chair in front of the television. My mother and Grandma were on the couch, watching a movie. Grandma paused it when I walked in.

"Did you see the tongue?" Grandma asked me.

It was no surprise that she knew about the tongue. My mom and Grandma were tuned in to the Burg gossip line. As soon as I left with Morelli, Grandma would have called her friend Mable Sheidig. Mable's daughter works police dispatch. After Grandma got the news from Mable, she would have called a bunch of other women who were related to firemen, cops, EMTs, and nurses. At this point, Grandma undoubtedly knew more about the crime scene than I did.

"I saw the tongue," I said. "It was in a baggie."

"That must have been something," Grandma said. "That's not the sort of thing you see every day."

"What kind of person commits such a horrible crime?" my mother said. "It's terrible."

"It could be worse," Grandma said. "At least he didn't have his face shot off like Lenny Gollinni. If you're just missing part of your tongue, you can still have a viewing with an open casket."

The ritual of death was important in the Burg. It was your last chance to look good.

"Your laundry is in the dryer if you want to wait for it," my mother said.

I shook my head. "I'll get it tomorrow. I just stopped by to say good night and get my car."

"Is Morelli out there?" my mother asked.

"No," I said. "Someone gave me a ride. Morelli is still working."

CHAPTER SIX

I parked in the lot to my apartment building, pushed through the back door to the small lobby, and took the stairs to the second floor. I looked down the hall and saw Melvin pacing in front of my apartment.

"I think I'm in trouble," he said. "Something bad happened to Clark."

"The bad thing that happened . . . did you do it?"

"No! I went to his house because I got a message from O.W. I needed to talk to Clark face-to-face, but when I got to his place Clark was on the floor. There was blood and I was pretty sure he was dead. I didn't get real close. I ran out and called the police. And then I watched from a block away. I saw all the emergency vehicles come and the crime scene tape went up. And I knew you were there because I saw you come out with Diesel. You went right past me on the motorcycle, but you didn't see me. Clark is dead, isn't he?"

"Yes."

Melvin was pale and his eyes were swimming in tears. "I think I might be next."

I unlocked my apartment door, ushered Melvin into the living room, and sat him on the couch. I got him a bottle of water and called Diesel.

"I'm having a situation," I said. "Melvin is here."

"Where's here?"

"My apartment."

"What's he doing in your apartment?"

"He's worried."

Ten minutes later, Diesel arrived. Melvin had some color back in his face, but he was still shaky.

"Let's take it from the top," Diesel said.

"I got a message from O.W. tonight," Melvin said. "It was sent to a private messaging account that only existed between me and Clark."

"What did it say?"

"Retribution," Melvin said.

"How do you know it was from Oswald?"

"He has a symbol that he uses with his inner circle. He signed the message with his symbol. I'm sure it was his way of telling me that he knows I hacked him."

"And then?" Diesel asked.

"I went to show Clark, but he was dead. I ran out and called the police and hid."

"Did you talk to the police?" Diesel asked.

"No! I'm a hacker. I have a record. I called them on a burner phone."

"Whoa," I said. "Why were you carrying a burner phone?"

"It's part of the business. I don't want my clients to know my identity."

"Or the police or the FBI?"

"Yeah, those, too."

"Understood," Diesel said. "Why are you *here*?"

"I'm afraid to go back to my loft. I thought I could, you know, hang out here until you catch Oswald."

"I appreciate your problem," I said, "but you can't stay here."

Melvin looked at Diesel. "How about if I hang with you?"

"Not gonna happen," Diesel said. "Can't you stay with a friend?"

"My friend is dead," Melvin said.

"Is he your only friend?"

"Yeah."

"What about the Baked Potatoes?" Diesel asked.

"I only know them online. I don't exactly know where they live. And if I did know where they live, I might not want to go there."

I exchanged a sideways look with Diesel.

"Do you want to elaborate on that?" I asked Melvin.

"Clark and I have known each other since high school. The rest of our group came together through various IRCs."

"What's an IRC?" I asked.

"Internet Relay Chat. Our goal was to hack the super hacker. It was a fun challenge. A game. We thought O.W. was a genius. We thought he would be impressed. We didn't know he was a homicidal maniac."

"Can you get in touch with the rest of the Baked Potatoes?"

"I've tried. The Baked Potatoes communicate through a super secure messenger app. Turns out it wasn't secure enough to keep out O.W. He's blocked my account. I'm sure I can break through the block, but I need a place to work."

My cell phone buzzed, and I saw that it was Lula.

"Hey, girlfriend," she said. "I've been out and about, and I got to talk to some of the Whip Bitches. So far, I haven't found anyone who had a business relationship with Oswald. How's it going on your end?"

"It's complicated on my end," I said. "Do you remember Melvin Schwartz?"

"No."

"He's a local hacker who was bonded out a couple times by Vinnie. It turns out he's remotely connected to Oswald. And it turns out that Melvin has a friend who was also remotely connected to Oswald, and this friend just got dead, not in a good way."

"There's almost never a good way to get dead," Lula said.

"True," I said, "but this was *really* not good. Anyway, Melvin is here in my apartment because he's afraid he might be next on the *to get dead* list."

"I'm obviously missing some key elements to this situation," Lula said. "There's more to the story, right?"

"Right. Bottom line is that he can't go back to his loft and he's looking for a safe place to stay."

"And?"

"And do you want him?"

"What does he look like?" Lula asked. "Does he look like a good time?"

"He looks like the Pillsbury Doughboy."

"Okay, what the heck. Throw in a bottle of wine."

I got off the phone, grabbed a bottle of red wine from my cupboard, wrote Lula's address on a scrap of paper, and handed it to Diesel. "Drop Melvin and the wine off at Lula's place. She's going to take him."

"Who's Lula?" Melvin asked.

"She works at the bail bonds office with me," I said. "You'll be safe with her . . . more or less."

Diesel and Melvin left and twenty minutes later Morelli arrived with Bob and the chocolate cake.

Bob snuffled me and bounded around the apartment, making sure nothing had changed and there were no cats in residence. Morelli gave me a quick kiss and took the cake into the kitchen.

"Anything new to report?" I asked Morelli. "Was the cause of death determined?"

"His throat was cut. No weapon was found."

"Horrible."

"Yeah." He got a bottle of beer from the fridge and chugged half of it. "Do you want cake?"

"Of course, I want cake."

I took the cake out of the cooler and set it on the counter. We each took a fork and dug in.

"Did you talk to Melvin Schwartz?" Morelli asked.

"Yes. He's rattled. He's worried that he's next."

"He thinks Oswald killed Clark Stupin?"

"Yes."

"What do you think?"

"I think it's possible. I get the impression from Diesel that Oswald is a bad guy."

Morelli stepped back from the counter. "We did some serious damage to this cake." He pulled me to him and kissed me. "I think we should move on to other activities."

"Television?" I asked.

"Not what I had in mind."

"I thought you might be out of the mood after dinner interruptus. That was a gruesome crime scene."

"It was and I don't want to fall asleep thinking about it. I want to fall asleep thinking about you."

I wrapped my arms around him. "So, I serve a purpose."

"You serve many purposes. Almost all of them are good. If you could learn to bake a chocolate cake, I might consider marriage."

"Seriously?"

"It crosses my mind from time to time."

"And it all hinges on chocolate cake?"

"Pretty much. You already excel at everything else that matters to me."

"Housekeeping?" I asked.

"No," Morelli said.

"Cooking in general?"

"No."

"Brilliant conversation?"

"No. Although you can hold your own when it comes to Rangers hockey and Giants football." His hand moved under my shirt and found my breast.

"I think I know where this is going," I said.

Some women might find it offensive to be reduced to chocolate cake and sex. I wasn't one of those women. Besides, I knew Morelli was being playful. It would take more than chocolate cake to get him to the altar. He ate in front of the television or in his kitchen because he had a billiard table in his dining room. This was not an indicator of a man ready for marriage.

"I have some unfortunate news," Morelli said.

My first thought was that in his current breast exploration he had discovered a lump.

"Oh crap," I said.

"I know this isn't a good way to start down the path to your bedroom, but I need to get it out there so we can move on."

"Tell me."

"It's my uncle Sergio's eightieth birthday Sunday and we have to go to his party."

"That's it? That's the unfortunate news?"

"Yeah."

Huge relief. No lump. On the downside, I had to endure a Morelli family party.

"Do I know Uncle Sergio?" I asked.

"Grandma Bella's brother."

"Is this the one who looks like a bald eagle? White hair, crazy beady eyes, hook nose, and walks hunched over?"

"Yep, that's him."

"He stares at my breasts."

"He can't help it," Morelli said. "He's only five feet four and the vertebrae in his neck are fused together. Anyway, if you've got to be stuck staring at something, your breasts are a good place to start."

"Any other bad news?"

"Isn't that enough?"

"Is there good news?"

"Give me ten minutes and I'll make you forget all about the bad news."

"Ten minutes might not be enough time," I said.

"How about twenty minutes?"

"You've got it. You're on the clock."

"It would help if you got naked," Morelli said.

It took me fifteen seconds to completely strip down in the kitchen. "Okay," I said. "I'm ready."

"Me, too," Morelli said.

That was stating the obvious. Morelli was way ahead of me.

A half hour later we had our clothes back on and we were watching baseball. I love going to the ballpark to see the Mets play, but watching it on television is like watching grass grow. Fortunately, Morelli had kept his promise and we were now feeling relaxed and mellow and didn't really care that the Mets had changed pitchers twice in the last ten minutes.

"I remember when we used to spend hours having sex," I said to Morelli. "What happened?"

"We got better at it," Morelli said. "Now we can have sex *and* still have time to watch baseball." Morelli wrapped his arm around me and cuddled me closer. "This is nice. It was good, right?"

"Yes." Good was an understatement. It was spectacular.

"We should do this more often."

"Like tomorrow?"

"Like in about forty-five minutes," Morelli said.

CHAPTER SEVEN

I woke up smiling, enjoying the feel of a warm body in bed with me. It took a few moments for me to realize it was Bob and not Morelli.

"G'morning," I said to Bob, and he thumped his tail in happiness.

Morelli sauntered in with a coffee cup in his hand. He hadn't shaved in celebration of Saturday, and he looked dangerous and sexy. He was wearing jeans and a plaid flannel shirt that was untucked.

"I promised Anthony that I'd help him install a fence in his backyard this morning," he said. "I should be done around noon, and I thought maybe we could do something together this afternoon."

"Sounds good. I was planning on working but I'd be happy

to cut it down to half a day. Call me when you're done with the fence."

Anthony is Morelli's brother. He's a fun guy with a big heart and a wandering dick. He has a pack of kids and a wife who keeps divorcing him and remarrying him. I like Anthony, but I wouldn't want to be married to him.

Morelli and Bob were gone by the time I was showered and dressed. My kitchen is small and unintentionally retro with Formica countertops and inexpensive dated appliances. This is okay with me because I don't actually cook. I defrost and reheat food from my mom, and I eat a lot of peanut butter. I haven't got room for a table in the kitchen and my dining room table serves as my office, so most of the time I eat standing at the sink.

I was currently at the sink, enjoying my coffee and leftover chocolate cake, when I heard someone fumbling at my door. Seconds later Diesel walked in.

"You could knock," I said. "It isn't necessary to always jiggle my doorknob, or whatever it is that you do to unlock a door."

He found a fork and tested the cake. "I like to stay sharp with my skills."

"You just missed Morelli."

"I passed him on the road. What are your plans for the day?"

"I have a low bond FTA that I'd like to clear off the books this morning and then I'm spending the afternoon with Morelli. What about you?"

"There's a car show downtown that I thought I'd check out. It sounds like something Oswald would like."

"When's the car show?"

"From one o'clock to four o'clock."

"I'll go with you," I said.

"What about Morelli?"

"I'll catch up with him for dinner."

Diesel grinned. "Can't resist spending the afternoon with me?"

"You got it. It would be a missed opportunity."

The missed opportunity would be capturing Oswald. Diesel was a good guy, but he had his own set of rules and code of conduct. His interests weren't so much about justice as about protecting the interests of his employer. This was a problem because this was no longer about an FTA who was charged with breaking and entering and assaulting a police officer. The stakes were higher now. It was possible that Oswald killed Clark Stupin. If Diesel immediately whisked Oswald off to Who-Knows-Where, Oswald's unexplained disappearance could leave Morelli with an open case and no closure for Stupin's family. Not to mention, I would be cheated out of my capture fee.

"I'll meet you at the bonds office at one o'clock," Diesel said. "Are you going to finish this cake?"

I pushed the plate over to him. "I'm done. It's all yours."

———

Connie was unlocking the office door when I arrived. She had a bakery box in one hand and the keys in the other.

"Looks like the bakery is open," I said.

"It's open but there are no cannoli until the new refrigeration case arrives." Connie crossed the room and set the bakery box on her desk. "I heard about Clark Stupin. My cousin Johnny was one of the EMTs that got called out. He said he saw you there."

"Johnny Ragucci? I didn't know he was your cousin."

Connie opened the box and took a doughnut. "Almost everyone is my cousin."

Lula shuffled in and went straight to the doughnuts. "Thank God," she said. "I need a doughnut real bad. I'm trashed. I had the worst night. Melvin doesn't sleep. Every now and then he naps and then he jumps up wide awake and goes on a rant. Sometimes he shouts *'eureka!'* and then he rushes over to his computer. What the heck's with that? And he talks all the time. He talks in his sleep. He mumbles when he's working. He paces and talks to himself. I got a small apartment. It's one room and a closet. It's not like I could get away from him. I tried locking him in the bathroom, but I could still hear him talking and tapping on his computer keys. Click, click, click, click all night long. And then he cracks his fingers. He's a nightmare. Look at me. I got bags under my eyes. It's not attractive."

Bags were the least of it. Lula had hair that was straight out of a horror movie. It was like her head had exploded but her hair was still attached to her skull. She was wearing an orange tank top, camouflage sweatpants, and two different-colored spike-heeled pumps.

"Your heels don't match," I said.

"Say what?"

"You're wearing two different shoes. One of them is neutral and the other is black."

Lula looked down at her feet. "Damn."

"Where's Melvin now?" I asked.

"He's in my car. You gotta take him back. He isn't even a good time, if you know what I mean. He takes geek to a whole new level."

I looked over at Connie.

"Don't even think about it," Connie said. "Bad enough I have to live with my mother."

"What are we doing today besides eating doughnuts?" Lula asked.

"I thought we would track down the duck roaster," I said. I pulled his file out of my messenger bag. "Andy Smutter. Age fifty-six. Homeless. Hangs out at Victory Park."

"That's by the college," Lula said. "It's a nice park. They got a jogging trail that goes through some woods. I tried it once."

"Only once?" Connie asked.

"I couldn't get into the whole pointless running thing," Lula said. "There should be something at the end of the run . . . like a deli or a shoe sale, you see what I'm saying? I bet if someone put up a running route that led to barbecue ribs it would be a big hit."

I put the file back in my bag. "Your car or mine?" I asked Lula.

"I'm not putting no homeless duck roaster in my baby. I just had her detailed. It would be better to take your car," Lula said. "Only thing is I'm not leaving Melvin in my car. He's gonna have to get transferred to someone else's car. Like, maybe yours. And I'm thinking he should ride in the trunk, so I don't have to listen to him."

"I have a hatchback," I said. "I don't have a trunk."

"So put him in your hatchback and turn the radio up," Lula said. "You got a radio, right?"

"Right."

Here's the thing, all the key tapping and clicking was to my benefit. Melvin was in overdrive working to find Oswald. I didn't want to live with Melvin, but I also couldn't just kick him to the curb.

A half hour later we were at the park.

"The pond is down the path," Lula said, getting out of the Focus. "There's usually not a lot of people there on account of the goose poop. You gotta be careful where you walk."

"I thought this was just a duck pond," I said.

"Nope," Lula said. "There's a bunch of nasty geese here, too."

Melvin was in the backseat with his computer, oblivious to what was going on around him.

"Hey, Melvin," I said. "You need to come with us. I don't want to leave you alone here in the parking lot."

He closed his computer and looked around. "What's going on?"

"We're looking for someone who missed his court appearance. He has to reschedule."

"And he's in the park?"

"He's homeless. He spends a lot of time here."

We walked down the path, reached the pond, and stopped to look around. There were a couple of geese in the water and several more waddling around on land. The ducks were on the far side of the pond. It was a nice Saturday and there were people in other parts of the park, but there weren't any people by the duck pond.

We followed the path around the pond and found Andy sitting in a camp chair, reading a book.

"Andy Smutter?" I asked.

"Yep," he said. "That's me."

"I represent Vincent Plum Bail Bonds. You missed your court date. We need to get you rescheduled."

"Sure," he said. "You go ahead and do that."

Melvin looked down at Andy. "You're reading Hemingway."

"He's a hoot," Andy said. "I've read everything he's written about a hundred times."

"Me, too!" Melvin said. "What's your favorite?"

"It depends on my mood. I'm reading *The Sun Also Rises* today because I woke up wanting to be vicariously decadent."

"I hear you," Melvin said. "You have a nice spot here by the pond."

"My pied-à-terre is a short distance away," Andy said. "I find it gets too damp by the pond at night."

"I used to live in a loft," Melvin said, "but it got too dangerous to stay there."

"Goodness," Andy said. "What sort of danger?"

"Someone might want to kill me."

"That's very dramatic," Andy said. "Hemingway would drink to it."

"Hemingway wasn't afraid of anything," Melvin said. "Although he had his demons."

"It made him even more interesting, don't you think?"

"Absolutely," Melvin said.

"Of course, he also had several concussions that might have affected his mental condition."

"I'd like to enjoy this discussion of Hemingway," Lula said, "but I didn't get a lot of sleep last night and I'm standing here in mismatched shoes, so could we get on with the bail bonds predicament?"

"Of course," Andy said. "I just need to put my book in my P-A-T and zip it up for the afternoon."

We followed Andy a short distance through a wooded area and came to a pop-up domed tent. There was another camp chair in a cleared area and a small fire pit with a spit.

"I guess this is where you do the ducks," Lula said to Andy.

"My finances are currently limited," Andy said. "And I do have a weakness for rotisserie duck. Fortunately, duck is in abundant supply here."

"It's also illegal," I said.

"You should barbecue a goose," Lula said. "Nobody would care if you barbecued a goose."

"I'm afraid of the geese," Andy said. "Sadly, I'm no Hemingway."

"Is this your tent?" Melvin asked.

"Yep," Andy said. "It was given to me by a city official who didn't want me camped out in front of his office on State Street. It's wonderfully roomy and it's only a short distance from the public restroom facilities."

"This is almost as good as my loft," Melvin said.

Lula elbowed me. "We got a match made in heaven here. You just stepped in a pile of good luck."

"I'm not sure this is secure," I said.

"It's totally secure. Who's gonna think to look for Melvin here?"

"We need a safe place for Melvin to stay for a couple days," I said to Andy. "Would you have room for him here?"

"Ordinarily I don't have houseguests," Andy said, "but I suppose I could make an exception for a Hemingway aficionado."

"I need to work," Melvin said. "Where can I charge my laptop and cell phone?"

"The public restroom has outlets," Andy said. "And I have an extra sleeping bag that you can borrow."

"See that," Lula said. "It's all perfect. We can bring Andy in any old time to get rescheduled. The important thing is that we have a home for Melvin."

"Do you like duck?" Andy asked Melvin.

"No!" I said. "No more duck. We'll bring food. No need to worry about food."

Melvin walked back to the car with Lula and me and got his backpack. "This will be fun," he said. "I've never camped out before."

"Make sure you keep your cell phone charged," I said. "Call me if you get information on Oswald."

CHAPTER EIGHT

I drove out of the park and found a supermarket. I bought two rotisserie chickens, a couple of bags of chips, and a couple of bags of cookies. I put them in an insulated grocery bag with a bag of ice and Lula and I left the store. We were almost to my car when two men ran at Lula, ripped her purse off her shoulder, and ran away with it. She took off after them and chased them around the side of the building. I dropped the bag of groceries and ran after Lula. When I rounded the building the men were scrambling into a car, and Lula was pounding on one of them with her shoe. The car started rolling with one man half in and half out and Lula running alongside. The car picked up speed and Lula was left behind.

"Did you see that?" she yelled at me. "They tried to take my purse."

"Did they get it?"

"No. I caught up to them and they panicked and threw it in the dumpster and ran for their car. Freaking amateurs."

"Did you get their plate?"

"No. Did you?"

"No."

Lula walked back to the dumpster and looked in. "There it is," she said. "Give me a boost up."

"You're going in the dumpster?"

"I gotta get my purse."

"It's disgusting in there. Maybe we can scoop it out with a net or something."

"It's on the top of everything. I can reach it if you boost me up."

She got her hands on the top rim of the dumpster and pulled herself partway to the edge. I got my hand under her ass and gave her a shove.

"I almost got it," she said.

And then she fell into the dumpster. I hoisted myself up and looked in at her. She was waste deep in rotting vegetables and fruit, thrashing around, trying to get to the side. She had her purse in one hand and a shoe in the other.

"Hang on," I said. "I'm going to get help."

A half hour later, the fire department had Lula out of the dumpster. They hosed her down and gave her a blanket. We walked back to my car, retrieved the insulated bag with the chickens, and I drove Lula to the bonds office so she could get her car.

"This just isn't right," she said. "These things aren't supposed to be happening to me."

Andy was in his camp chair by the pond and Melvin was in the camp chair by the tent when I got back to them. I gave Melvin the grocery bag and told him I'd be back in the morning. I'm not sure he heard me. He was busy on his computer. It was too early to meet Diesel, so I went to my parents' house to retrieve my laundry.

My mother and Grandma were in the kitchen. My mother was making egg salad for lunch and Grandma was at the small kitchen table, texting on her phone.

"Marilyn Kreger just told me that there's going to be a viewing for Clark Stupin on Monday night, and the funeral is Tuesday morning," Grandma said. "The viewing is going to be a big event. It's open casket but I guess his mouth will be closed. Nobody's saying if he'll be buried with his tongue. Personally, I think the tongue should at least be in the casket with him."

My mother gave a small shudder and kept mashing the hard-boiled eggs.

"Did you know the Stupins?" I asked Grandma.

"I think I might have met the mother in the bakery once a while ago," Grandma said. "They live in north Trenton, but they go to the church here."

According to Burg protocol, it isn't necessary to know the deceased or the grieving family to enjoy the social aspects of the viewing. Mob celebrities and mutilated corpses draw especially large crowds.

I called Morelli to see how the fence project was going. There was a lot of shouting in the background.

"What's going on?" I asked.

"Anthony and his wife are having a discussion about a fence

boundary," Morelli said. "I might be here later than planned if we have to move the fence."

"That's okay," I said. "I have a lead on Oswald, and I'd like to follow it through. Let's plan to get together for dinner."

"It's Saturday," my mother said as I put my phone away. "You shouldn't be working on Saturday. You should be spending the day with your boyfriend. You're never going to get him to marry you this way."

"He's helping Anthony put up a fence," I said. "It's okay."

"You aren't getting any younger," my mother said. "What happens if Joseph moves on? Where are you going to find another boyfriend?"

"There's the internet," Grandma said. "And I heard Stanley Puccinni is getting a divorce. He would be a good catch. He's not as hot as Joe Morelli, but he's got a Toyota dealership."

"He's also got two other ex-wives and seven kids," I said.

"I guess you could look at it like he's had practice wives," Grandma said.

"I'm not interested in Stanley Puccinni," I said.

"How about Walter Dimmit?" Grandma asked. "I saw him at the grocery store. He was working in the produce section, and he asked about you."

"I'm not interested in him, either," I said. "He's eighty years old."

My mother put the egg salad on the table. "Are you staying for lunch?" she asked me. "Your grandmother got some little rolls from the deli this morning. You can make a sandwich."

"I got coleslaw too," Grandma said, going to the refrigerator. "Gina Giovichinni just made it. And there's some macaroni salad."

I set the table and took a seat. "Where's Dad?" I asked my mom.

"He's at the track with your uncle Lou."

"Are you going to the Stupin viewing?" Grandma asked me.

"Probably," I said. Unless I caught Oswald in the meantime. Another reason to stick to Diesel. If we snagged Oswald, I could avoid the viewing.

"I wouldn't mind a ride if you're going to the funeral home on Monday," Grandma said. "It's a long way to walk in heels and now that I'm a single woman again I have to look attractive. You never know when you're going to meet Mr. Good Enough."

———

Diesel was waiting in front of the bonds office when I drove up and parked. Lights were off inside the building and the office looked closed.

Diesel opened the door to the passenger's seat of my Ford Focus and slid in.

"Where's Connie?" I asked.

"She left about ten minutes ago. She said she was bonding someone out and then she was done for the day."

I cruised down Hamilton Avenue and followed Diesel's directions to downtown Trenton, where the car show was being held in a parking lot.

I saw the food trucks and merchandise stands before I saw the rows of cars being exhibited.

"This is huge," I said to Diesel. "How are we going to find Oswald in this crowd?"

"We're going to walk around and hope we get lucky."

After two hours we were still meandering without having

an Oswald sighting. We'd passed through the Porsche and other luxury car sections several times. We looked at a couple of monster trucks. We spent some time with the exotic cars. Diesel was alert, scanning the gawkers, but clearly not especially interested in the cars.

"You aren't a car guy," I said.

"They're a convenience. Transportation."

"What kind of an exhibit would get you excited?"

"Hammocks, drinks in coconuts, maybe pool floaties."

"What about sports? Do you get excited about sports?"

"Rugby."

His phone buzzed with a text message. "It's from Oswald," Diesel said.

"What's the message?"

"'So nice to see you again,'" Diesel read. "'I very much like your pretty little assistant.'"

Where are you? Diesel typed in.

I'm directly in your line of sight, Oswald answered. *You look but you don't see.*

Diesel stared straight ahead and typed in his reply. *I didn't recognize you. You've put on some weight. You're looking a little chubby.*

Diesel's screen went blank.

"Are we going after him?" I asked.

"No. He's too far away and there are too many people here. We'll cover the exits to the parking lot. There are only two."

The exhibits shut down at four o'clock and the crowd dispersed. Diesel was at one exit, and I was at the other. The parking lot was mostly empty by five o'clock and Oswald hadn't passed through either exit.

I called Diesel. "Now what?"

"Now we go home. Stay where you are, and I'll pick you up."

"You don't have a key to my car," I said.

"Not a problem."

A couple of minutes later Diesel pulled up next to me in my Focus.

"Would it be a waste of time to ask how you unlocked the doors and got the car started without a key?"

"I'm special," Diesel said.

I wasn't sure if this was good or bad, but I had to concede that it was true. And I suppose it was a comfort to know that if times got tough, Diesel could always support himself by stealing cars.

"At least we know Oswald's here," I said.

"He didn't walk past us," Diesel said. "If he exited in a car, he wasn't the driver or a passenger in the front seat. There were some cars with tinted back windows and there were a couple of vans."

"If he was on foot, he could have escaped the area by going around or through one of the buildings."

Diesel rolled out of the lot, onto the street, and I spotted Oswald walking two blocks ahead. Black ponytail, chubby guy wearing a black shirt, black messenger bag hung cross-body.

"It's him," I said.

Diesel cranked the Focus over. "I'm on it."

Oswald entered a parking garage and Diesel idled out of sight of the garage exit. Five minutes later a black 911 Porsche turbo with New York plates motored out of the garage and turned right.

"Two options," Diesel said. "Either I run him down or we follow him at length and hope he doesn't make us."

I was afraid if we followed Oswald we'd lose him and I really didn't want that to happen. I was super close to avoiding Clark Stupin's viewing.

"My vote is to run him down," I said.

Diesel got on the bumper of the 911. Oswald ignored a red light and Diesel followed him. The 911 cut into a side street, made two quick right turns, and got onto the freeway. In seconds the Porsche was up to 90 mph. Diesel stayed with it. I held tight and regretted my decision to run Oswald down. We were weaving in and out of traffic and passing cars as if they were standing still. The Focus was sounding wound out and it was vibrating. I was afraid we were going to lift off the road.

Oswald took an off ramp and rocketed through an industrial area. I had no idea how this was going to end, but I expected that it would end badly. Oswald skidded into a U-turn and came at us. Diesel avoided him by inches, wheeled the Focus around, and was back on Oswald's bumper. Oswald returned to the divided highway at high speed and entered, going in the wrong direction.

Diesel stopped at the beginning of the off-ramp. "I draw the line at this one," he said. "He's driving flat out against traffic."

We circled around to the on-ramp and made our way back to the office.

Diesel looked at the Focus with the pink spray paint and mismatched wheel covers. "What about you?" he asked. "I'm guessing that cars aren't your passion. So, what is your passion? Do you play the guitar? Do you collect bottle caps? Is it yoga? Bowling? Unicorns?"

I was stumped. "It isn't anything," I said.

"Darlin', everyone has something that they love to do."

"I like to walk Bob, except when he poops."

"I guess that's a start," Diesel said. "What else do you like? What makes you happy?"

"Birthday cake with white icing and pink and yellow roses. And wind. I like wind."

Until that moment I didn't know that I liked wind. It just popped out of my head in a burst of desperation to have a passion.

Twenty minutes later I pulled into the parking lot to my apartment building and parked next to Morelli's green SUV. Here was another thing that I liked. It was nice to come home to Morelli and Bob. Maybe not every day, but sometimes.

Morelli was in the kitchen, unpacking a large to-go bag, when I walked into my apartment.

"I felt like having Chinese," he said. "I hope that's okay."

"That great. What did you get?"

"I got everything."

We took all the boxes of food into the living room and turned the television on.

"What do you want to watch?" I asked.

"Anything but news."

I surfed around and settled on a golf tournament. It wasn't anything either of us was interested in, so it wouldn't interfere with eating.

"Have you ever played golf?" I asked Morelli.

He mixed fried rice with ginger chicken. "I played a few times with Marty Stackhouse. I liked it okay, but it takes all day, and I don't have that kind of time."

"So, it's not your passion?"

"No."

"What is your passion?"

He stopped eating and grinned at me.

"Besides that," I said.

"I guess it's sports. Hockey, football, baseball. I like to play pool and poker. Is this about my birthday present? It's not for a couple months."

"Diesel asked me what my passion was, and I said wind."

"Cupcake, you're always saying how you hate wind because it messes up your hair."

"I know. I panicked! I didn't have an answer. I haven't got any hobbies. I don't play sports. I can't cook or knit or tap-dance. I'm passionless."

"You like superheroes," Morelli said. "You're an Avengers junkie."

"That's true!"

I cracked open a beer and felt much better about myself. I wasn't boring. I just didn't have a lot of space in my life right now for my passion. Always living on the edge of financial disaster tended to put the Avengers low on the list of priorities. Catching lawbreaking morons was high on the list. Although it probably wouldn't hurt to channel Thor when I was trying to get cuffs on an angry 250-pound bad guy.

"Did you have any luck with Oswald today?" Morelli asked.

"I got a glimpse of him twice, but he got away both times."

"Do you have an address for him?"

"No, but he drives a black 911 Porsche Turbo with New York plates."

Morelli finished the Kung Pao Chicken and moved on to the fortune cookies. "How's Melvin doing?"

"I had him stashed with Lula, but she kicked him out, so he's camping in the park with the duck roaster."

"Do I want to know any of these details?" Morelli asked. "For instance, who is the duck roaster?"

"Homeless guy who got arrested for barbecuing the ducks in the park. It turned out that he has a nice tent and he agreed to let Melvin stay there with him." I looked at my watch. "I should check in with Melvin to make sure everything is okay."

I called Melvin and there was no answer.

"Maybe his phone is dead," Morelli said.

"He was supposed to keep his phone charged. The duck roaster had a hookup in the public restroom."

I waited a couple of minutes and tried again. Still no answer.

"I don't like this," I said. "We need to go to the park."

"My fortune cookie told me I was going to get lucky tonight. It's bad luck to mess with a fortune cookie."

"We can deal with the fortune cookie after we check on Melvin."

"Sounds like a plan," Morelli said. "Bob likes the park."

CHAPTER NINE

The sun had set but the sky was still light when Morelli parked his car in the lot by the path to the duck pond. A fire truck and an EMT truck were also parked in the lot. My stomach went hollow at the sight of the trucks, and I had my hand on the door handle before Morelli killed the engine. I ran down the path and followed it to the camp chair by the water's edge. I could hear voices and activity back by the tent site. I hurried along the short trail to the tent and was relieved to see Melvin standing off to one side. He was holding his computer and looking dazed. Andy was on the ground with first responders clustered around him.

"What happened?" I asked Melvin.

"I'm not sure," Melvin said. "I think he might have food poisoning. He started throwing up around six o'clock. It was like *The Exorcist*. Vomit was exploding out of him. He stopped for a short time and then it started again, and it looked bloody. I didn't know what to do, so I called 911."

"You did the right thing," I said. "Are you feeling okay?"

"Yeah. I didn't eat the chicken. I ate the cookies."

Morelli and Bob ambled over. "I talked to one of the EMTs," Morelli said. "They have him stable and they're going to take him to the medical center."

"Who's this?" Melvin asked.

"Joe Morelli, Trenton PD," I said. "And the dog is Bob."

"You brought the police?"

"He was at my house when I tried to call you. He's my boyfriend."

It always felt uncomfortable when I referred to Morelli as my boyfriend. I had boyfriends when I was a teenager and the term felt childish now. The problem is that there are no good words to describe an adult relationship. Lover was limiting. Partner was too vague. He was much more than a friend or a date. So, for lack of a better word, he was a boyfriend.

I walked over to Andy. He was on a stretcher, and he looked very pale.

"I'm sorry," I said. "I hope you feel better."

They rolled him down the trail to the path, and I went back to Morelli and Melvin.

"Get your backpack," I said to Melvin. "You can't stay here."

"Where am I going to stay?" he asked.

"You can stay with me tonight," I said. "I'll figure it out in the morning."

My hope was that he'd crack Oswald's code and start pulling information that would lead me to Oswald. If I could catch

Oswald, I could get rid of Melvin, I could pay my rent for next month, I could avoid Clark's viewing, and Morelli might be able to solve his case. The reasons for catching Oswald were adding up. I suspected Diesel had reasons for wanting Oswald that were a lot more serious, but that was his problem and I had mine.

We waited for Melvin to gather his things and we returned to Morelli's car. The fire truck had already rumbled away and the EMTs were getting ready to leave.

"I have Andy's Hemingway library in my backpack," Melvin said. "I figure the parks department will come in and clean out his campsite. I didn't want him to lose his books."

"I'll make sure he gets them," I said.

We put Melvin in the backseat with Bob, and we left the park.

"Are you getting any closer to tapping into Oswald's network?" I asked Melvin.

"I'm making progress but it's slow."

"Have you been able to contact the other five hackers in Baked Potatoes?"

"No. I haven't been able to get past the block. I've been looking on IRCs we originally met on, too."

"I don't suppose we could just take you home to your parents' house," Morelli said to Melvin.

"They sort of kicked me out," Melvin said. "And they converted my room into a home gym."

"Sisters or brothers or cousins?" Morelli asked.

"None in the area," Melvin said. "We're a small dysfunctional family."

Morelli parked in my building's lot, walked Bob around a little so he could lift his leg, and we all trooped up to my apartment.

"Have you had anything to eat today besides cookies?" I asked Melvin.

"I don't think so," he said. "Not that I can remember."

"We have leftover Chinese, Froot Loops cereal, and peanut butter. Does any of that interest you?"

"The peanut butter."

"Good choice," I said. "You can't go wrong with peanut butter."

I put the bread, a jar of peanut butter, a jar of strawberry jam, pickles, olives, and potato chips on the kitchen counter. I looked for Melvin and found him at my dining room table, setting up his computer. No problem, I thought. I can't cook but I'm a master at making peanut butter sandwiches. I made peanut butter and jelly, peanut butter and olives, peanut butter and pickles and potato chips, and peanut butter and banana sandwiches. I set them next to Melvin with a can of soda and left him to eat and work. Morelli, Bob, and I settled on the couch and found a ball game to watch.

At ten o'clock the sandwiches were all eaten, and Melvin was pacing and mumbling. The ball game was over, Bob had gone out for his last leg lift of the night, and Morelli handed me the slim strip of paper from his fortune cookie that told him he was going to get lucky. I put an extra blanket and pillow on the couch for Melvin, but I suspected it wouldn't get used.

"Melvin," Morelli yelled from the bedroom door, "we're going to bed."

"Okay," Melvin said.

"If you come into the bedroom, I'll shoot you."

"Okay," Melvin mumbled back.

I crawled into bed wearing panties and a T-shirt.

"I was hoping you'd be looking a little sexier than this," Morelli said

"What did you have in mind?"

"Nakedness, but it's not a problem. I can work with the T-shirt." He slipped in next to me and ran his hand over the shirt.

"I don't think we should be doing this," I said. "It's uncomfortable."

"Is it that time of the month?"

"No! Melvin is in the next room."

"I can lock him out. He can wait in the hall."

"He would know we were doing it."

"And?"

"It's awkward," I said. "It's like doing it with people watching."

"And?"

"Wouldn't that bother you?"

"It would depend on the people. If they were a couple hot women . . ."

"Omigod!"

Morelli grinned. "We could be quiet. He would never know."

"Yes, but I know!"

"You do realize that for eons people have performed this activity with other people in close proximity. Sometimes those other people were in their very own family."

"Melvin isn't family. He's Melvin."

"I can't argue with that," Morelli said, "but it's bad juju to screw with a fortune cookie."

CHAPTER TEN

I woke up to rain on Sunday morning. "Do you think it's the fortune cookie telling us something?" I asked Morelli.

"It's not too late to set things right," he said. "I'm ready to do whatever it takes."

Morelli was always ready. He had testosterone oozing out of his pores.

I sat up in bed. "I hear Melvin. He's stomping around in the living room." I got out of bed, pulled on jeans, and went to see what Melvin was doing.

"My leg fell asleep," he said. "I was sitting on it, and I fell asleep, and when I woke up my leg was dead." He stomped from one side of the room to the other. "It's feeling better. It's pins and needles now. That's a good sign."

Morelli ambled out of the bedroom. "I'm going to let Bob

check out some tires in the parking lot and then we're heading home." He gave me a friendly kiss. "I'll pick you up at three o'clock for the disaster."

I waved him and Bob away and I went into the kitchen for coffee.

"What disaster?" Melvin asked.

"Family birthday party," I said. "Morelli's Uncle Sergio."

"Is he old?"

"Eighty."

"I bet he's cranky. The old people in my family are cranky."

I ate a handful of cereal while I waited for my coffee. "How's the hacking going?"

"Okay. It would be going faster if I had Clark to help me. We shared ideas."

I passed the cereal box to him. "Help yourself to cereal. There's milk in the fridge, and I just made coffee."

"Good. My synapses need coffee."

"I'm going to take a shower. I want to be at the hospital at eight o'clock to see Andy. You need to come with me. After Andy we're going to stop at my parents' house. They have an extra bedroom, and they might be willing to let you stay there."

"I'm like a man without a country," Melvin said.

"It's temporary. As soon as we track down Oswald, you can go back to your loft."

———

Andy was sitting up in bed eating breakfast when we walked into his room. He was hooked up to an IV, but he had color in his face, and he seemed happy to see us.

"I brought your Hemingway," Melvin said, handing him the books in a plastic bag. "I was afraid they might disappear if I left them behind."

"That's a fact of life when you live in a park," Andy said. "Things disappear all the time."

"How are you feeling?" I asked him. "Was it food poisoning?"

"I'm feeling much better," he said. "I'm getting fluids and some antibiotics. They think it was food poisoning, but it might not have been the rotisserie chicken. I tend to be lax about refrigeration. They thought it might have been the dead squirrel I found the day before. I had leftovers for breakfast."

"I'm no kind of homemaker," Melvin said, "but I know enough not to eat a dead squirrel."

"Will you get discharged today?" I asked Andy.

"Not today," he said. "Probably tomorrow."

I stopped at the nurses' station on the way out and told them I would be taking Andy home and needed to be notified when he was ready to leave. This was a small fib because I would actually be taking him to the courthouse to get a new court date. And probably he would remain in jail until he went before the judge. He secured his bail bond with a watch the first time around. I doubted he had anything valuable enough to secure a second bail bond.

––––––––––

My mom goes to Mass Friday night and Sunday morning. Grandma goes to bingo Friday night and the bakery on Sunday morning. This seems like the perfect arrangement to me because my mom's devotion to God is rewarded by fresh baked jelly doughnuts when she comes home from church. This morning was no exception. Three white bakery boxes were open on the counter when I brought Melvin into the kitchen. I knew the contents without looking inside. One box contained assorted doughnuts. The second box was filled with Italian cookies. The third box held cannoli.

My mom and Grandma were huddled at the small kitchen table. The church and bakery partnership also worked from the point of view that multiple sources of gossip were superior to one.

"We were wondering if you would stop around this morning," Grandma said to me. "I got an extra chocolate chip cannoli just in case. And we have enough for your guest."

"This is Melvin Schwartz," I said. "He's helping me find an FTA."

My mother was on her feet, getting two plates and napkins. "Help yourself," she said to Melvin and me. "Would you like coffee?"

"What FTA is this?" Grandma wanted to know. "Is it Oswald Wednesday? I know you've been stumped by him."

Melvin looked overwhelmed, not sure if he wanted a doughnut or a cannoli. I put one of each on his plate, added a couple cookies, and sat him at the table.

"I saw Joseph's mother at church this morning," my mother said to me. "She said you were going to Sergio's party. Did you get a card?"

"No," I said. "Do I need one?"

"I have a box of them. I'll get one for you before you leave."

"I think there's more than meets the eye with Oswald

Wednesday," Grandma said. "He broke into a cop's apartment. Who does that? And he's from out of town."

Melvin still had his computer case hung on his shoulder. He slipped it off and put it on the floor by his backpack.

"Is that your computer?" Grandma asked.

"One of them," Melvin said. "I have another computer in my backpack."

"Are you one of those IT people?"

"More or less," Melvin said.

"Is that how you're helping Stephanie?"

"More or less."

"I'm pretty good at a computer," Grandma said. "I'm good at tracking down criminals. I've had some experiences."

"Melvin is looking for a place to stay while he helps me," I said to my mom. "I was wondering if he could use my room for a day or two. He needs a quiet place to work."

"I should discuss it first with your father," my mom said. "He's at the lodge. They're having a pancake breakfast for one of their charities."

"What lodge does he belong to?" Melvin asked. "My father belongs to a lodge and they're always having pancake breakfasts. His name is Philip Schwartz. He's a pharmacist."

"A pharmacist!" Grandma said. "That's a wonderful profession. And I bet you're a college graduate."

"More or less," Melvin said.

"It would help if I could leave Melvin here temporarily," I said. "I can come back to check on how things are going after the party."

"I don't see any harm in it," Grandma said to my mom. "His

father is a pharmacist, and Melvin is more or less a college graduate."

"I suppose it would be all right," my mom said.

"I'll get you all set up," Grandma said to Melvin. "There's even a little desk in Stephanie's room."

"I have to go," I said. "Things to do."

I took a couple Italian cookies, my mom gave me a birthday card for Uncle Sergio, and I drove off. I parked in front of the bail bonds office and called Diesel.

"I've got Melvin stashed at my parents' house and I'm free until this afternoon," I said. "Do you have any new leads?"

"No, but I was thinking we should take a look at Melvin's loft."

"I was thinking the same thing. I'm at the bonds office."

"I'm in the area. I'll pick you up."

"In case you haven't noticed, it's raining."

"It's not a problem. I have a car."

Ten minutes later the rain had slowed to a drizzle, and Diesel parked behind me in a yellow and black Ford Bronco.

"This looks brand-new," I said.

"Yeah, right out of the box. I've got a good fixer."

"Did he also fix you a place to live?"

"She," Diesel said. "Ana."

"So, where do you live?"

"Wherever I want. Right now, it's in your parking lot. It's a motor home."

"Omigod! I was wondering who owned it. It looks like it belongs in a NASCAR lot. Is it wonderful inside?"

"It has all the necessities," Diesel said. "And some luxuries."

I buckled in and Diesel headed across town to Deacon

Plumbing. The lot was empty when we drove in. Diesel parked close to the building, and we went to Melvin's door.

"Someone's been here," Diesel said. "They didn't have a key and they aren't as talented as I am at uninvited entry. There are visible scratches." He opened the door and we walked in and went upstairs to the loft.

We stood very still for a moment, taking everything in. Drawers were slightly ajar from being searched, couch cushions had been removed and cut open, the refrigerator door had been left open. In the center of the room, on Melvin's desk, two giant monitors had been smashed beyond recognition. *Retribution* had been written across them in yellow mustard from a squeeze bottle. The remainder of the bottle emptied out onto the carpet.

We walked through the loft and returned to the stairs.

"Doesn't look like Oswald took anything," I said.

Diesel nodded. "I'm sure he was disappointed at not finding Melvin at home. He spent some time looking for something, though. Melvin's computer would be at the top of my list."

"There are a lot of possibilities. Oswald could be a computer hoarder. You can never have too many computers. Or he could be sentimental and collect computers as mementos when he trashes someone's loft. Or he could be worried that the Baked Potatoes accessed something sensitive, and it was stored on Melvin's computer."

"Yeah, I'm going with the last one."

"You know what it is, don't you?"

"I don't know the details. I just know the big picture. My job is to capture Oswald. I'm only interested in Melvin's computer if it leads me to my man."

"What if Melvin's computer has nothing?"

"Then I look elsewhere. Right now, it's what I have, so we should go back to your parents' place and talk to Melvin."

"Yes, but it will have to wait. I'm tied up for the rest of the day."

"Let me know when you aren't tied up," Diesel said.

CHAPTER ELEVEN

I was downstairs in my building's lobby, waiting for Morelli, when he arrived at three o'clock. The sun was making a halfhearted attempt to struggle out through the cloud cover, but the rain was still at a drizzle. I was wearing an extra layer of mascara, heels, and a cranberry-colored knit dress for the occasion. I accessorized with a tan raincoat.

"My mother gave me a card to give to Uncle Sergio," I said to Morelli.

"My mother gave me a present to give to him," Morelli said. "I have no idea what it is."

Morelli drove out of the parking lot and turned onto Hamilton Avenue. "What's new?" he asked.

"Andy looks a lot better. They're keeping him in the hospital one more day. Melvin is staying with my parents. Grandma has adopted him. And Diesel and I went snooping in Melvin's loft. It looks like someone broke in and searched the place."

"Oswald Wednesday?"

"That's what I'm thinking."

Sergio's party was being held at his daughter's house in the Burg. It looked a lot like my parents' house, but it was more Catholic. There was a plaster Madonna on the front lawn and there were Madonnas and crucified Jesuses in every room in the house.

We left our card and present on a table that was already filled with cards, presents, and bottles of wine. The table was by the front door and Morelli looked like he was thinking about sneaking out.

"Too late," I said to him. "Your mother spotted you. She's making her way through the crowd."

Moments later, his mother wrapped her arms around him and gave him kisses. "You wore the new sweater," she said. "It looks nice. Did you give Uncle the present?"

"It's on the table by the door," Morelli said.

His mother turned to me and gave me a hug and kisses. "You always look so pretty!" she said. "It was nice of you to come to our party. We think of you as family." She looked over her shoulder at Morelli when she said it. It was as good as *When are you going to marry her and get her pregnant?*

Morelli's crazy Grandma Bella followed in his mother's wake.

"Joseph!" she said, hugging and kissing Morelli. "My favorite. My favorite. Did you give Uncle his present? He doesn't deserve anything. He's worthless."

"A fine way to talk about your brother on his birthday," Morelli's mother said.

"He's lucky I don't give him the eye. It's only because we're blood."

Bella has been in this country for more than fifty years, but she speaks broken English and she dresses like a Sicilian extra in a Godfather movie.

"Who's this?" Bella said, looking at me. "I know who you are. I know your family. The women are gypsies. Hungarians."

"They're good women," Morelli's mother said. "And Stephanie's father is Italian."

"Poor man," Bella said. "They cast a gypsy spell on him. They're all gold diggers." She shook her finger at Morelli. "You stay away from this one. Look at her, she wears slut clothes."

"Not yet," Morelli said, "but I have high hopes for later tonight."

"You should visit the food table," Morelli's mother said to him. "There's meatballs in red sauce and macaroni. I think Bess got the antipasto at Giovichinni's but it's still good. And your aunt Lou made the ricotta cake that you like."

Morelli draped an arm around me and steered me to the food table. "You handled that really well," he said. "You didn't even punch Grandma in the face."

"Do you think this dress is slutty?"

"No, it's pretty and a little sexy. If you told me that you weren't wearing underwear it might approach slutty."

"Sorry to disappoint."

"There's still time," Morelli said, surveying the food. "The lines are getting blurred in my family between a birthday buffet and an after-burial party buffet. They're all looking the same."

"There's a cake with candles at this one."

"There's the difference. I missed the cake. It's hiding behind Mrs. Mazzerella's noodle casserole."

Morelli's phone buzzed. He looked at the text message and stepped aside to make a phone call. I went to help myself to a dinner roll and came breast to eyes with Uncle Sergio.

Uncle Sergio took a dollar bill out of his pocket and jammed it into the low neckline of my dress. "I was wondering when the strippers would get here," he said.

My mouth dropped open and I looked over at Morelli. He was in full-on cop mode, nodding and listening, serious.

"I'm not a stripper," I said. "I'm Joseph's girlfriend."

Sergio squinted his eyes and looked as if he was trying to raise his head to make eye, or at least chin, contact. "What's that, chicky?"

"I'm Joseph's girlfriend," I yelled.

Sergio's eyes widened at the revelation. "Oooooh. I didn't know." He took another crumpled bill out of his pocket, shoved it into my dress with the first bill, and winked at me. "High class," he said.

Joe disconnected and returned to the food table. Under the serious cop face, I could detect some excitement. He looked at Uncle Sergio and then at the cash flow coming out of my chest. He removed the bills and handed them back to Sergio. "Happy birthday, Uncle Sergio," he said. "Afraid we have to leave. Something came up at work."

Uncle Sergio looked disappointed. "What? No stripper? Please tell me someone at least hired the mooner."

We were out the door and running through the drizzle to Morelli's car before his mother could object.

"And?" I asked.

"That was a courtesy call. There's a dead guy in Hamilton Township, and he's missing part of his tongue. They think the dog might have eaten it."

I felt the dinner roll stick in my throat.

"Are you okay?" Morelli asked.

He thumped me on my back, and I coughed up the chunk of bread.

"I want to go take a look," he said. "The guy was just discovered. The ME hasn't gotten there yet. Bucky Schmidt was the first on the scene and he knew I'd want to see it."

"You aren't faking this just to get out of the party, are you?"

"No, but I'm not unhappy about it, either."

Fifteen minutes later Morelli angle-parked behind an EMT. We ducked under crime scene tape and went through the open door to a ground-floor garden apartment. The front room was filled with cops and med techs. A man was facedown on the floor. Shoulder-length gray hair. Looked like he spent more time in the bakery than the gym. He was wearing baggy jeans, sneakers, and a T-shirt. Blood was pooled under him. I didn't look too closely.

"Where's the dog?" Morelli asked.

"It was a neighbor's dog," one of the uniforms said. "The door was left open, and the dog ran in. From the blood on his paws and nose and what was left on the floor, we figured he had dinner here. He's back with his owner."

I wandered around while Morelli helped with evidence collection in the immediate area of the body. It looked to me like the man lived alone. It was a two-bedroom apartment but only one bedroom was furnished, and only one side of the bed had been slept in. There was one toothbrush in the bathroom. The table in the dining alcove was being used as a desk. It held a printer, a stack of Spider-Man comics, assorted gizmos that were alien to me, pads, pens, sticky pad notes, some empty soda cans, and an empty bag of Chips Ahoy cookies. There was a power strip under the table with several cords attached. I didn't see a computer. I also couldn't remember seeing a backpack or a computer bag anywhere in the apartment. I returned to the bedroom and looked in drawers and under the bed. No computer. I pulled the rumpled bedding back and found the computer. A ThinkPad X1. It was the same kind of computer I'd seen Melvin using. There was also a notepad and felt-tip pen by the computer and a large ink spot on the bedsheet.

I didn't want to risk the computer being collected by the CSI crew. I wanted to hand it over to Melvin first. When he was done with it the police could have it. I buttoned and belted my raincoat and shoved the computer and the notepad inside. I pulled the linens back over the ink splotch and I called Diesel.

"I'm at a crime scene in Hamilton Township and I need a ride," I told him. "The sooner the better."

"Are the police after you?" he asked.

"Not yet," I said. "I'll text you the address."

I went back to the front room and told Morelli that Diesel was going to pick me up and take me home.

Morelli looked at the slight bulge in my raincoat and raised an eyebrow. I gave him a smile and he gave his head a single small shake.

"I'll be here for a while," he said. "I'll call when I'm ready to leave."

I buckled myself into the Bronco and removed the laptop from my raincoat.

Diesel grinned. "Is this stolen evidence from a crime scene?"

"Yes. I want Melvin to look it over. There's a very dead man back at the apartment complex. He's missing part of his tongue, and I'm guessing he's one of the seven Baked Potatoes."

"And this is his laptop?"

"It was in a jumble of bed linens. I think Oswald overlooked it. I swiped it before the police got to it. I thought it might be helpful."

"I underestimated you," Diesel said. "You have real potential."

I found myself smiling again. I agreed with him. I had my moments.

Grandma and Melvin were at the kitchen table when Diesel and I walked in. My mom had the dining room table set for dinner and she was at the stove, watching the potatoes boil and basting the two chickens that were roasting in the oven. Sunday was roast chicken day. She always made two because Monday was leftover chicken day. Melvin was at his computer and Grandma was lurking. My mom and Grandma stopped what they were doing and stared at Diesel.

"Diesel!" Grandma exclaimed.

"Yep," Diesel said. "I'm back."

"He's helping me find Oswald Wednesday," I said.

"Seems like you've got a lot of people helping you find him," Grandma said. "It's getting hard to keep track of them all. Melvin's working hard to help you, too. And he's teaching me how to be a hacker."

My mom gave me a warning glare not to encourage this. She made the sign of the cross, and she took a hit of her version of *iced tea*.

"Melvin has software and gadgets that are amazing," Grandma said. "His backpack is filled with all kinds of things. And his computer is the bomb. I never heard of that brand before but it's supercool."

"It's important to have good hardware and software," Melvin said.

"Are you staying for dinner?" Grandma asked me. "I'll set extra plates."

"Dinner would be great," I said.

"Agreed," Diesel said. "Dinner would be great."

"How about Morelli?" Grandma asked. "What happened to him? Did you leave him at the party?"

"He's working," I said. "He got called out on a homicide. He said he would get in touch when he was done."

"A homicide!" Grandma said. "Anybody I know? Did you go to the crime scene?"

"I was there briefly. I don't know the man's name," I said. "He looked to be in his sixties. A little overweight. Lived alone. He had part of his tongue cut off."

Melvin's eyes opened wide, and he sucked in some air. "No way."

My mom put a hand on the counter to steady herself and chugged more tea from the big-gulp glass.

"Another tongue murder!" Grandma said. "This is big. This is going to make national news. We need to go to the funeral home early tomorrow or we won't get in. It's going to be packed."

I motioned for Melvin to meet me in the dining room. So far as I knew, the connection between the tongue murders and Oswald wasn't common knowledge. Nothing remained a secret for very long in the Burg, but I didn't want to be responsible for this going public.

I handed Melvin the laptop. "I found this in the victim's bedroom. It might eventually get turned over to the police as evidence, but I wanted you to look at it first. It's a ThinkPad X1."

"There were two more Baked Potatoes who I thought might be local," Melvin said. "One was an older dude who went by the handle of Mushy2. I know he worked on a ThinkPad like me."

"When the Baked Potatoes hacked into Oswald's network, did you see or download anything?" Diesel asked.

Melvin shook his head. "No reason to download anything. It was just about getting in. I was so surprised and excited when it happened, I don't remember seeing much of anything. Maybe some basic info about hardware and software, and some directories."

He returned to the kitchen table with the new computer and tried a series of passwords, with no success. He plugged something that looked like a large flash drive into the computer and after several seconds a home page appeared.

"I'm in," Melvin said.

"Go to his mail account," I said.

Only one item came up. RETRIBUTION. The word was repeated in an endless scroll. Melvin clicked a few keys and the scrolling stopped.

"This is bad," Melvin said. "I really hate this."

"It's boring," Grandma said. "Especially in comparison to a

homicide." Grandma's attention turned to me. "Did you get to see the tongue?"

"No," I said. "The neighbor's dog ate it."

"For real?" Diesel asked.

My mom had the chickens out of the oven, and she was making gravy. "Someone needs to mash the potatoes," she said.

Grandma went to the stove, drained the potatoes, and added butter and milk to the pot. "I like a lot of butter," she said. "It's the trick to making good mashed potatoes."

My father walked into the kitchen. "Hey," he said to Diesel. "How's it going?"

As if Diesel hadn't been gone for two years.

"It's going okay," Diesel said. "And you?"

"I'm hungry. I smell chicken." He looked at me. "When did you get here?"

"A couple minutes ago," I said. "You were asleep in your chair."

"I wasn't sleeping," he said. "I was resting my eyes." He looked at Melvin. "Who are you?"

"He's Melvin," Grandma said. "He's living here."

"How long's he been living here?" my father asked. "Why don't I know about this?"

"Stephanie dropped him off this morning," Grandma said. "He's a hacker."

My father perked up at this. "A hacker!" he said. "No kidding?"

"He's the one who replaced the TV news with a porno movie," Grandma said.

"Way to go, kid," my dad said. "That caused a stir at the lodge.

We thought Marty Bloomfeld was going to have to get another stint after he watched that clip. Good thing it didn't last any longer or Marty might have thrown a clot."

"The station cut it off before it got to the end," Melvin said.

"It didn't bother Marty," my dad said. "He's used to not getting to the end. He's getting on in years. He's happy if he can have a couple minutes in the beginning."

"We're ready to eat," my mom said, slightly slurring her words.

My dad went to the dining room and took his seat at the head of the table. He helped himself to a wing and a drumstick and a mound of mashed potatoes and drowned it all in gravy.

"So, what have you hacked lately?" he asked Melvin. "Have you ever blacked out a grid or taken down a bank or a slaughterhouse?"

The rest of us were gobsmacked because my father never talked at the table. He always concentrated on eating and ignoring Grandma.

"Right now, I'm helping Stephanie break into a private network," Melvin said.

"It's the Oswald Wednesday case," Grandma said. "I'm helping with it."

"Oswald has a network?" my father said. "Go figure."

I turned to my father with my fork midway to my mouth. "Do you know Oswald Wednesday?"

"Yeah, sort of short, roly-poly guy with a black ponytail, right?"

"Right," Diesel and I said in unison.

My father chewed a chunk of meat off the drumstick and some gravy dripped onto his shirt. "I picked him up with the cab a couple times and took him to the train station." He dabbed at his shirt with his napkin. "He seems like a nice guy. Always gives me a good tip."

"Where do you pick him up?" Diesel asked.

"Different places," my father said. "Always downtown by the capital buildings. I figure he lives in one of the high-rises. What's he done?"

"For starters, he broke into an apartment that was being rented to a cop."

"It was probably a mistake," my father said. "He doesn't look like he needs to rob apartments. He dresses nice and he said he has a Porsche, but he doesn't like to leave it at the train station. Afraid it won't be there when he comes home."

"If you pick him up again, call me," I said. "His recovery fee will pay my rent for next month."

"Sure," my father said. "I don't have any stuffing. I missed the stuffing."

Grandma passed him the stuffing and poured herself a glass of wine. "Isn't this nice," she said. "I like when the table's filled with people."

There was a knock on the front door and Morelli walked in. "I thought I'd find you here," he said to me. "I called but you didn't answer."

"My phone is in my messenger bag," I said. "I didn't hear it."

"This gets better and better," Grandma said, getting to her feet. "Pull up a chair and I'll get you a plate."

Diesel was sitting on one side of me and Morelli took the chair on the other side. Grandma gave Morelli a place setting and a glass of wine.

"I guess you just came from the murder scene," she said to him. "Stephanie said she didn't get to see the tongue. Did you at least get to see the dog that ate it?"

Morelli filled his plate. "I did. He belongs to a neighbor."

"What kind of dog was it?" Grandma asked.

"Black Lab," Morelli said. "Very friendly. We decided not to charge him with evidence destruction." Morelli cut his eyes to me. "Usually when people and animals tamper with evidence there are repercussions."

"But not always?" I asked.

"Sometimes there are extenuating circumstances," Morelli said.

"Like when a fortune cookie is involved?" I asked.

"Yeah," Morelli said. "A fortune cookie could make a difference."

Two people to a side at my mom's table was comfortable. Three to a side was a tight fit. I was squashed between Diesel and Morelli and the best I could say about my position was that it kept them from challenging each other to arm wrestling.

Diesel excused himself after the apple pie. Morelli waited until I'd helped clear the table before he pulled me aside.

"I'm assuming that was a laptop under your raincoat," he said.

"How did you know?"

"It had corners."

"If I left it in the apartment, it might have sat in evidence storage without getting opened. I have Melvin here and he was able to plug one of his gizmos into the laptop and get it working."

"Has he found anything?"

"An email message that said RETRIBUTION and was signed

with Oswald's special mark. Melvin got a similar message, but he wasn't home when Oswald visited."

Morelli smiled at me. "Nice work. Not legal, but nice."

"Melvin's hacker group is called Baked Potatoes. Out of the seven Potatoes, two are dead with their tongues cut out."

"What about the other four group members?"

"Melvin only communicates with them online and his ability to do that has been blocked. He doesn't know where they live or their real names. They could be anywhere on the planet."

"I can have a search sent out for homicides with the same MO," Morelli said. "If these murders are connected to hacking, the feds should get involved. They should also get involved if we have a serial killer."

"Melvin has a record and a business to protect. He might not be a good match-up with the feds."

We looked through the dining room to the kitchen, where Melvin was back to working at the little table.

"He's motivated," I said to Morelli.

"And he won't leave this house?"

"Grandma's watching him."

Melvin shook his head and mumbled something. He got up and walked around his chair and sat down again.

"Is he any good?" Morelli asked.

"He's good enough to be able to hack the super hacker. Apparently, he's not smart enough to have seen the downside, which might be death. Melvin said hacking Oswald was like a game to the Baked Potatoes. Melvin's exact quote was *We thought he was a genius. We didn't know he was a homicidal maniac.*"

Melvin was on his feet again, walking around, waving his arms in the air, talking to himself.

"I need to go to my house to feed Bob," Morelli said. "Are you going to stay here and watch him pace, or are you coming with me?"

"I'll come with you. I want to be around when you cash in on your fortune cookie luckiness."

CHAPTER TWELVE

My smartphone alarm went off at 8:00 a.m. and I had a moment of disorientation. The moment passed and I figured it out. I was in Morelli's bed and the day had started without me. As usual, Morelli had gotten up at the crack of dawn and was already at work.

Bob was sitting beside the bed, watching me.

"Hey," I said, "how's it going?"

There was a note on the bedside table that told me Bob had eaten his breakfast and gone for a short walk. If I let him out in the backyard for five minutes, he'd be good.

Forty-five minutes later, I was back at my apartment, showered and dressed in my usual work uniform of jeans and a T-shirt. I ran out of my apartment building with my hair still damp and jumped into the Focus. I hadn't taken the time to make coffee because I was behind schedule. I wanted to get to the hospital before Andy checked himself out.

I bypassed the reception desk at the hospital and went straight to Andy's floor. I stopped at the nurses' station and told them I was there to collect Andy.

"He left last night," one of the nurses said. "He disconnected his IV, got dressed, and left."

"How could that happen?" I asked. "That's not supposed to happen."

"True," she said, "but every now and then we get a sneaky old guy who doesn't want to be here anymore and finds a way to leave. He's one of those guys."

"Did he leave anything behind? Like a wallet?"

"No. He took everything. There wasn't much. Some spare change and a couple books."

This was my fault. I could have checked him into the locked-down prison ward at the hospital, but I thought he wasn't a flight risk and he'd be more comfortable on a normal floor.

I returned to the Focus and drove the couple of blocks to the office. Connie and Lula were already there.

"We've been waiting for you," Lula said. "Did you hear about the second tongue murder?"

I waved her away and went straight to the coffee machine. I filled my mug and hit up the doughnut box on Connie's desk.

"I was there," I said. "I went with Morelli."

"We heard it was an older guy," Lula said.

"I didn't get a good look at him," I said, "but he had gray hair and he was a little paunchy."

"Police report says his name is Gerard Gouge," Connie said. "Single. Self-employed computer repair."

"He was a hacker," I said.

"Yeah," Lula said. "We figured. How's Melvin doing? Does he still have his tongue?"

"He's okay. He's staying at my parents' house. I'm going over there to check on him."

"I guess the duck roaster didn't work out," Lula said.

"He ate a squirrel and had to be hospitalized," I said. "I couldn't leave Melvin in the park alone. Worst part is the roaster snuck out of the hospital last night and took his books with him."

"Are you sure the roaster skipped?" Lula asked. "Maybe he made it look like he left, but he's really hiding out in the park, behind a tree or something."

It was possible. Homeless people tended to return to comfort spots. He could have gone from the hospital back to the park.

"I'll tag along with you," Lula said. "I haven't got much else to do today. I couldn't get a hair appointment until four o'clock. I wouldn't mind saying hello to Grandma."

Lula was wearing a fluffy white angora knit cap over her hair. Her scoop-necked sweater was also white angora, and when she moved, she shed wisps of angora. She looked like a giant rabbit squished into a short black leather skirt and over-the-knee black leather boots with five-inch spike heels.

My father was making his morning cab runs when Lula and I got to my parents' house. Grandma and Melvin had their computers set up on the dining room table.

"We moved in here because we needed more room with all

the equipment we got now," Grandma said. "I'm taking notes for Melvin, so he doesn't forget important things."

"Have there been any eureka moments?" Lula asked.

"There were a couple," Grandma said, "but we still haven't got answers like we want. At least we know the name of the second murder victim."

"Melvin was able to get it off the computer?" I asked.

"No," Grandma said. "I got it from Mary Jane Kuleski at the deli this morning. Her daughter lives in the same apartment building as the victim, Gerard Gouge. She said he was nice but kind of a loner. He helped get her computer straightened out once. She said the dog that ate the tongue was real nice, too. He wasn't usually running around loose but he broke away from the owner when he saw the open door. I guess Gerard used to give him treats."

"Have you heard from Andy?" I asked Melvin.

"No," he said. "I haven't heard from anyone. I don't know where my phone is."

"I got it charging in the kitchen," Grandma said.

I went to the kitchen to say hello to my mom. She was at the counter, making meatballs.

"There wasn't enough chicken for leftovers," she said. "So, I thought I'd make some spaghetti for dinner."

The marinara sauce was simmering on the stove and the kitchen smelled like sautéed garlic and onions mingling with assorted herbs and tomatoes.

"You're starting early," I said.

"I like when the meatballs get to soak in the sauce for a while."

"How is it going with Melvin?"

My mom rolled a glob of meat mixture around in her hand and placed the meatball onto a cookie sheet. "He's no trouble. He's a little eccentric but that's not a problem. If your father and I could learn to live with your grandmother, we can learn to live with anyone."

I went back to the dining room and looked over Melvin's shoulder for a couple of minutes. There were numbers flashing on his screen. They would stop and Melvin would type something, and the numbers would resume scrolling. I had no clue what he was doing.

"I'm heading out," I said to Grandma. "Call me if anything important happens."

"You bet," Grandma said. "You'll know as soon as we do."

"And don't let him out of the house or out of your sight."

"No worries," Grandma said. "I'm on it."

Lula and I got into the Focus, and I headed for the park.

"I could never be a hacker," Lula said. "Melvin just sits in front of a computer all day and night with nothing but numbers to look at. I'd go nuts doing that job. Truth is the most stimulating job I had was when I was a pleasure facilitator. I met a lot of interesting people. Every night it was something different trying to figure out how to get the job done."

"Being a bounty hunter isn't so bad," I said. "There's a lot of variety to it. And we do a service for the community."

"I guess that's true, but my wardrobe has gotten boring," Lula said. "And when I was working on the street, I never got a bat stuck in my hair."

I pulled into the lot by the duck pond and parked. Lula and I got out and followed the path to where Andy had his camp chair.

"His chair is gone," Lula said. "And it looks like the area's been cleaned up. I don't see any candy wrappers or cigarette butts."

We walked through the clump of shrubs and flowering trees and came to Andy's campground. The tent and the camp chair were gone. A guy in a green parks uniform was raking up debris.

"What's going on?" Lula asked.

"General cleanup," he said. "Someone was squatting here, but I guess he moved on. Or maybe he got kicked out."

"Hey, Andy!" Lula yelled. "Are you out there somewhere?"

No one answered.

"Just checking," Lula said to the cleanup guy.

We walked back around the lake and got into the car.

"That was a bummer," Lula said. "He was gone one day, and they took his home away."

"It wasn't really his home," I said. "He wasn't supposed to be there. And he wasn't supposed to be eating the ducks."

"I guess that's true, but I'm feeling sad all the same. I could use a burger with cheese fries to cheer myself up. Besides, it's almost lunchtime, give or take an hour or two," Lula said.

"Do you have someplace special in mind?"

"If we head back to the office, I could get a Clucky Burger at Cluck-in-a-Bucket."

———

I was in the Clucky parking lot, waiting for Lula, and my dad called.

"I just dropped Oswald Wednesday off at the train station," he said. "I thought you'd want to know. I would have called you sooner, but I didn't get a chance. I didn't want to talk with him listening."

"Thanks," I said. "You did the right thing."

I hung up, called Diesel, and told him I'd meet him at the train station. I beeped my horn for Lula to hurry and moments later she hustled out with a giant soda and a large takeout bag.

"What's going on?" she asked, buckling in.

"Oswald's at the train station."

"Good deal. I'm ready. How are we doing this? Are we going in guns drawn?"

"No. We're going in like normal people and we're going to look around without making a fuss."

"No worries. I'll have my gun handy if you need some firepower."

"I won't need firepower, and you don't want to go flashing your gun around in a train station. You're carrying concealed without a permit."

"It's okay," Lula said. "It's like common-law marriage. After a certain amount of time, it gets to be legal, and you don't need the paper. I've been carrying since I was nine years old. That's gotta count for something."

I reached the train station and parked in the parking garage. We hurried inside and looked at the train schedule. The train to New York was running late. It was due in five minutes. Lula and I strolled through the waiting areas, looking for a pudgy guy with a black ponytail.

"He's not in here," I said to Lula. "Let's split up. You stay inside, and I'll go out to the platform."

Lula kept wandering and I went outside. People were

congregating at the designated train stop. Some were sitting on benches, but most were standing, queuing up to get a good seat. I spotted Oswald standing off by himself at the end of the platform. I wasn't sure he would recognize me, but I kept my head down just in case and tried to stay hidden in the crowd. I texted Diesel that I had Oswald in view on the outside platform. I had cuffs in my back pocket and a key chain stun gun in the front pocket of my jeans. I took the stun gun in hand and crept closer to Oswald. I hated to make an apprehension like this. I would be the center of attention, probably the police would be called, and I'd end up on the evening news.

I did a fast check on my ponytail and wished I'd spent more time on my makeup. At least I was wearing a nice shirt with a V-neck. Plus, it was blue, and I knew I looked good in blue. The worst part of the apprehension would be if it didn't go well, and I looked like an idiot. This happened a lot.

I moved next to Oswald and did my bounty hunter thing, so it was all by the book.

"Oswald Wednesday?" I asked.

"Ah," he said. "Stephanie Plum, correct?"

"I represent your bail bondsman and I need you to reschedule your court date."

"I'm thinking you need me for more than that," he said. "You're working with Diesel."

"He has his own issues," I said. "Mine are strictly in connection to your bail bond."

"It's a pity that we have an adversarial relationship. I find you to be attractive in spite of your rather drab clothes. In another time we might have enjoyed a relationship."

"It would be great if you would come with me and we didn't have to make a scene," I said.

"Sorry, that's not going to happen. I have other plans for the day."

Mental sigh. It was never easy. I had the cuffs in one hand and the stun gun in the other. "I'm asking you one more time."

There was an announcement that the train was approaching. I glanced at the track and Oswald used the opportunity to pull a canister of pepper spray out of his pocket and spray me in the face. Instantly I couldn't see, and I was having difficulty breathing.

"Goodbye, Sugar Cookie," Oswald said.

I felt myself get shoved backward and fall off the platform. I landed hard on the tracks, momentarily stunned. My eyes were burning, and I still couldn't see, but I could feel the vibration and the noise of the approaching train. I tried to stand and stumbled. I went down to hands and knees, completely disoriented. I had no thoughts in my head beyond pain and panic.

Hands grabbed me, and I was hauled back onto the platform. People were shouting. The train rumbled in. I could feel the heat rolling off it.

My eyes were swimming in tears, and a massive amount of mucus was pouring out of my nose. I was being held close by someone. Diesel. He had his arms wrapped around me and his voice was in my ear.

"It's okay," he said. "You're okay. I've got you."

I was shaking and struggling to take normal breaths. I got myself under control after a couple of minutes and was able to relax in Diesel's arms.

"Shit," I said, "my nose is running. It's going to be all over your shirt."

He walked me off the platform and into the lobby. I still couldn't see. Blurry images. A big blob of blue that I recognized as being a cop. Diesel sat me down on a bench. Someone handed me tissues. Two EMTs arrived and applied a cold compress to my face and eyes.

Diesel answered everyone's questions.

"I was a short distance away," he said. "I saw a man pepper-spray her and shove her off the platform onto the tracks. I was able to grab her and pull her back onto the platform before the train rolled in. I don't know what happened to the man who sprayed her. Maybe he got on the train."

There were more questions and answers, but I was finding it difficult to focus on them. I had a gash on my arm, just above my elbow, and I had scrapes on both hands and knees. An EMT was cleaning and patching me up, asking if I was in pain.

The compress was removed from my face and a gel was applied. Drops were put in my eyes. I was feeling better. I was asked if I wanted to go to the hospital and I declined.

A large fluffy white thing rushed at me. It was Lula.

"What's going on?" she asked. "What happened? What did I miss?"

"I got pepper sprayed and pushed off the platform," I said.

"That's horrible. That's terrible. What's this world coming to when a woman can't even go about her business," Lula said.

The EMTs were packing up and the cop had gone off in search of Oswald. Diesel got me up on my feet and Diesel and Lula walked me out of the building.

"She can't see well enough to drive her car," he said to Lula. "I'll take her home and you can leave the Focus at the office."

"I hope they catch the guy who pushed you," Lula said to me.

I handed her my car keys. "It was Oswald. He had the pepper spray hidden in his pocket. I got distracted for a nanosecond and he sprayed me. And here I am," I said.

"Damn," Lula said. "That's a whole bitch and a half."

Lula walked off to the parking garage and Diesel led me down a short ramp to a lot where police cars were parked. It was mostly empty. One unmarked car, two squad cars, and Diesel's yellow and black Bronco.

He helped me in, and he slid behind the wheel.

"How do you get to park here without getting towed?" I asked.

"I have diplomat plates on this car."

"I never noticed."

"They're new."

"Should I ask how you happened upon them?"

"No. You've had enough trauma for one day. Let's just say they're mostly legal and leave it at that."

Morelli called. "Are you okay?" he asked.

"I guess you heard about my train episode."

"Six different people called me. One of them was my dentist who had the day off and was waiting for the train to the city."

"I have some scrapes and bruises and I'm waiting for my eyes to clear, but nothing serious. Diesel is driving me home."

"Do you know who pushed you?"

"Oswald."

There was no reason to keep Oswald's role in it secret. Morelli would have access to the security cameras on the platform.

I disconnected with Morelli and Ranger called.

"Babe," Ranger said.

Ranger was my mentor when I was an inexperienced bounty hunter. He's close to my age in years but he's way ahead of me in life experience. He's former special forces, and while he's lost his military standing, he's kept his skills and perfectly toned body. He's six feet of awesome, brown-eyed sexiness. He was working as a bounty hunter when we met and he's since progressed to owning a high-tech, exclusive, under-the-radar security firm. He's my friend and on a few memorable occasions he's been my lover. He's also decided that it's his job to keep me alive, so his monitoring system goes into red alert when my name pops up on police chatter.

"I'm okay," I said. "I was trying to make an apprehension and it didn't go as planned."

"Do you need help with anything?"

"No. Diesel is here and he's driving me home."

"Babe," Ranger said, and he disconnected.

Babe has many meanings in Ranger speak, depending on the inflection. His final Babe wasn't a question like his opening Babe. His final Babe was more of a warning to be careful.

CHAPTER THIRTEEN

Diesel got me into my apartment, and I took stock of myself. There were bloodstains on my shirt and my jeans, and my jeans had been cut off above the knee so the EMT could clean the cinders out of my scrapes.

"I'm a mess," I said. "Good thing I'm still partly blinded, or I'd probably be twice as horrified. That was freaking scary. I thought I was going to get run over by the train. I wasn't able to see enough to get myself off the tracks."

"It could have been a lot worse. The train wasn't that far away when I grabbed you. The engineer must have been in a panic. I'm sure he saw you fly off the platform."

"Oswald was calm. Smiling. Not at all agitated. He said, 'Goodbye, Sugar Cookie' when he pushed me. It was creepy. Do you think he got on the train?"

"Probably not. It would have been too easy to locate him. He would have been trapped."

"I'm surprised no one stopped him."

"There was a large crowd and a lot of confusion." Diesel grinned. "I had to knock a couple people over to get to you."

"Thank you. I appreciate it. I'm going to change into clean clothes, and then I'm going to get something to eat. I'm nauseous from the pepper spray."

"Do you need help with your clothes?"

"No!"

Another grin. "Too bad. I'm good at undressing women."

There was no doubt in my mind.

"Since you don't want help with your clothes, I'll get us takeout lunch," Diesel said.

He returned a half hour later with smoothies.

"No dairy," Diesel said. "Just fruit and vegetables and a protein and mineral supplement."

I took a sip. "It's like a frozen slushie. It's not bad."

"I couldn't see you choking down peanut butter and white bread after getting pepper sprayed."

"This is perfect. Who would have thought you'd turn out to be a sensitive guy?"

"Don't get used to it. It takes too much effort."

"I screwed up. I almost had Oswald."

"He's going back and forth to New York but he's not going to his condo," Diesel said. "And he's not driving. He's leaving his car with the New York plates here."

"Mail," I said. "Maybe he has a PO box in New York. He goes in to check it and then he hops back on the train. Or maybe he's buying drugs. Or getting romanced by a girlfriend. He was wearing a backpack. He probably had his computer in it so he can work on the train."

"Good to see that your brain is operating," Diesel said. "How's your eyesight coming along?"

"Not perfect, but much better."

"Are you okay to be left alone? I have some leads I want to look into."

"Anything really promising?"

"No, but I'll run them down anyway."

"I'm okay. I'm going to take a nap and rest my eyes. I promised Grandma I'd take her to the Stupin viewing tonight."

"I should go to that, too," Diesel said. "It's unlikely that Oswald will show up, but he's psycho, so anything is possible."

———

My car was parked at the bail bonds office, so Grandma and I hitched a ride to the viewing with Diesel. I was wearing navy slacks with flats, a white sleeveless sweater, and a short red jacket, all designed to hide my Band-Aids. Not that it mattered, because pictures of me getting rescued seconds before the train rolled in had already been splashed all over the internet, and a short clip made the six o'clock news.

"How's Mom doing with my latest disaster?" I asked Grandma.

"She's not speaking to your father and she's in the kitchen ironing to calm herself. Melvin is keeping an eye on her. I told him if she irons the same shirt more than fourteen times, he should pull the plug on the iron."

"Melvin didn't want to go to Clark Stupin's viewing?"

"No. He said he's not into stuff like that. He said he already talked to Clark about it, and Clark said he didn't want to go to the viewing, either."

"Good to know he's communicating with Clark," I said. "Did Clark have any inside information about Oswald? Maybe he told Melvin how to crack Oswald's network?"

"Melvin didn't mention anything," Grandma said.

We were fifteen minutes early, but a crowd had already gathered outside the funeral home. Diesel dropped Grandma and me off and went in search of a parking space.

"We have to get up on the porch so when they open the door we can rush in and get a good seat," Grandma said.

I knew the drill. This wasn't my first viewing with Grandma. My mother refused to go with her, so I frequently ended up with the chore. As gratitude I got free laundry services and desserts of my choosing.

I followed Grandma as she pushed her way to the front.

"Excuse me," Grandma said, "old lady coming through. Excuse me, pregnant woman. Excuse me, I got diarrhea."

More often than not, people would see that it was Grandma, roll their eyes, and step aside.

The doors opened and Grandma jumped in and went straight to Slumber Room #1. She put her purse down on a chair in the first row, set me next to it, and got in line to give her condolences. This was the tricky part because I knew she would look for an opportunity to search the casket for the tongue. If security was lax, there was a good chance she'd try to pry the deceased's mouth open for a quick peek. This was where I earned my free laundry and dessert.

It took twenty minutes for Grandma to inch her way up to the casket. She did a very slow pass, scrutinizing the white faux silk interior. She nodded to the stoic parents and studied Clark Stupin's face.

"He looks good," she said to the parents. "You'd never know he didn't have a tongue. Did they put it back where it belongs?"

I jumped up and swept Grandma away before the Stupins could answer. I grabbed her purse and steered her up the nearest aisle to the lobby.

"I need a cookie," I said to Grandma. "Don't you need a cookie?"

"I suppose," Grandma said. "They're going to go fast what with this crowd."

We reached the hostess table, and a ripple of excitement went through the lobby.

"Someone important must have just walked in," Grandma said. "I can't see through all these people. There are some men in K of C regalia here. And I spotted a couple Elks. It might be the big cheese of some lodge."

Marjorie Schneck was standing at the table next to Grandma. "It's the hero," she said. "I just caught a glimpse of him. He's even more rugged and handsome than his pictures. Everyone is talking about him online. He's a total hottie." Marjorie spotted me next to Grandma and leaned in. "What's he like? Do you know him? It must have been amazing to have him rescue you."

The hero broke though the cluster of women who were surrounding him and walked toward us.

"Next time you get pushed off a train platform I'm going to let the train run over you," he said to me. "The hot hero thing is a nightmare. Some woman just grabbed my ass."

"Have a cookie," I told him. "The night is young."

"I didn't see the tongue in the casket," Grandma said to Marjorie. "I thought they might have put it in a little box or something."

"Betty Lukach does hair and makeup for the funeral home, and she said in cases like this they usually stuff it into a convenient cavity like you would for a turkey. Of course, she didn't know about a tongue because that's so unusual. She was talking mostly about fingers and toes."

"Makes sense," Grandma said. "I didn't get a chance to look in any cavities."

Diesel was grinning. "Would she really check out the cavities?"

"In a heartbeat," I said.

Diesel took a couple of cookies and looked around. "I don't see Oswald. I imagine he's gone underground. The police and half the country have seen him on the transit security feed."

Grandma had her big patent leather purse in the crook of her arm, and she was balancing a cup of tea and a small paper plate filled with cookies. Women were swarming around us, and Grandma was getting jostled. Some tea sloshed out of her cup onto her hand, and cookies slid off her paper plate onto the floor.

"What the heck," Grandma said. "What's wrong with these people? It's like they never saw a cookie before."

"It's not the cookies," I said. "It's Diesel."

"Okay, I guess I can understand that," she said. "He's something to look at."

I tugged Grandma away from the hostess table, toward the door. "We should go home and check on Mom and Melvin," I said.

"That's fine with me," she said. "They didn't have any of my favorite cookies anyway."

Diesel followed us out and led us across the street to his Bronco. It was parked on the sidewalk with two red cones in front of the car and two behind it.

"Where did you get the cones?" I asked him.

"They were marking a pothole in front of the hospital. It was well lit. I didn't think they were necessary."

My mother was still ironing when we walked into the kitchen. Melvin was at his computer, making notes in a steno pad.

"You're home early," my mom said.

"It was a bust," Grandma said. "They had the deceased's mouth clamped shut and there was no sign of the tongue. Then it was so crowded you couldn't even see who was there. And if that wasn't enough, I got bumped and spilled my tea and cookies." Grandma filled the teakettle with water and turned it on. "I'm having a cup of tea and some of that leftover applesauce cake." She pulled the cake out of the refrigerator. "There's plenty for everyone, and we got whipped cream for it."

"Sign me up," Melvin said.

"Are you making any progress?" I asked him.

"I was able to access some older emails and messages from Mushy2's computer. I found some embarrassing nude selfies and it looks like there's another local Baked Potato. Mushy2 and Charlie Q. seemed to know each other. Mushy2 sent messages to Charlie Q. through a different messenger app than the group used."

"Oswald was able to track down at least three Baked Potatoes and learn who they were and where they live," I said. "Why can't we?"

"I suspect he traced us through the secure messenger app service we used. At least we thought it was secure," Melvin said. "Pretty impressive. And the Baked Potatoes were so privacy oriented that we never shared our real identities. It turned out to work against us because now I can't warn anyone."

"Can you send a message to Charlie Q. through Mushy2's messenger app?" I asked.

"I already tried. Charlie Q has wiped his account and trail clean. I suspect he heard about Mushy2."

"What do you know about Charlie Q.?"

"Almost nothing except that he's brilliant. It would be a terrible loss if Oswald got to him. I think some of the Baked Potatoes might have been evil. Charlie, Clark, and I were on the fence. If we did something bad it was for a good reason, and we didn't take money for it."

"How did the Baked Potatoes get to be a club?" Grandma asked.

"Shared interests online," Melvin said. "I've been communicating with some of the Baked Potatoes since high school."

"That's nice," Grandma said. "Good for you. It's important to have friends, even if you don't know who they are."

My mom unplugged the iron.

"You still have a shirt left in the ironing basket," Grandma said. "And you only ironed the one on the board seven times."

"I'm out of steam," my mom said. "I'm switching to my new hobby. I've taken up knitting."

"Since when?" Grandma asked.

"Since this afternoon. I got some yarn and needles and a

knitting book. There was a woman on television who said knitting was like yoga for your mind."

"I might try that, too," Grandma said. "I always wanted to take up yoga, but it seemed like a lot of fuss. You have to carry a mat around with you and you have to get into all those awkward positions. All you have to do is move your fingers with this knitting yoga. And I can see where carrying knitting needles in your purse would come in handy. I imagine you could do some damage with a knitting needle. If a man attacks you, you could give him a poke in his one-eyed snake."

Diesel winced and Melvin looked confused.

"Gotta go," I said. "I need to pick my car up at the bail bonds office."

My mom pulled a plastic container from the fridge. "I put some spaghetti aside for you. And there's some grated cheese with it." She put it in a paper grocery bag with half a loaf of Italian bread. "The bread is from the bakery. Fresh today." My mother gave me a kiss and shook her finger at Diesel. "Make sure she gets home safe."

Diesel was back on his heels, smiling. "Yes, ma'am."

"And thank you for not letting her die on the train tracks."

———

Diesel drove to Hamilton Avenue and idled behind my car. "I'm going to follow you home, not only because my motor home is parked in your lot, but because I promised your mother that I'd keep you safe. And honestly, your mother and grandmother can be a little scary."

This was fine by me. I wasn't so liberated that I didn't appreciate a man protecting me from spiders and maniacs. Diesel's headlights in my rearview mirror were comforting. The comfort started to fade when I got closer to my neighborhood and saw an ominous red glow in the direction of my building. I turned onto the side street that led to my parking lot and was relieved to see that my building wasn't on fire. The fire was in the parking lot. Probably the dumpster, I thought. Again. Impossible to see past the fire trucks and EMTs.

I parked on the street, and Diesel and I walked into the lot and stared at the drenched but still smoldering remains of his motor home.

His phone buzzed; he looked at the screen and muttered, "Oswald." He did a fast scan of the area. He went to speakerphone mode and answered.

"Where are you?" he asked. "It's hard to spot you sneaking around in the dark."

"It's quite easy to spot you," Oswald said. "What do you think of my handiwork?"

"It's disappointingly boring. Mundane, actually."

"Perhaps, but I liked the symbolism. Your rescue this morning robbed me of the pleasure of seeing Ms. Plum get turned into train smash. Now I've robbed you of your home away from home."

"It was a rental," Diesel said. "Not enough hot water. Do you have anything else to tell me?"

"Don't underestimate me. I'm having some fun playing with you and Ms. Plum right now, but that will soon end. I'm sure that you and the organization that employs you are aware of the extent of my power. I don't make frivolous threats. When I send a ransom request I'm always capable of carrying out my threat. In this case the threat is significant. You can relay this message to your organization. It's only begun. As Sherlock would say, 'the game is afoot.'"

"Yeah," Diesel said. "Game on."

Diesel hung up and put his phone away. "The guy is seriously sick. He's gone from genius hacker and closet psychopath to complete nut job."

"He sounded serious."

Diesel nodded agreement. "He was right about his threat being significant, but he's still a complete nut job."

"Sorry about your motor home. Did you lose a lot of stuff in there?"

"Nothing that can't be easily replaced. I travel light. My backpack is in the Bronco. Everything I need is in the backpack."

"Where are you going to stay tonight? Can your fixer get you another motor home?"

"Another motor home isn't necessary. I can stay with you."

"Oh no. No, no, no. That won't work."

"It's the obvious solution. You don't have all the creature comforts of the motor home, but I can make do."

"You can't stay in my apartment."

Diesel draped an arm across my shoulders. "Darlin', I *did* save your life. Not that I would ever hold that over your head, but I'm just sayin'."

Crap. Crap, crap, crap, crap, crap.

"Okay, just for tonight," I said, trying to stifle a giant sigh, not being successful.

Diesel called Ana and gave her the high points.

"She'll take care of everything," he said. "Let's get the spaghetti out of your car. I'm hungry."

"Do you think we should try to find Oswald?"

"In the dark?"

"Do you have something better to do?"

"I have a laundry list of things that are better to do. Eat spaghetti is at the top. You probably wouldn't agree to number two so we can skip over that one."

I felt another sigh organizing in my chest.

"I'm having second thoughts about not bringing the feds in to find Oswald," I said. "They have resources that aren't available to us."

"I have resources that are as good, if not better," Diesel said.

"Are you a fed?"

"Sort of. Just not for this country. They don't pay enough. And the perks suck."

"What country do you work for?"

"It's not exactly a country. It's more of a loosely organized entity. I'm thinking about recruiting your grandmother."

We got the spaghetti and Diesel's backpack and retreated to my apartment.

"Do you carry a gun?" I asked Diesel.

"Not usually," he said. "I don't need one."

"How about a knife?"

"I carry a knife. I use it to open beer bottles and shrink-wrapped packages."

I had my laptop on the dining room table. Diesel dropped his backpack on the floor and established himself across from me.

I reheated the spaghetti dinner and set it on the kitchen

counter. We filled our plates and took them into the dining room so we could eat while we were working.

"This is great," Diesel said. "I have a late night ahead of me and I'd be starving at midnight without this spaghetti. This will carry me through."

"Why such a late night?"

"I need to talk to some people who are half a world away and aren't available until after midnight. In the meantime, I need to catch up on world events and I can stream soccer." He mopped some red sauce up with his bread. "And you?"

"Facebook," I said. "And then I'll watch *Dumplin'* for the fifteenth time, or the *Somebody Feed Phil* show. I need a life-affirming experience after the train track incident."

————

I closed my computer at eleven o'clock. Diesel was still at the table, slouched in a straight chair. He was wearing wireless earbuds, surfing around on his computer. He looked up when I stood, and he nodded at me. I did a little finger wave and trudged off to bed.

I didn't approach the subject of where he was going to sleep. I expected to find him naked in my bed when I woke up. I would try to overlook this fact and think of Diesel as a pet. If I had a very large dog, he would sleep on the bed, and he wouldn't wear pajamas. Even if the dog woke up with a woody I wouldn't be offended because this happens sometimes. It's a natural body function. As long as he stayed on his side of the bed it would all be good. And to add an extra degree of security I'd go to bed fully clothed in sweatpants and a sweatshirt. Truth is, I was less afraid that he would try to get friendly with me than I would wake up in a state of hormonal need and attack him. The man was sex walking.

———

I was jolted out of sleep by a clap of what sounded like thunder. I looked at the bedside clock. Four a.m. Diesel was beside me, propped up on one elbow.

"Clever," Diesel said. "I know you're here. What's up?"

A soft light went on at the foot of the bed and I recognized Diesel's cousin, Wulf. His full name is Gerewulf Grimoire and he lives up to the name in a diabolically handsome sort of way. I pulled the covers over my head and inched closer to Diesel.

Diesel looked under the covers at me. "It's just Wulf," he said. "I believe you met a couple years ago."

I peeked out and gave Wulf a little finger wave. "Hi."

Wulf smiled. He was the same size as Diesel, but he appeared slimmer, less Thor Ragnarok, more Dr. Strange. He was dressed in black. Custom-tailored suit. Black dress shirt, open at the neck. And he was wearing a cape. Black on the outside. Blue satin on the inside. He had black hair pulled into a low ponytail.

"Hello, cousin," Wulf said.

Doesn't anyone in this family ever use a doorbell, I thought. Do they have no sense of time or what's inappropriate?

"You've made your entrance," Diesel said. "Now what?"

"Now I wait. Auntie sends her best wishes."

I looked at Diesel. "Auntie?"

"Don't ask," Diesel said.

There was another flash of light and some green smoke and when the smoke cleared Wulf was gone.

"Where'd he go?" I asked.

"Who knows, who cares," Diesel said.

"What's with the green smoke?"

"He's always been the theatrical member of the family. He read *Magic for Dummies* and Harry Potter and decided he was a wizard."

"Can he help us?"

"Hard to say. Wulf does what he wants."

"Obviously 'Auntie' thought he might be useful."

"Wulf is the magician. He makes things disappear. I'm sure he was brought in for the endgame."

"Whenever and whatever that is?"

"Yeah, whenever and whatever that is."

Diesel adjusted his pillow, wrapped his arm around me, and went back to sleep.

I was wide awake. I was living in a Marvel comic book.

CHAPTER FOURTEEN

The sun was shining behind my bedroom curtain. Diesel was asleep next to me. His hair was more tousled than normal, and he had a beard that went a couple days beyond five o'clock shadow. He was adorable and desirable and more trouble than I needed. I slipped out of bed, grabbed some clothes, and locked myself in the bathroom. I stepped into the shower and I was half afraid there would be a crack of thunder, some green smoke, and Wulf would appear. I knew even less about Wulf than I did about Diesel. I knew nothing about Auntie.

I was out of the house a little before eight o'clock. Diesel was still asleep, and Rex was also asleep in his soup can den after a long night of running on his wheel. I'd given Rex fresh water and filled his food bowl before I left. Diesel was on his own.

The parking lot to my building had somewhat returned to

normal. The fire trucks and cop cars were gone. Tenants were
parked in their usual spots. The motor home was in a far corner
of the lot. It was cordoned off with yellow police tape and there
were puddles of sooty water surrounding it. Not much was
left. Some twisted metal structure and the rest was a big lump
of smoky-smelling charred mystery remains. It was sad and
depressing. If it was still here when I returned tonight, I was going
to have to watch double episodes of *Feed Phil* or *Queer Eye in
Japan* to cheer myself up. Lucky me that I had Phil and the Fab
Five in my life. Six men who were a slap in the face to gloom and
doom.

I skipped the bonds office and went straight to my parents'
house. I was having a hard time shaking the trauma of the train
experience. It wasn't so bad that I wanted to hide under my bed.
It was more like a general feeling of foreboding. It was a *what
next?* piece of baggage that I couldn't get rid of. What would
Oswald do next? Who would he target? Hopefully, it wouldn't
be me. Hopefully, I was just a victim of a convenient opportunity.

So, what's the deal with the foreboding? PTSD? Maybe a little,
but mostly I thought it was acknowledgment of too many rescues.
I'd reached the conclusion awhile ago that I must have a guardian
angel. I know this is a crazy idea because I never go to church and
I'm not even sure how I feel about God. You would think that one
thing would go with the other, right? Problem is, there's no other
way to explain the fact that I'm still alive. I've survived a bunch of
life-threatening experiences, and I'm pretty sure someone besides
Ranger is looking out for me. I don't say this out loud because
people look at you funny if you credit an angel. And not to take
anything away from Diesel, but the timing of his rescue smacks

of heavenly intervention. This would make one more mark on the chalkboard of angelic interference. How many marks does a screwup like me get? At some point the angel is going to get fed up with me and move on to a better Catholic. What if it's now? What if the train thing was the last straw?

This was all going through my mind as I parked in my parents' driveway and went into the house. Once in the house the foreboding was pushed aside by the smell of bacon and pancakes.

"Pull up a chair," Grandma said to me. "Melvin wanted pancakes this morning."

I got coffee, snitched a piece of bacon, and sat at the table. My mom brought a stack of pancakes and bacon and we all dug in.

"This is real maple syrup," Grandma said to Melvin. "We don't fool around with the fake stuff."

"How's it going?" I asked Melvin.

"I penetrated his network this morning," Melvin said. "I'm downloading now. I'm not sure what I'm going to get. I've gotten this far before and then it suddenly cut off. He has some kind of a fail-safe system that I haven't figured out."

"Melvin hasn't got any clothes here," my mom said. "If he's going to continue to stay, he needs clothes."

"Maybe I should go home," Melvin said.

"Not while you're making progress hacking Oswald," I said. "And not while he's still out there."

"Besides, we're having meat loaf tonight," Grandma said. "You don't want to miss that."

"I'll get clothes for you," I said. "Is there anything else you want from your loft?"

"No. I've mostly got what I need," Melvin said.

I took Melvin's key and went to the office.

"I smell bacon on you," Lula said when I walked in. "I bet you had breakfast at your mama's house."

"I wanted to check on Melvin."

"How's he doing?"

"He's good, but he needs clothes," I said.

I was trying not to stare at Lula's hair. It was a strange shade of blond with undertones of green and it was puffed up into a teased bouffant.

"So, what do you think?" Lula said. "I tried a new salon."

"It's not suburban soccer mom," I said.

"Yeah, but what *is* it?" Lula asked.

"It's 1970 double-wide," Connie said. "It's *Hairspray*."

"I guess I could live with that," Lula said. "It's just a hard color to coordinate with. For instance, I couldn't do pastels with this, but then I don't own any pastels so it's all good."

"I got two new FTAs in this morning," Connie said. "One of them is Mary Jane Merkle. She had an accelerated court date, and she didn't show."

"That's the bakery shooter, right?" Lula asked.

"She's in the Burg and she probably just forgot the date," Connie said. "It's a low bond, but it shouldn't be a lot of effort."

I took the two files and shoved them into my messenger bag.

"I heard the viewing was packed to overflowing last night," Connie said. "Everyone is talking about Diesel. He's being called Hero Hottie."

"They got that right," Lula said.

And I wore sweatpants to bed and left before he even woke up. Mental head slap. He was so tempting and so wrong.

"I'm going to Melvin's loft first," I said to Lula. "Are you on board?"

"Hell yeah. I'm ready to rock. I hope we come across that Oswald guy. I'd like to punch him in the face and stomp on him."

"Okay, that might be fun but what we really want to do it get him in cuffs without leaving bruises or drawing blood."

"Sure," Lula said. "I get that."

———

There were two pickup trucks and four cars parked in the lot in front of Deacon Plumbing. Lights were on inside and I could see people wandering around. Deacon was open for business. A young woman walked out and got into one of the cars. She backed out of her space and drove around the building toward the loading dock.

"I bet she's going to pick up a refrigerator," Lula said.

"She's driving a Kia," I said. "It would have to be a very small refrigerator."

I followed the Kia and stopped at the edge of the loading dock apron where several cars were parked.

"This looks like employee parking," Lula said. "These look like plumbers' cars."

"I'm hanging here until I see what's up with the Kia."

"She's parking by Melvin's front door," Lula said. "Did Melvin mention having a girlfriend? She looks to be about his age."

"He didn't say anything about a girlfriend."

"We for sure know he doesn't have someone coming in to clean."

The woman got out of her car, went to the door, and knocked. She waited a couple of beats and knocked again.

"This is the first time she's been here," I said. "She went into the store to ask about Melvin just like we did."

The woman turned from the door and looked around. She didn't seem to notice us or maybe she didn't care. Two women sitting in employee parking didn't interest her. She hammered on Melvin's door one last time and left when there was no answer.

"What do you make of this?" Lula asked. "Do you think Oswald could have sent her? She doesn't look like a killer. She looks like someone who's fashion challenged. Her clothes are too big for her, and she has her hair pulled back in a braid that's messy."

I followed her out of the parking lot and onto the highway. I kept a decent distance back and eventually she took the turnoff to Quaker Bridge Mall.

"Go, girl," Lula said. "Makeover time. I'm thinking she needs to start with undergarments."

She parked near the Macy's entrance, and I was able to snap a photo of her when she got out of the Kia. Lula and I followed her into the mall, to the food court. She bought a coffee, took it to a small table, and pulled her laptop out of her tote bag.

"She's here to use the Wi-Fi," I said to Lula.

"That's a bummer," Lula said. "I thought we were going to see some self-improvement. Do you know what this food court needs? Mac and cheese. Somebody could clean up if they opened a place that sold mac and cheese."

I watched the woman for a long moment trying to decide if I wanted to approach her. She was intent on whatever she had on the screen. Her coffee was sitting untouched, getting cold.

An older man walked close to her table on his way to the public restroom and she automatically shielded her work.

"Something going on there," Lula said.

I called Connie and gave her the plate on the Kia. "See what you can find," I said to Connie. "Sooner would be better than later."

I got a soda and Lula got two chili dogs and a large curly fries. Lula was finishing up her fries when Connie called me.

"Charlotte Huck," Connie said. "Twenty-five years old. Self-employed MIT graduate. Single. No derog. No litigation. Good credit. Graduated Trenton High School. Parents are divorced. No siblings. I'll text her address to you."

Huck abruptly slipped her laptop into her tote, stood, and power walked out of the food court. Lula and I scrambled to keep up with her.

"She's leaving," Lula said. "What are we going to do? Do you want me to take her down?"

"No. I want to see where she goes."

We followed her to her car and back to the highway. She drove toward the center of the city, and I lost her at a traffic light on State Street.

"We should have taken her down when we could," Lula said. "Now we lost her."

"We had no reason to take her down," I said. "I know who she is, and I know where she lives. That's enough for now. I want to show her photo to Melvin. She's probably just a friend."

"So now what?"

"Now we go back to Deacon Plumbing and get clothes for Melvin."

I parked in the employee area so my car wouldn't be conspicuous.

It was possible that Oswald was returning periodically, hoping to catch Melvin at home or to get at hint at his hiding place. Seeing a car parked by Melvin's front door might encourage Oswald to break in with the hopes of tongue removal. In Melvin's absence, Oswald might be temporarily satisfied to mutilate *me*.

The loft looked untouched since my last visit. One of the laundry baskets seemed to be filled with clean clothes. Underwear, socks, T-shirts, jeans, pajamas, and sweatpants. I grabbed a sweatshirt and a pair of sneakers off the floor and added them to the basket.

"Do you see anything else that you think Melvin might need?" I asked Lula.

"It looks like he sleeps with a teddy bear," she said.

I put the bear in the basket, carted the basket down the stairs, locked the front door, and stowed the basket in the Focus.

"If we take the basket to Melvin now, we could have the added advantage of lunch at your mama's house," Lula said.

That worked for me. I wanted to ask Melvin about Charlotte Huck and show him her picture. And when we were done with lunch, we would be practically next door to Mary Jane Merkle.

———

I set the laundry basket on the floor beside Melvin and took the seat across from him at the dining room table.

"There was a woman at your front door today," I said. "She knocked several times and left when no one answered."

"A woman? What kind of woman?"

"Your age."

"I've never had a woman visit me," Melvin said. "Was she pretty?"

"Yes. In a natural kind of way." I showed him the picture on my phone. "Do you know her?"

"She looks familiar, but I don't think I know her. Maybe I've seen her around."

"Her name is Charlotte Huck."

He shook his head. "Nope. What did she want?"

"I don't know. I didn't get to talk to her."

"She has nice hair," Melvin said. "It looks silky."

Beauty is in the eye of the beholder, I thought. And her hair did indeed look silky.

"How's the hack going?" I asked him.

"Not so good. Turned out to be a red herring. I only had access to a bunch of fake files and directories. Every other directory was named *idiot* or *loser* and all of the files just say 'retribution' over and over. They looked legit at first. Some of them gave me bogus financial information. Cryptocurrency accounts. If the information was real and we were inclined, we could make millions, maybe billions, in blackmail."

"Are you inclined?"

"No," Melvin said. "I wouldn't know what to do with the money. I have almost everything I need."

"What are you lacking?" I asked.

"A girlfriend," he said. "I'm not good with girls. I like them but I never know what to say. And I might like to have a cat someday."

"We brought your teddy bear," Lula said.

"Mr. Bumbum!" Melvin said. "He's my best friend. I tell him everything."

Grandma set a platter of sandwiches on the table. "We got egg salad, ham and cheese, roast beef with horseradish, and chicken salad," she said.

My mom set plates and napkins out. "Help yourself," she said. "We have more in the kitchen."

I took an egg salad sandwich and Morelli called.

"I got three hits on my query about murders involving tongue mutilation," he said. "A nineteen-year-old male in North Dakota, a thirty-two-year-old male in Connecticut, and a thirty-six-year-old male in North Carolina. In each case computer equipment was missing and the crime was written off as a homicide committed during a burglary."

"Wow."

"Yeah," Morelli said. "That was my reaction, too. How's it going on your end?"

"Nothing I can talk about right now, but it's good."

"Understood."

"What about you?" I asked Morelli. "Are you making any progress with Stupin and the other hacker?"

"Gerard Gouge," Morelli said. "Nothing I can talk about right now, but it's going sucky."

"Understood," I said.

I finished my sandwich and took my plate to the kitchen. My mom was at the table, knitting.

"That looks great," I said. "What are you making?"

"A scarf," she said. "I started it last night."

"She's been working on it all morning," Grandma said. "At this rate we're going to have to go out and get more yarn."

"I have to get back to work," I said. "If you go shopping for yarn, leave Melvin at home. I don't want him seen out of the house."

CHAPTER FIFTEEN

Mary Jane Merkle lived in a small two-story house positioned on a small lot in the middle of the block. The house was bookended by two driveways that led to single-car garages. One of those garages belonged to Mary Jane. I parked in front of her house, and Lula and I went to the door. I rang the bell and Mary Jane answered on the fourth ring. She looked more like her booking photo than Mary Jane the prom queen I remembered from high school.

She had a baby strapped to her chest and I could see two toddlers watching television in the living room. The volume on the television was deafening.

Mary Jane rotated her head and yelled over the television. "Benjamin Ryan Merkle! Turn the sound down or I'm taking the remote away. And stop eating those biscuits. They're for the dog." She turned back to Lula and me. "Omigod, Stephanie Plum?"

"Mary Jane? Holy cow, how many kids do you have?"

"Four. Dillon James is in first grade. Benjamin Ryan is four, Ethan Dale is two, and Samantha Louise on my chest is four months." Mary Jane took a step back. "You have to come in the house. If the door stays open the dog will run out."

I closed the door and a fat Chihuahua waddled in from the kitchen. It stopped inches from Lula and growled.

"I got a way with animals," Lula said.

"Lula and I work for Vinnie," I said to Mary Jane. "He wrote your bail bond when you got arrested for the bakery thing."

Mary Jane looked like she was drawing a blank.

"You know," Lula said. "When you shot up the bakery case with the cannoli and the éclairs. What the heck were you thinking? Why didn't you just shoot up a loaf of bread?"

"I needed an éclair, and the bakery was closed," Mary Jane said. "It wasn't supposed to be closed. They closed early."

"I didn't know that," Lula said. "That might make a difference."

Mary Jane rocked back and forth with the baby. "I gave up smoking and drinking and coffee to have this baby. And now I'm breastfeeding so I'm still off smoking, drinking, and coffee. Do you know what's left? An éclair. All I wanted was a stinking éclair. My mother-in-law came over to babysit, so I could go to my ob-gyn appointment, and after my appointment I had ten minutes left to go to the bakery and get an éclair."

"And the bakery closed early," Lula said.

"Exactly," Mary Jane said.

"That's outrageous," Lula said. "They had no business doing

that. Still, I had to eat a bagel on account of you shot up the éclairs and the custard-filled doughnuts."

"I was able to get the front door open, but when I got inside, the refrigerator case with the éclairs was locked. *Locked!* I mean it was the last straw. What the Hellman's Mayonnaise do I have to do to get an éclair?"

"You could have just stolen some cookies," Lula said. "Nobody would have minded. They're usually stale anyway."

"I wanted an *éclair*," Mary Jane said. "I *needed an éclair*. I totally freaked when I couldn't get in the case. I found a gun behind the counter and I just started shooting."

"You had bakery rage," Lula said.

"Yes!" Mary Jane said. "Bakery rage!"

"I hear what you're saying," Lula said. "I get rage at the drive-thru when they short me on the fries. That's why I don't go to the drive-thru anymore. You always get forked at the drive-thru."

A tear rolled down Mary Jane's cheek. "I've got too many hormones. I'm a mess. It's not easy having a baby and I've pushed out four of them."

"I never pushed out a baby," Lula said. "I had hemorrhoids once and that wasn't a treat."

"And look at my hair. Look at my nails," Mary Jane said. "I haven't had a salon appointment since before the baby was born. My breasts leak milk when I walk past the baby food section in the supermarket. A woman shouldn't be expected to be rational in this condition."

"The thing is, you missed your court date," I said to Mary Jane. "We have to take you downtown so you can reschedule."

"Okay," Mary Jane said. "When?"

"Now?"

"Are they going to take my picture again? Can you do it without me?"

"No and no," I said.

"I don't have a babysitter."

"Lula can babysit," I said.

"Say what?" Lula said.

"I'll call Connie. We can pick her up on the way and immediately get you bonded out again."

"I guess that would be okay," Mary Jane said, "as long as I can take the baby. She's due for a feeding."

Connie had the office locked and was waiting at the curb when I drove up in Mary Jane's minivan. We went straight to the court and a half hour later we were back on the road to rescue Lula. I stopped for a light in town and spotted someone who looked like Oswald a block away. He'd cut his hair, but I was pretty sure it was him. Under any other circumstances I would have gone after him, but the baby was fussing in its car seat and Mary Jane was on the phone with Lula explaining how to change Ethan Dale's diaper.

"Make sure he's clean," Mary Jane said. "Use the baby wipes, and if he's irritated you can put some baby butt salve on him."

I called Diesel and gave him the news. "I think Oswald is still in Trenton," I said. "I just saw someone who looked like him. He was walking down State Street, a block from South Broad. The guy I saw had short hair, but he still resembled Oswald."

"I'm on my way," Diesel said. "I talked to Melvin right after you left. He's trying to hack in again, and he gave me what he downloaded just in case there is something legit in it."

"Morelli got bad news on his national inquiry. Three more victims. Same MO. All out of state."

"Three problems off our desk," Diesel said. "Catch you later."

———

Ethan Dale and Benjamin Ryan were watching television when we walked into Mary Jane's house. Lula was wearing rubber gloves, and she had Lucky Charms stuck in her hair. Considering her latest color and style, I thought the Lucky Charms were an okay addition.

"I'm understanding why you shot up the bakery," Lula said to Mary Jane. "You had every right to do that. I've never seen anything like what was in that diaper. It smelled terrible. It was a smell I'm never gonna be able to forget. I'm gonna have nightmares."

"You get used to it," Mary Jane said.

"Nuh ah, honey. Not me. If I have a baby, it's not getting born until it's at least ten years old."

Lula stripped off her rubber gloves and handed them over to Mary Jane and we headed for the door.

"Your new court date is Friday," I said to Mary Jane. "Connie will call to remind you."

We got into my car and Lula powered her window down. "I need air," she said. "I need aromatherapy. I swear to God, I looked for a hazmat suit, but I couldn't find one."

"It looks like you gave them a snack."

"Cereal and gummy bears. They got into an argument over who had more. The two-year-old threw some at his brother and then the big kid threw some at the little kid and then the little kid pooped his pants and that was the end of it."

I didn't have any of those problems with a hamster. My life was almost perfect.

"I think I saw Oswald in town when I was on the way back from the courthouse. I couldn't stop but I thought we could go back and look around."

"Sounds like a plan," Lula said. "And I'm glad you didn't stop because if I had to last much longer, I might have felt like shooting up a bakery. Except I wouldn't take out the éclairs. That's the thing about rage. You gotta have selective rage. You don't shoot things that are valuable like people and éclairs. If you gotta shoot up something, you go for the gluten- and dairy-free zucchini bread. Vegans always give you a pass."

"Something to remember."

"You bet your ass."

I drove out of the Burg, crossed the railroad tracks, and took South Broad to State Street. Two blocks in I saw Oswald exit an office building and turn left. I got as close to him as possible, pulled to the curb, and parked in a no-parking zone. Lula and I jumped out of my car and ran for Oswald.

Lula was clattering down the sidewalk in her five-inch heels, waving her gun and shouting, "Stop, or I'll shoot" to Oswald. Oswald looked over his shoulder at us and took off.

"No shooting," I yelled at Lula.

"Don't worry," she yelled back, "I got him in my sights."

Oswald turned down a side street and we ran after him. He was surprisingly fast for a pudgy little guy. Lula sounded like a steam engine with asthma, chugging beside me.

"Damn," she gasped, "the son of a bagel can run."

I wasn't gaining on Oswald, but I wasn't dropping behind,

either. He entered a building and took the stairs. One floor, two floors, three floors. My lungs were burning, and my legs were failing me. Lula was still on the street. Oswald took a door and disappeared. I was cautious at the door. I didn't know if he was armed. I opened the door and jumped to the side. No one shot at me so I peeked out. The door opened to a hallway and an elevator. No Oswald in sight. I carefully walked into the hall and looked at the elevator. It was going down.

I called Lula to tell her to monitor the elevator. No answer. I went back to the stairs and ran down. I got to the first floor and heard gunshots below me. I had an adrenaline surge that had my heart rate at stroke level. I burst out of the door at ground level and almost knocked Lula over.

"What happened?" I asked Lula. "I heard gunshots."

"I was standing here catching my breath and next thing he came out of the elevator. I had my gun in my hand and I said, 'Stop, or I'll shoot.' He did one of those kung fu moves you see on television and knocked me on my ass. I fired off a couple shots, but he got away."

This wasn't a surprise to me. I've seen Lula fire point-blank at a target and miss it. Lula was the worst shot ever.

We walked back to the car, keeping watch for Oswald. We didn't see Oswald and when we got to the car it had a police boot on the left front tire and a ticket on the windshield.

"What the heck?" Lula said. "The police truck must have been sitting around the corner waiting for someone to park here."

I called Morelli and told him about Oswald and the parking problem.

"I'll see what I can do," Morelli said. "Stay with your car."

An hour later, the boot got removed but the ticket stayed on my windshield. I didn't see Diesel cruising around. I didn't see Oswald waltz by. And Lula had already taken an Uber back to the office. It was after five o'clock when I drove into my apartment building's parking lot. The remains of the motor home had been removed and the blacktop had been swept clean. I bypassed the stairs and took the elevator to my apartment.

Diesel was in the kitchen pulling containers out of a grocery tote bag. Green salad, steak fries, cheeseburgers, seven-layer carrot cake with cream cheese frosting. "Ana brought us dinner," he said. "I told her I was in a burger mood."

"I've never met her, but I love her," I said.

I went into the dining room to dump my messenger bag by my seat at the table and looked into the living room. My furniture was gone and in its place was a new overstuffed, arctic gray couch in a soft chenille fabric, two matching swivel chairs, a new iron and glass coffee table, and a large flat-screen television.

"Excuse me," I said to Diesel.

"What?"

"The furniture."

"Ana got it. I told her I needed a television and she sort of ran with it."

"What was wrong with my television?"

"It was fuzzy and there's a game I want to watch tonight."

"This is why you can't stay here," I said. "You have no boundaries. You come in and take over."

"Do you want your stuff back?"

I gave up a sigh and acknowledged that I was doing way too

much sighing. The sighing was getting old. "No," I said. "I don't want my stuff back. Thank you."

"Problem solved," Diesel said.

How could I possibly want my stuff back? My stuff was old and horrible.

I returned to the kitchen, filled a plate with food, and took it to the table. "Did you have any luck finding Oswald today?"

"No," Diesel said. "I cruised around for about an hour and gave up. I needed to go back to the apartment to do some computer work."

"I never pictured you as a computer guy."

"It's hard to avoid it. How do you picture me?"

"Beach bum."

"That's the guy I *want* to be. How was your day?"

"After I got my FTA rebonded, Lula and I went into town to look for Oswald. I saw him come out of an office building and I chased him and lost him."

"I've never been instructed to apprehend him before," Diesel said, "but he's been a bad actor in other projects where I've been involved. He's unpredictable because everything is a game to him. He doesn't always do what's expected or logical. He's like a cat that enjoys playing with a mouse before eating it. I'm sure he loved having you chase him just like he got off on our car chase three days ago."

I finished eating and opened my laptop. First up was an email from Grandma.

You made local news, she wrote. *There was an article on the viewing last night and the size of the crowd. They had a picture of the mob scene in the lobby and you're right up front. It's a real nice picture of you. I read the paper online, and I took a screen shot for you. I attached it to the bottom here.*

I looked at the picture, and what caught my attention more than the photo of me was the woman standing a couple people behind me. She was just a face in the crowd, but I was almost certain it was the woman I'd seen at Melvin's door, Charlotte Huck.

"This is interesting," I said to Diesel. "Grandma sent me a photo that was taken at Clark Stupin's viewing. I'm almost positive that this woman in the photo was at Melvin's door this morning. Lula and I went to Melvin's loft to get him fresh clothes and we saw her knocking on his door. When he didn't answer, she left. I took her picture and when I showed it to Melvin, he said that he didn't recognize her."

"Maybe she was a hooker and Melvin didn't want you to know. Maybe she was selling Girl Scout cookies."

"Maybe she was sent by Oswald," I said. "He likes pretty women and she's kind of pretty. They could be a couple."

"Do you have a name? An address?"

"I have both."

"Let's go for a ride," Diesel said.

Charlotte Huck lived on a quiet side street in downtown Trenton. There were two blocks of narrow two-story attached town homes and they all looked the same. Her house was in the middle of the block.

"This is it," I said, "108 Spruce Street."

"I don't see a Porsche parked anywhere on the street," Diesel said.

"She drives a Kia, and I don't see it here, either."

Diesel drove to the end of the street and turned the corner. A one-lane alley divided the block of town homes. He took the alley and counted off houses. He stopped at the fifth house.

"This is the back of her house," he said.

There were no garages, but cars were parked in pull-off areas behind all the houses. No Porsche or Kia in sight. Diesel parked two houses down and we walked back to Charlotte Huck's house. No lights were on. No sign of activity. Diesel knocked on the back door. No answer. He carefully opened the door. We stepped inside and looked around.

"Bail bonds enforcement," I said, just to make things legal.

"The air smells stale," Diesel said. "I think this place has been closed up for at least a week. No mess in the kitchen." He opened the refrigerator. "Not a lot in here."

We walked through the house, looking in closets and dresser drawers. Everything was neat and organized. Clothes were minimal. Mostly casual, leaning to oversize cotton. All clothes were female.

An upstairs bedroom had been made into an office. Desk, chair, printer. No computer.

"She's not out of town," I said. "She was at a viewing last night."

"She's staying with someone," Diesel said, "but after looking in her closet and going through her drawers, I find it hard to believe she's with Oswald. I can't see him doing someone who wears granny panties. My guess is she's staying with a less demanding boyfriend or girlfriend."

"Why was she knocking on Melvin's door?"

"I don't know the answer to that."

"And why was she at Stupin's viewing? I think there's a connection. Charlotte Huck, Melvin Schwartz, and Clark Stupin. They're local. They're all around the same age and they all went to Trenton High."

"Maybe she was Stupin's girlfriend," Diesel said.

"Melvin would have recognized her. Suppose she's the fourth Baked Potato?"

"Then she's smart to be hiding."

Diesel locked Charlotte's back door and we walked to the Bronco.

"Now what?" Diesel asked.

"Carrot cake," I said.

"Works for me."

"When is your game on?" I asked him.

"It starts at three o'clock."

"Tomorrow?"

"Three in the morning. New Zealand is playing Argentina."

"I get that game?"

"You do now," Diesel said.

"Have you heard any more from Wulf?"

"No, but I got a call from Auntie. Oswald is still creating havoc within the organization, overriding security systems and shutting down energy sources, projecting doomsday videos on monitor screens."

"Why is he doing this? Has he made ransom demands?"

"No ransom demands yet. It appears to be a show of force leading up to something serious."

"The something 'big.' "

"Yeah. The details are on a need-to-know basis," Diesel said, "and I don't need to know. Oswald hacked in about four weeks ago and the worst was expected, but it's turned into a show of gamesmanship. Not sure why he's charting this course, but it's given us time to track him down. Maybe that's part of the thrill for him. Maybe he enjoys increasing his own personal danger."

"Or maybe the Baked Potatoes hacked Oswald and screwed something up?"

"The timing fits," Diesel said.

CHAPTER SIXTEEN

I woke up feeling energized. I was sure Charlotte Huck was a piece of the puzzle. And I had a strong suspicion that she was a Baked Potato. She had a degree from MIT. She was hiding out somewhere with her computer and she had an interest in Melvin and Clark.

I was enjoying leftover carrot cake for breakfast when Diesel walked into the kitchen. He was barefoot and tousled, wearing jeans that were sitting low on his hips. I suspected he was commando under the jeans. I was making an effort to look him in the eye, but the temptation to stare at the perfect ripped part of him between navel and denim waistband was undeniable.

"Carrot cake for breakfast is going to go straight to your hips," Diesel said. "Of course, that's only conjecture since I never get to see your hips."

"Did your team win?"

"Yeah, they always win."

"Do you have plans for the day?" I asked him.

"No. I thought I'd sleep for most of it. How about you?"

"I have plans but they're vague."

"Let me know if they involve me."

I finished my cake and went out to the parking lot. Diesel's Ducati and Bronco were parked side by side at the edge of the lot. The Ducati looked like it had been run over by a steamroller. It was squashed flat, and a note had been pinned to it. The message on the note was "*hahahahahahaha! O.W.*"

Bad Stephanie wanted to laugh along with the note. I told myself that would be inappropriate and quickly walked to my car. I debated telling Diesel but decided there was no reason to ruin his morning. He'd find out soon enough.

I drove to my parents' house, and I could smell the coffee brewing the instant I opened the front door.

My mom was knitting at the little kitchen table and Grandma was setting out pastries on a platter. Melvin was working at the dining table.

"We got a new coffeemaker," Grandma said. "It can do all kinds of fancy things except we don't know how to do them, but the coffee is real good. It's got something called crema on top of it. It's like being in Italy where they have all those special coffee shops. I know about it because I watch the travel channel. I like the ones on Italy, and I like the one with Stanley Tucci. He's hot."

The pastries looked tempting, but I'd just had carrot cake, so I bypassed them and got a cup of coffee with crema.

"The scarf looks like it's coming along," I said to my mother.

"I don't know why I didn't take this up sooner," she said. "It's so satisfying."

"It's nuts," Grandma said. "All you do is knit all day. You got a scarf that's seven feet long."

"I'm perfecting my stitch," my mom said.

I took my coffee into the dining room. "How's it going?" I asked Melvin.

"Okay, I guess," he said. "I'm making progress and I think I've figured out some of O.W.'s tricks. If the fake files are any indication of what's in the real files, I'm kind of sorry I can't do something with the downloads when I get them. But that's not the deal."

"What deal is that?"

"The deal with Diesel and then I have a deal with the police guy, Morelli."

"Morelli talked to you?"

"Yeah. He's okay. He has a job to do. I get it. And he's been good to me and not turned this over to the feds. Except I'm sure at some point the feds and who-knows-what will be involved."

"Why do you think Oswald is killing Baked Potatoes?"

Melvin shrugged. "Crazy? A show of strength? Pissed off at being hacked?"

"Is it possible the group saw something they shouldn't have during the initial hack?"

"I guess it's possible O.W. thinks we did, but I didn't see anything."

I broke down and ate a cheese Danish.

"Remember I showed you a picture of Charlotte Huck yesterday?"

"Yeah."

"She was at Clark's viewing. She's around your age and she went to Trenton High School. Are you sure you don't remember her?"

"I didn't know a lot of girls. Clark and I mostly hung together and looked at girls, but we didn't get to talk to them."

"Is Clark still talking to you from the great beyond?"

"No, he checked out. I guess he's talking to someone else."

"You must miss him."

"Yeah. Clark was cool. He was a good friend. It's lonely without him."

"Maybe you need to spend some time with your family."

"I've been thinking about that, but I'd have to do a lot of changing. I don't fit into their adult son image. And the thing is, I'm comfortable with myself the way I am right now. My life was okay until O.W. decided he had to kill me."

I left Melvin and drove to the office. Connie was at her desk, and Lula was pacing in front of the big plate glass storefront window. Lula's hair was still retro seventies, but it had chunks taken out of it at random places.

"How's your life?" Lula asked.

"It's good," I said.

"Mine's crap," Lula said. "I've totally lost my mojo. Something happened in the universe, like an asteroid passed too close and sucked out my mojo, and I'm pretty sure it got transferred over to you. Now you've got my mojo, and I'm a walking disaster waiting to happen. Just think about it. Who had the bat get stuck in her hair? Me. Who got their purse snatched and ended up in a dumpster? Me. I was the one who did an overnight with Melvin Stupin. I was the one who got hosed down by the mooner. I was the one who had to babysit the toxic pooper. I'm the one in hair hell. And it keeps getting worse. Those things always happen to you, you see what I'm saying? They're supposed to happen to *you* and not to *me*. It's all topsy-turvy. You're even the one with a hottie sleeping at your house."

"She has a point," Connie said.

"I've got to get to the bottom of this," Lula said. "I made an appointment to have my stars read. There's some kind of voodoo bull-dookie going on."

"I have my own problems," I said. "I want to find Charlotte Huck."

"Why is she important?" Lula asked.

"I think she's connected to Melvin and Clark. And since I have no clue where to look for Oswald beyond *downtown*, I'm going to search for Charlotte Huck."

"Did you try her home address?" Connie asked.

"Yes. I went through the house, and it looked deserted."

"We could take another look," Lula said. "You never know when people decide to go home. I'm meeting my astrologer this afternoon, but I haven't got anything better to do this morning."

I drove into the downtown area, turned onto Spruce Street, and found #108. I recognized a plainclothes cop car parked next door. I could see motion beyond the sheers on the downstairs front windows.

"Hunh," Lula said. "Somebody must have a problem. Or else Officer Woody is doing an early nooner."

I parked across the street, and we sat in the car and watched both houses. Nothing was happening. Lula checked her email on her phone, and I kept watching.

"How long are we going to wait here?" Lula asked. "Are we going to bust into her house or what?"

"I'm reluctant to bust into her house when I think there's a cop next door."

"Here we go," Lula said. "The front door just opened."

A man stepped out with a dog on a leash. He closed the door, and the man and the dog went to the sidewalk and turned left.

"That's a cop if I ever saw one," Lula said. "And he's taking his dog for a walk."

"Oh boy," I said. "Hold on."

I snatched Oswald's file out of my bag and thumbed through it. I found the police report and my heart did a little jump when I read that Oswald Wednesday had been apprehended by an officer in residence at 106 Spruce Street. I felt like my whole body was smiling.

"Oswald got caught breaking into 106 Spruce Street," I said to Lula. "He had the wrong house. He was looking for Charlotte Huck next door. He even said he was in the wrong house."

"How could he do that if he's supposed to be so smart?"

"All these houses look alike. And in the dark, it would be easy to misread 108 for 106. I think it's possible that Charlotte Huck is Charley Q, the fourth Trenton Baked Potato."

"I could see that," Lula said. "She looks like the lady version of Melvin. Can we bust into her house now?"

"It's not necessary. I know she's not there. I want to go back to my parents' house and talk to Melvin."

"Yeah, but it's too early for lunch."

"I'm sure there will be leftover pastries from breakfast."

"I guess I could settle for that," Lula said.

Melvin was gaming on his computer when we walked in.

"Whoa," Lula said. "Is that Fortnite you're playing? Dude, you've got a setup. What kind of keyboard is that?"

Melvin shut down and took his headset off. "It's a Corsair K95 RGB Platinum. And I go with a Hyper X Cloud Alpha headset. The headset is a little old school, but in my opinion it's still the best."

"Not having any luck getting back into Oswald's network?" I asked him.

"I need to reset my head," Melvin said. "I switched to Fortnite to energize."

I moved to the kitchen, where my mom was still knitting and Grandma was at the table, watching her.

"Melvin's playing Fortnite," I said to Grandma. "I'm surprised you aren't in there with him."

"I can't keep up with him," Grandma said. "I got a ladies' group I play with when there's no bingo. We're ruthless but some of us have a touch of arthritis, so our fingers don't move so fast."

Lula peeked into the bakery box on the counter. "Looks like you got a bunch of leftovers in here," she said.

"Help yourself," my mom said. "Would you like coffee or tea?"

"One or two of these pastries will be enough, thanks," Lula said.

"What are you girls up to?" Grandma asked. "Anything exciting going on?"

"I couldn't stop thinking about Charlotte Huck," I said, "so Lula and I went to check out her house. It turns out she lives next door to the house Oswald broke into. We saw the cop leave to walk his dog and I figured it out. At the time, Oswald said it was all a mistake, that he was in the wrong house. No one believed him and he was charged with breaking and entering and assaulting a police officer. I think he was telling the truth. I think Oswald was looking for Charlotte Huck. It's possible that Charlotte Huck is Charley Q."

Grandma sucked in some air. "You think Charley Q is a girl?"

I pulled her credit report and photo out of my bag. "I don't have much on her," I said. "She probably wipes her profile."

Grandma looked over at the photo. "That's Jean Barkolowski's girl."

It took a couple of beats for my brain to catch up to what I just heard. "Do you know her?" I asked Grandma.

"She worked at the dry cleaner for a while when she was in high school and summers when she was home from college. She was always polite when I stopped at the dry cleaner. And she's smart. She went to MIT. Jean's real proud of her."

"Where does Jean live?"

"She's on Garret Street, behind the church. She got the house after the divorce. That was a bunch of years ago. She's remarried now. She married Harry Barkolowski. I think he taught you algebra."

"I hated him!"

"Isn't this something," Grandma said. "You never know about people. Are you going to tell Melvin?"

"Not yet," I said. "I want to find Charlotte first and make sure I'm right."

I looked at my mom. "Is that still a scarf? It looks long."

"We measured it a half hour ago," Grandma said. "It was eleven feet."

"That's a lot of scarf," I said.

"It might not be a scarf," my mom said. "It might just be a *thing*. If it's a thing it's more relaxing. I don't have to worry about making a mistake. I can add a couple stitches or take away a couple stitches and it doesn't matter. And if I run out of yarn, I can tie a knot in the end and keep going with any color I want. It doesn't have to match."

"That's genius, Mrs. P.," Lula said. "That's profound. I think you hit on something. Craft projects that have no use and are endless. Somebody could clean up on that idea. We could take it to QVC. I could sell the heck out of that idea."

"In the meantime, I'm going to pay a visit on Charlotte's mother," I said.

"You can't miss the house," Grandma said. "She painted it lime green and ran out of paint, so some of it is tan."

Lula followed me out and we went in search of the green and tan house.

"It doesn't look too bad," Lula said when we found it. "It's more interesting like this and the colors are totally Zen."

The woman who answered my knock reminded me of my mom. Her brown hair was cut in a short bob and everything about her was age appropriate. She was wearing sneakers and jeans and a tailored shirt with the sleeves rolled.

I introduced myself as Edna Mazur's granddaughter.

"Of course," she said. "You're Stephanie Plum. You're famous in the Burg. We all enjoy your exploits."

You can run, but you can't hide, I told myself.

"I'm looking for Charlotte," I said. "Is she at home?"

"I hope she's not in trouble," her mother said.

I gave her a reassuring smile. "Not at all. I'm actually looking for a boy she knew in high school, and I thought she might be able to help me."

"Have you tried her house on Spruce Street?"

"Yes. She wasn't there."

"Sometimes she goes to the mall or a Starbucks to use the Wi-Fi. She started doing that a couple weeks ago. I told her she could come here, but she doesn't get along with her stepfather."

"Thanks," I said. "You've been helpful."

"I guess next stop is the mall," Lula said. "It could be a problem for me if you plan on staying past lunchtime, because I don't want to miss my appointment pertaining to my celestial alignment. Madam Eileen gets booked up. I was lucky she could squeeze me in."

"It's hard to say how long I'll be there. I can drop you off at the office and catch up to you later, after you have your stars examined."

CHAPTER SEVENTEEN

Charlotte Huck was sitting at a small table in the Quaker Bridge Mall food court. She was hunched over her computer in deep concentration. She looked rumpled and unkempt. I walked over and sat at the table with her.

"Charlotte Huck?" I asked.

She looked up. Startled. "Yes?"

"I'm Stephanie Plum and I'm friends with Melvin Schwartz."

"I don't know Melvin Schwartz."

"You know HotWiz."

"Oh gosh," she said. "How do you know that?"

"It's a long and complicated story. The short version is that I'm trying to help you and Melvin avoid Oswald and stay alive."

"We thought Oswald was brilliant. We didn't suspect that he was a monster. I received a message from him that said

Retribution. I didn't know how to take that, but later that night he broke into my neighbor's house. It was really scary. The police were there and when they took him away, he saw me standing on my front porch, watching. As soon as I saw him, I knew it was Oswald. I'd seen pictures of him. He would go to conferences and be a celebrity. Sometimes he would be with a beautiful, glamorous woman. I saw him look at me, and his expression was terrifying. I packed up a few things and left. I was afraid he'd get out of jail and come back."

"What did you think he would do to you?"

"I didn't know. He looked crazy when they were taking him away."

"I saw you at Melvin's door and at Clark's viewing. You knew they were Baked Potatoes?"

"I suspected from the beginning. They were friends and I'd been lurking on them since high school. They didn't know I existed. I was always frump girl."

"Why were you lurking on them?"

She fidgeted with her single braid. "I sort of always thought Melvin was kind of cute. And he was smart. And he never made fun of me. And I guess I wanted to, you know, meet him someday."

"Why were you at his door?"

"I wanted to warn him. I heard about Clark on the news. Poor Clark. He was a good person. I didn't know for sure if it was Oswald who killed him, but it wasn't a normal murder. And it was weird that Clark of all people would have that happen to him. It was hard to believe at first that Oswald would get so freaked out over being hacked that he would track us down and kill us."

"Maybe there was more to it than just getting hacked," I said.

"Like what?"

"There were rumors that Oswald had something big in the pipeline. Your hacking could have put that in jeopardy."

Charlotte sat back a little. "I don't know anything about that," she said.

I wasn't going to push her on it, but I felt in my gut that she was keeping something from me.

"You did the right thing when you tried to warn Melvin," I said.

"I had a really hard time finding him. Oswald shut down everything. I knew Melvin wasn't living at home, and I didn't feel comfortable exposing my identity to Melvin's family. In hindsight, I shouldn't have been so protective of my privacy because two people are dead, and I might have prevented that. Even after I saw Oswald taken away in handcuffs and I was scared, I didn't think he was capable of doing such horrible things."

"Where are you staying?"

"In my car. And I come here during the day to work. I have a number of cybersecurity accounts that I need to monitor."

"How can you live in your car?"

"It's awful. I'm tired and I'm scared. I don't want to die, and I don't want someone cutting my tongue out because I was stupid and hacked them. We didn't mean any harm. We thought Oswald might be impressed and let us into his inner circle. It was exciting."

A tear rolled down Charlotte's cheek. She wiped the tear away and pressed her lips together. "Sorry," she said.

"Nothing to be sorry about," I said. "Pack up your computer. We need to get out of here."

"What about Melvin? Is he someplace safe?"

"He's with my parents. I'm going to see if there's room for you to stay there, too."

"Omigosh," Charlotte said. "I can't see Melvin like this. I look even worse than usual. I've gone from frump girl to street person."

"Don't underestimate Melvin," I said. "He sees beauty that others don't recognize."

Charlotte smiled. "He's special, isn't he?"

"Yep," I said. "He's special."

I walked Charlotte out of the mall, to my car.

"What about my car?" she asked.

"I don't want your car parked in front of my parents' house. I'll have someone pick it up and garage it in a safe place. Is there anything in the car that you need?"

"No. I left my house in a hurry. I took equipment I knew I would use for work and one change of clothes. It's all in my backpack."

"I'm not sure I could have survived on a change of clothes and sleeping in my car for as long as you have."

"It's been awful. Once a week I get a room in a hotel. I've been holding out on relocating, praying Oswald would get caught. I don't get along with my stepfather, but my mom is here. I don't want to leave her."

I'm not a touchy-feely person. I think I'm loving and affectionate and I'm okay with moderate hugging of friends. I've never been entirely comfortable with the cheek-kissing thing. I mean, what's the deal? Do you just air kiss? Do you make a kissing sound? Do you actually plant one on the other person?

Anyway, I was wanting to hug Charlotte, but I held back. I didn't know if I could pull it off in the food court.

I parked in my parents' driveway and hurried Charlotte into the house. Melvin was no longer gaming. He was at his computer, in his zone. I sat Charlotte opposite him and he never looked up.

Charlotte looked like she was on the verge of a panic attack. Her hands were clenched in her lap and her eyes were darting around, focusing on everything but Melvin.

"Melvin!" I shouted.

Melvin jumped in his seat and looked up at me. Grandma and my mother ran in from the kitchen.

"This is Charlotte Huck," I said to everyone. "She's the fourth Trenton Baked Potato, Charley Q."

Melvin blinked about twenty times in rapid succession. "What?"

I gestured with my hand. "HotWiz, meet Charley Q."

"She's a girl," Melvin said.

Charlotte nodded. "Yes," she said softly. "Correct."

"That would make her a Hot Potato," Grandma said.

Charlotte smiled and two pink splotches appeared on Melvin's apple cheeks.

"Um, gosh," Melvin said.

"We went to high school together," Charlotte said. "Do you remember me? We were in the chess club senior year, but we never played each other."

"Maybe I remember," Melvin said. "Your hair was different. It was short."

Charlotte nodded. "I grew it out in college. It's easier to keep this way."

"I like it this way," Melvin said. "It's pretty."

Charlotte froze for a beat, and it occurred to me that this might be the first time anyone had told Charlotte that anything about her was pretty. She dipped her head, hiding her smile, and she fidgeted with her braid. "Thanks," she said. "I like your hair, too."

Melvin rolled his eyes up into his head, as if he could see his hair. "I think it might be too thin." He put his hand to his head and felt his hair. "It feels thin. The men in my family lose their hair early."

"Grass don't grow on a busy street," Grandma said. "Better to be smart than to have hair."

"I was hoping Charlotte could stay here for a couple days," I told my mom. "She's in a similar predicament as Melvin."

"I'd like to help but I don't know where we'd put her," my mom said. "We don't have any extra bedrooms."

"She can have my room," Melvin said. "I don't sleep a lot and I can nap on the couch."

That sealed the deal for Charlotte. Melvin was her hero. She was breathlessly besotted. I swear I could see stars in her eyes. Melvin looked like he'd just won the million-dollar lottery and was worried he might be dreaming.

"I guess it would be okay then," my mom said.

"I understand why you chose Charley," I said to Charlotte. "It's from Charlotte. Why the Q?"

"It's my favorite letter in the alphabet," Charlotte said. "It's an oval with a swirly tail. It's elegant."

———

I didn't stay for lunch. My mom now had two extra people to feed. I didn't want to add to the burden. I let myself into my apartment and saw that Diesel was in the kitchen, talking on the phone. He signaled me that he'd be off in one minute, and he told the person at the other end that it wasn't necessary to replace the bike. I assumed he was talking to Ana.

He hung up, got a beer out of the fridge, and chugged half. "You saw the bike?" he asked me.

"Yep. Smush city."

"He's losing his edge," Diesel said. "The *Hahahahaha* was middle school."

I got bread and peanut butter and made myself a sandwich. "Do you want one?" I asked Diesel.

"I'll pass. Ana brought me a salad. There's some left if you want it."

"I'll pass." I added slices of banana and took a bite. "I found Charlotte. She was living next door to the house Oswald broke into. The home invasion was a mistake just like Oswald said. He was actually after Charlotte. She's Charley Q."

"The fourth Trenton Baked Potato."

"Yeah. She was hiding out, living in her car and using the Wi-Fi at the food court in the mall. I stashed her with Melvin at my parents' house."

Diesel grinned. "How's that working out?"

"They're a perfect match, but it would be good if we could catch Oswald sooner than later. I don't know how long my parents are going to tolerate having two houseguests."

"I have someone watching the train station and I have someone walking the streets downtown. My IT guy hasn't been able to ping Oswald. He's changed all his devices. Melvin got in and was able to download information but nothing that helped us get to Oswald. And what really pisses me off is that Oswald's been playing with us while he continues to evade us. He's making me look bad."

"Not to mention, he's killing people."

"Yeah, that, too."

"When I asked Charlotte about hacking into Oswald's network she hesitated and sat back a little. Maybe Melvin got out right away and didn't see anything, but I think Charlotte hung in there for a while."

"It would make more sense if Oswald was killing Baked Potatoes for some reason other than retribution for hacking."

"Exactly. Like he's been killing people to keep them from talking. And the tongue thing would be appropriate."

Diesel nodded. "So, you aren't just pretty, you're smart, too."

That caught me by surprise. My self-image ran more toward pleasantly ordinary. Pretty is definitely a couple notches above pleasantly ordinary. I must be having a good day.

"We should capitalize on the pretty," Diesel said. "Suppose we dress you up in a skimpy little skirt and put some socks in your bra and set you on a street corner in downtown Trenton. See if Oswald takes the bait."

Obviously, my prettiness fell short of the mark when it came to breasts. "You think I need to put socks in my bra?"

"Not for me. I think you're a nice handful, but Oswald likes big boobs."

"How about if we dress you up in drag and see if that turns him on?"

"I've tried that in the past. I make a really ugly woman."

"Okay, suppose I go out there as bait and he grabs me. You're going to step in before he cuts my tongue out, right?"

"I saved you from the train, didn't I?"

I looked around to see if there was a sign that my angel was getting all this.

"I don't suppose you have any other ideas?" I asked him.

"Not at the moment."

"Wonderful. I'm going to the office to see if any new FTAs came in. I'll be back at dinnertime and maybe you'll have some other ideas by then."

"There's something that never fails to give me ideas," Diesel said.

"No!"

"I was talking about pizza. Do you want me to have Ana get it or do you want to bring some home?"

"I'll get the pizza."

I finished my sandwich, grabbed a bottle of water from the fridge, and drove to the office. I stopped for a light and glanced down at my breasts. I thought they were perfectly okay. They aren't centerfold breasts, but I can run up and down a flight of stairs without a bra and not rupture something.

CHAPTER EIGHTEEN

Connie was cleaning her gun and Lula hadn't returned from her session with the astrologer when I got to the office.

"Anything new?" I asked Connie.

"No, but Vinnie called in and he's not happy that Oswald Wednesday is still in the wind."

"I'm not happy about that, either," I said. "I've turned my parents' house into a safe house, and I've got a strange man sleeping in my bed."

"If you want to get rid of him, I'd be happy to have him in my bed," Connie said.

"If only it was that easy."

Lula burst in. "What's happening? Did I miss anything?"

"I found Charlotte Huck, and she's with my parents," I said. "That's about it."

"How did it go with your reading?" Connie asked.

"I don't remember all the details but there's a moon that's out of orbit and it's creating a disturbance in my energy zone. And Stephanie's moon is taking its place where my moon should be, so she's getting all my good juju and I'm keester cakes out of luck."

"That sounds about right," Connie said.

"Yeah, it made sense to me," Lula said. "There isn't much I can do about it until my moon gets back on track."

"Charlotte gave me the key to her house," I said. "I'm going to get some clothes for her."

"I'll go along," Lula said. "You might need some muscle. There could be squatters in her house. It happens when you leave a house empty. Or Oswald could show up. I bet he looks in on that house all the time."

I drove past Charlotte's house on Spruce and cut through the back alley. I didn't see Oswald's Porsche. I didn't see anything that might look like a cop car. I didn't see any random suspicious-looking vehicles.

I parked behind Charlotte's house, and Lula and I went in through the back door.

"This is a nice house," Lula said. "You could see nobody's been here for a while. It's still all tidy."

We went upstairs to Charlotte's bedroom, and I pulled some clothes out of her closet and went through her drawers.

"This is terrible," Lula said. "This girl needs the queer guy, Tan France. Get his number. Is he in the book? She don't need birth control with underwear like this. We need to do an intervention."

I put the clothes and some toiletries in a laundry basket and carted it downstairs.

"I need to use the powder room," Lula said. "I'll be right out."

I took the basket to the car and stashed it in the back. I turned around and was face-to-face with Oswald.

"Hello," Oswald said. "We meet again. I see you have the puzzle figured out. You've obviously found Charley Q. And I suspect you also are harboring HotWiz. Are they in your apartment? Doubtful. Diesel is living there. I can't see him tolerating two geeks day and night. So where are they? Your parents' house? I don't think so. You aren't that dumb."

A lot he knew. I was absolutely that dumb.

"I have no idea," I said. "Diesel sent me to this address to get clothes."

"I almost believe you. Not that it matters. You're going to make a nice hostage."

I reached for the pepper spray in my pocket, and he pointed a gun at me.

"Just call me Quick Draw," he said. "Don't worry, I won't kill you. Not immediately anyway. I'll shoot you in a horribly painful spot and make sure you hang on long enough for me to accomplish my task."

"What is your task?"

"To demolish the Baked Potatoes. Silenced forever. A favor to the world. If you're going to be a hacker, you need to be smarter and better than whoever you're hacking. They're not. They're just plain-ass potatoes. No butter, no sour cream, not even a sprinkling of chives."

"Has it occurred to you that you are insane?"

"Of course. All true geniuses have a touch of insanity. I happen to be criminally insane and that makes me much more interesting."

"Diesel thinks you're boring and childish."

"Diesel doesn't even have a last name."

He had me there.

"Keep your hands where I can see them and walk down the alley," Oswald said.

"Which way?"

"To the right, toward town."

Lula came out of the house and yelled at me. "Do you want me to lock the door?"

Oswald stepped out from behind my car, and Lula's eyes almost popped out of her head when she saw him.

"It's *you*!" Lula shouted. "Stay where you are, or I'll shoot." Lula was wearing a big cross-body hippie hobo bag. She had her hand in the bag, trying to locate her Glock, which was mixed in with her hair care products, makeup, a bottle of water, and all the other junk she needed to get through the day. She pulled the gun out and before she could fire, Oswald shot her, twice. Lula froze for a beat in stunned disbelief before crumpling to the ground.

I've never found the time for martial arts training, so what I lacked in skill I made up for with rage. I lunged at Oswald and took him down to the ground. We rolled around for a couple seconds, and he lost his grip on the gun. It skidded across the dirt road and we both went after it. I got there first, one-handed the gun, and fired a warning shot. Oswald got to his feet and ran. I fired again and tagged him in the arm. He spun around, grabbed his arm, and continued to run.

"That sonovabitch shot me," Lula yelled. "Big woman down."

I ran to Lula with my phone in my hand, calling 911.

"I see spots and stars," Lula said. "I'm going. Lordy, this is it. I'm gonna die and I never even had a dog."

"Where are you hit?" I asked. There was blood on her leg, her skirt, her hobo bag, her hands.

"I don't know," Lula said. "I can't think. Okay, it's my leg. It hurts like a bitch."

"I've got help coming," I said. "There's a firehouse two blocks away. They should get here fast."

"If I don't make it, I'm leaving my wigs and special occasion clothes to you and Connie," Lula said. "You can divide them up."

"You're going to make it," I said. "I don't see any gunshot wounds other than your leg."

"Yeah, but I'm bleeding. I'm probably already down a quart."

A Trenton cop car drove down the alley and two guys got out and ran toward us. I could hear a fire truck on the road in front of the house.

"Is that sirens?" Lula asked. "I must be in real bad shape if they're using the sirens."

I stepped back and let the first responders take over. I called Morelli and told him what happened. I got off the phone with Morelli, and Ranger called.

"Babe," he said. "We got an alert that your car is parked in an active shooter area."

"Lula got shot in the leg and the paramedics are taking care of her. I'm okay. I'll stop by when I'm done here. Are you in your office?"

"Yes. I'll be here for the rest of the afternoon."

Diesel was next on my list. "We ran into Oswald at Charlotte's house," I said. "He shot Lula and tried to abduct me. I got the gun away from him and shot him in the arm, but he ran away."

"Is Lula going to be okay?"

"Yes, I think so. He shot her in the leg. The paramedics are with her, and the place is crawling with police. Morelli is on his way. As soon as I'm done here, I'm going to talk to Ranger about housing Charlotte and Melvin. It's too dangerous for them to stay with my parents."

"I'll poke around town and see if I can pick up Oswald's scent."

"One last thing. What's your last name?"

"Diesel."

"What's your first name?"

"Diesel."

"So, you're Diesel Diesel?"

"I'm the last kid in a large family. My parents didn't have a lot of time to think of a name."

I hung up and thought the name suited him. He was big and powerful and hard to stop once he got going. An EMT truck drove in, and a stretcher got rolled over to Lula. I went to see how she was doing.

"This is because of my moon," Lula said. "I'm not leaving my house until my juju changes. Did you get shot? No. Do you know why? It's because you've got my good juju." She looked up at the attendant. "What have you got in your bag for pain. I want it all. Load me up."

I called Connie and gave her the short version. "They're getting ready to put Lula in the truck and take her to the medical center," I said. "Can you meet her there? I'd go with her, but I need to take care of Charlotte and Melvin."

"I'm on it," Connie said. "I'll close up shop."

———

Rangeman is located on a quiet side street in downtown Trenton. The seven-story building is unremarkable on the outside and a state-of-the-art security operation on the inside. I pulled into the underground garage and parked in one of Ranger's primo spots by the elevator. I waved at the camera and pushed the elevator button for the fifth floor. The fifth floor holds the control room, a dining area, and private offices, one of which is Ranger's.

I worked for Ranger for a short time, and I've occasionally stayed in his seventh-floor apartment, so I know my way around. I walked through the control room and made a fast stop in the dining area to grab a to-go chicken salad sandwich.

The door was open to Ranger's office, and he was at his desk. He was dressed in the standard Rangeman uniform of black cargo pants and black long-sleeved dress shirt with the Rangeman logo on the sleeve. I pulled a chair up to his desk and unwrapped my sandwich.

"Do you want half?" I asked him.

"I had something earlier," he said. "How's Lula?"

"She'll be okay. They took her to the medical center. Oswald Wednesday shot her twice. Both times in the leg."

"Should I know Oswald Wednesday?"

I gave him the long, detailed version that included Diesel's and Morelli's involvement.

"I assume you want to get this guy before Diesel takes him away and you're out the recovery fee," Ranger said.

"I don't care about the recovery fee. I want him stopped. No more hacking. No more killing. My problem right now is keeping Charlotte and Melvin alive. I can't leave them with my parents. It's too dangerous for them and for my parents and Grandma."

"I can put them in one of my safe houses, or I can give them dorm rooms on the third floor. They have en suite baths and small sitting areas. They can eat here on the fifth floor."

"Dorm rooms would be great. I'll get Charlotte and Melvin packed up and bring them over."

"Out of morbid curiosity, where is Diesel staying?"

"With me."

"I'm sure Morelli loves that arrangement."

"He doesn't know," I said. "It hasn't come up in conversation."

Ranger almost smiled. He walked me down to the garage, gave me a kiss that was slightly more than friendly, and watched me leave.

I called Connie on the way to my parents' house to check on Lula.

"She's in surgery to remove the two bullets," Connie said. "If they discharge her today, I'll take her home with me. I don't think she'll be able to manage the stairs to her apartment."

"Let me know how it goes. I'm moving Charlotte and Melvin into Rangeman."

CHAPTER NINETEEN

Charlotte, Melvin, and Grandma were all at the dining room table, working on their computers. My mother was in the kitchen, knitting.

"That's a big thing," I said to my mom. "How long is it?"

"I don't know exactly," she said.

"We measured it this morning," Grandma yelled from the dining room. "It was fourteen feet long."

"It's pretty," I said to my mom. "It's colorful."

"We're gonna have to send her to Knitters Anonymous," Grandma said. "It's an addiction."

My mom didn't respond. She was concentrating on her knitting.

"I'm moving you out to stay with a friend of mine," I said to Melvin and Charlotte. "You'll be safer there. Pack up your things, and I'll drive you over."

"Where are you taking them?" Grandma asked.

"Rangeman."

"Darn," she said. "I wish I could go with them. I was just getting the hang of hacking."

"It's only for a couple days," I said, "and then you can all get together again."

"Will I be with Charlotte?" Melvin asked.

"You'll have your own rooms, but you can be together as much as you want."

"They're like two peas in a pod," Grandma said. "I don't even know what they're saying half the time when they're talking about computers and codes and passwords."

"We were in two classes together in high school and we didn't even know each other," Melvin said.

"And chess club and robotics club," Charlotte said.

Melvin went upstairs to get his clothes and Charlotte stuffed her computer into her backpack.

"He's very smart," she said. "And he can be funny. I never saw that side of him as a Baked Potato."

"He's got a crush on you," Grandma said. "I could tell by the way he looks at you."

"No one's ever had a crush on me before," Charlotte said.

"You just had to wait for the right person to come along," Grandma said.

"Do you think Melvin is the right person?"

"That's something you have to figure out," Grandma said.

Melvin came down with his laundry basket of clothes. "I'm all set," he said.

I grabbed his backpack, yelled goodbye to my mom, and

wasted no time getting Melvin and Charlotte into my car. I drove to Rangeman and was relieved when we were safe in the garage.

Ranger met us on the third floor.

"This is a residential floor for guests and employees who need a place to stay," Ranger said to Charlotte and Melvin. "You will have complete privacy while you're in your room, but the rest of the building is constantly under audio and video surveillance, including the elevators and stairwells. For your own security we ask that you don't leave the building until your problem is resolved. We have laundry service and food is available on the fifth floor all day, every day. The control room is also housed on the fifth floor." Ranger handed me two keys. "I'd like to talk to you after you get them settled in."

Charlotte and Melvin had rooms next to each other at the end of the hall. The rooms were pleasant and immaculate. Queen-size beds with white linens and comforter and a tan blanket folded at the footboard. Nightstands with lamps, a desk and chair, a two-seater couch and comfy chair, coffee table, television, window with impact glass that looked out at the street. There was a small refreshment area with an under-the-counter fridge. Bathroom with walk-in shower and a walk-in closet.

"This is really nice," Melvin said. "This is like a hotel but better."

I gave them their room keys and took them up to the fifth-floor dining area. There were several small tables with chairs and there was a serve-yourself buffet that was continuously restocked with salads, soups, sandwiches, fresh fruit, cereal, breads, dinner entrees, juices, tea, coffee, and whatever else was needed. Only occasionally were there cookies. There were no fat Rangemen.

"Only use the third floor and the fifth floor," I told Charlotte and

Melvin. "Call me if you have problems or questions or you have information we can use. I'll check in on you a couple times a day."

I left them staring at the buffet like it was Christmas morning and walked down the hall to Ranger's office.

"Do you need extra security?" Ranger asked.

"No," I said. "I think I'm okay."

"My apartment is available."

I smiled at that. "Tempting, but no."

And it was truly tempting because not only was his apartment perfect and fantastic, but it came with Ranger, who was close to perfect and pretty darn fantastic. Problem was I had a relationship with Joe Morelli, and while I could keep Diesel at arm's length, I would have no luck doing that with Ranger. Ranger was a guilty pleasure that was hard to resist.

I left Rangeman and drove back to Charlotte's townhouse. The fire truck and the EMTs were gone. Morelli was still there with a single squad car. I parked and went to talk to him.

"I have Charlotte and Melvin staying at Rangeman," I said. "Were you able to track down Oswald?"

"Not yet. The blood stopped at the end of the alley, where he must have parked his car. I put out an alert to hospitals and clinics. Haven't gotten any response yet. The blood trail was minimal, so it's possible he was able to take care of himself. I have one of the men looking for your round. Did you fire off more than one?"

"I'm not sure. I was flustered. I'm shocked that I hit him. I fired on instinct."

Morelli grabbed me, hugged me to him, and kissed me on the top of my head. "You've always had good instincts."

This is why I'm not staying at Rangeman, I thought. I love

Ranger and Morelli and maybe even Diesel, but there's a comfort level with Morelli that I don't feel with anyone else. We have a long history and a lot of shared interests. When I'm with him it feels like a marriage without the paperwork and cohabitating. Even when it involves blood and fear and craziness, he has a calming effect. This is probably one of the reasons he's such a good cop.

"It's hard to believe this guy is still out and about," Morelli said. "There are a lot of people looking for him."

"It's only a matter of time," I said. "He's obsessed and he's in the red zone on the narcissistic psychopathic killer meter. It's going to make him careless."

"I hope you're right. I don't like you involved in this. Why don't you move in with me until we catch this guy?"

"It's Wednesday. Poker night at Squigie's house. You won't even be home until midnight."

"I could skip poker."

"It's not necessary. I feel safe in my apartment. Diesel is there."

"I thought he was sleeping elsewhere."

"He had a motor home, but Oswald torched it. It's okay. He's on the couch."

"What's your plan for the rest of the day?"

"I'm going to call Connie to see how Lula is doing and maybe I'll stop by to see her. What's your plan?"

"I'm heading back to my desk," Morelli said. "I have paperwork."

I went to my car and called Connie.

"Lula's out of surgery," Connie said. "They're keeping her there overnight, and she seems to be feeling okay, considering she got shot twice. I'm on my way back to the office."

Twenty minutes later I was at the medical center. I got a pass from the front desk and went in search of Lula's room. I found her propped up in bed looking cranky.

"How's it going?" I asked.

"It's been going better. All I got to wear is this unflattering hospital gown. Plus, I'm never gonna get the blood out of my skirt, and it was one of my favorites."

"Connie said the surgery went well."

"Yeah, if you get shot, this is the place to go. They have a lot of practice. I still can't believe that little turd shot me twice. One of the bullets just ripped some skin off me, but the other one had to get dug out of my upper leg. They said I was lucky that I have a lot of thigh. Otherwise, I might have had bone damage.

"Are you in pain?"

"Hell yeah. I've been freaking shot."

"Is there anything I can get you?"

"I'd like a bucket of extra crispy chicken and a pizza with the works, but I'm not supposed to eat anything yet."

"I'll pick you up tomorrow and we can stop at Cluck-in-a-Bucket on the way home."

"They said I'd get discharged at nine o'clock."

I left the medical center and drove to Target. Lula was going to need something comfortable to wear tomorrow. Everything in her closet was skintight and she needed something loose over her stitches. When I left Target an hour later, I had a tent dress for Lula, two throw pillows for my new couch, a new lipstick, and two bags of groceries. The groceries included ice cream, so I bypassed the office and went straight to my apartment.

Rex came out of his soup can den to say hello while I was

unpacking the groceries. I told him about Lula and gave him a corn chip and half of a walnut.

"Have you noticed how quiet it is?" I asked Rex. "That's because it's just you and me. No Diesel. No Morelli. No Bob Dog."

I got a bottle of water and took it to the dining room. Diesel's side of the table was cluttered with notepads and pens, coffee cups, his computer, his headset, and an iPad. My side of the table had my laptop on it. I opened mail and found a hundred messages from Oswald that all said the same thing. *Retribution.* No other emails. My account had been wiped clean. I guess he didn't like getting shot.

I called Diesel.

"What's happening?" I asked him.

"I found someone at a CVS pharmacy that recognized Oswald's picture. He said he came in and loaded up on gauze and bandages and first aid cream. Paid with cash."

"It sounds like I wounded him but not badly."

"I canvassed the neighborhood, flashing his photo, but I didn't get any hits other than CVS. It's only been a few days, but I feel like this has been going on for years," Diesel said.

"The problem is that we aren't making any progress. He's able to find us but we can't find him. We think he's downtown somewhere, and we think he might still be driving a black Porsche. The only thing we're sure of is that he's gone off the rails."

"He's always been off the rails. This time he's *way* off the rails."

"It all seems so silly. He could be working on something productive like destroying the Russian grid."

"Vengeance, greed, and lust for power are some of life's great motivators," Diesel said. "They're also self-destructive obsessions."

"I wish Oswald would self-destruct faster. He's freaking me out. I just checked my email. It's been wiped clean, with the exception of a bunch of one-word messages from Oswald."

"Let me guess the message."

"Yeah, it's not hard. I'm now officially on the retribution list."

"That could be a good thing," Diesel said. "It would be a way to flush him out. We just dangle you in front of him. You wouldn't even need to do the sock thing."

"Jeez, that makes me feel so much better."

I could sense Diesel smiling at the other end.

"I'll be home around six," Diesel said. "What do you want for dinner?"

"I'm feeling Italian. Do you know where Pino's is located?"

"I do."

"Bring me anything from Pino's."

At five thirty I got a call from Lula.

"They said I could go home," Lula said. "Can you come pick me up?"

"They don't usually discharge patients at this time of the day."

"Well, they're discharging me."

"Can I talk to a nurse?"

"Sure," Lula said. "I got one standing right here."

"Is she really okay to go home?" I asked the nurse.

"As long as she has help," the nurse said. "She's insisting on leaving and the resident doctor has signed her release. How soon can you get here?"

"Fifteen or twenty minutes," I said.

"We'll meet you at the emergency entrance."

"Doesn't she need clothes?"

"We've got her in a bathrobe. She'll be fine. We don't want it back. Ever."

Oh boy.

Fifteen minutes later I rolled up to the emergency entrance. Lula was in a wheelchair and an attendant was standing behind her. He helped Lula into the passenger seat, handed her a plastic bag, and stepped back.

"Let's go," Lula said. "I don't want them changing their mind and wheeling me back in there."

"I'm guessing things weren't wonderful."

"First off there was a cheap-ass television in my room that was from 1950 or something. I couldn't get anything on it, and it was all fuzzy. And there are bells going off all the time and carts clattering down the hall. And then there were people talking, and people coming into my room when I'm trying to get a nap, taking my blood pressure and testing to see if I'm dead or not. And they told me I was getting chicken broth and crackers for dinner, and I told them my insurance company would want me to have steak and mashed potatoes, but I don't think they were listening. And on top of that I asked for ice cream, and no one ever brought it to me. I asked a lot of times in a polite voice, and I still didn't get any ice cream. I mean, what's the big deal about getting a Dixie cup of vanilla and chocolate? I'd been through a lot. I was shot. I deserved a Dixie cup."

"So, you decided to leave?"

"It was one of those mutual decisions. They said I was demanding and disruptive. Can you imagine? Have you ever known me to be demanding and disruptive? I don't think so. I might have a strong and assertive personality, but I consider that to be a positive attribute."

"The nurse said you shouldn't stay alone tonight."

"Yeah, I thought I could stay with you. Plus, you got an elevator. If I go home, I have to walk up some stairs with my stupid gunshot leg."

I called Diesel and told him to bring a lot more food.

"What's in the bag?" I asked Lula.

"My clothes and my purse and my meds. They said I didn't have time to get dressed. They put everything in that plastic bag and got me into a wheelchair. The wheelchair was the good part. I liked getting wheeled around. We should stop at a drugstore and rent me a wheelchair so you can get me up to your apartment."

"Really?"

"A motorized one would be even better," Lula said. "I could take it to Walmart and Target."

"You're planning on walking sometime soon though, right?"

"Heck yeah, I can walk now, but why walk when you can ride? Only thing is, if I'm always in the chair no one is going to fully appreciate my superior derriere."

"That would be a shame."

"Damn skippy. I got a whole wardrobe based on boobs and booty."

"So, I guess we should skip the wheelchair?"

"It was just one of those thoughts," Lula said. "I was weighing the merits."

"What about clothes?" I asked. "I got you a comfortable dress yesterday but that's it."

"I'll be okay until tomorrow. I always carry an extra thong in my purse in case I get an IBS attack, and I'm wearing the hospital gown and robe, so I don't need sleep clothes."

CHAPTER TWENTY

I found a parking place close to the back door to my apartment building and Lula and I slow-walked to the elevator. I got her into the apartment and stretched out on the couch.

"Do you want ice cream?" I asked her. "Or would you rather wait for dinner?"

"What's for dinner?"

"I'm not sure. Diesel is bringing it."

"Say what?"

"He's temporarily living here."

"I thought he was in a motor home."

"Oswald toasted it."

"Lucky you," Lula said. "What's Morelli got to say about this?"

"He's cool."

"Uh oh."

"What uh oh?"

"Morelli should be nuts. He's Italian. He's supposed to be doing a lot of arm waving and yelling about you living with another man. You know what this means, right?"

"That he trusts me?"

"Heck no. It means he's cheating on you."

"He's not cheating on me."

"How do you know?"

"I guess I don't exactly know," I said, "but I'm pretty sure."

"Aha!" Lula said. "There you have it."

This had me doing a mental head-slap. It was becoming more and more clear why they kicked her out of the hospital.

"Do you want ice cream, or not?"

"Sure, I'll have some ice cream."

I gave her a pint of ice cream, a spoon, and the television remote.

"Is this a new television?" Lula asked. "I don't remember you having a big television like this. You had one that was a step away from rabbit ears."

"Diesel bought it."

"Uh oh!" Lula said.

I wasn't buying into the *uh oh* this time. I went to the dining room table to see if my email was still All Oswald All the Time. I opened my laptop and wasn't disappointed.

I was still at the table when I got a call from Grandma.

"The strangest thing just happened," she said. "Your mother ran out of yarn, so she did a yarn run before your father came home for dinner."

"Where was he?"

"He had to fill in with the cab. Willie Small came down with a bursted appendix and they were short a cab for the commuter rush hour at the train station. Anyway, I was in the kitchen and there was a knock on the front door, and I opened it without thinking. I was making gravy, and you know how you have to keep stirring it while it cooks down. You'll never guess who it was?"

"Oswald?"

"Yes! I recognized him from his picture. He pushed past me and rushed in, looking all around. And then he ran through the house, out to the kitchen and upstairs, opening doors and slamming them shut.

"I'm calling the police," I said to him. "I gotta make gravy."

I guess Oswald decided I was dumber than he originally thought.

"If I wasn't so caught off guard, I could have snagged him, but my gun was upstairs. I thought about whacking him with the fry pan, but I had gravy going in it. It was the good cast iron one. I suppose I could have gone after him with the carving knife, but I've never been good with a knife. And he was moving fast like a crazy person. His eyes were squinchy and his forehead was frowny.

" 'They aren't here,' he said to me. 'Where are they?'

" 'Who?' I asked him. 'What are you talking about?'

"And he ran out and got into his car and drove away."

"Did you see the car?"

"Yes. It was a blue sedan. I don't know what kind. I'm thinking I should keep this between you and me," Grandma said. "Your mother isn't good at dealing with these dramatic episodes."

Diesel rolled in at six o'clock with bags of food.

"I smell Pino's," Lula yelled from the couch.

Diesel looked in at Lula and then at me. "Can it get any worse than this?" he asked.

"It can almost always get worse. They kicked her out of the hospital. She's only here for one night and then I can take her home."

"We've got meatball sandwiches, pizza with the works, vodka rigatoni, and chicken parm. Plus, a bunch of sides. What do you want?" I asked Lula.

"Just fill a plate," she said. "I'm starving. They wouldn't feed me in the hospital."

I piled food onto a plate, grabbed a bottle of water, and took it all to Lula. Diesel and I ate standing in the kitchen.

"How's your internet?" Diesel asked me.

"I just checked a little while ago. It's nonexistent."

He helped himself to a second slice of pizza. "Mine's wiped out, too. He crashed my computer. At least I didn't get pages and pages of *retribution*."

"Did he cut you off without sending you any kind of message?"

"His message was *HAHAHAHAHA!*"

"He might be a genius hacker, but he has no imagination when it comes to anything else. He visited my parents' house a half hour ago. Grandma just called to tell me. She was alone in the house. She said Oswald ran through the whole house, asked her where '*they*' were hiding and left. She said he drove away in a blue sedan. Grandma said she would have hit him with the iron fry pan, but she was making gravy in it."

Lula made her way into the kitchen. "That was real good," she said, setting the plate on the counter. "I appreciate that you're helping me out in my time of need. I'm sure I'll be better tomorrow, but right now I'm wiped out. Where do I sleep? I don't mind sharing a bed or I can sleep on the couch."

"Not the couch," Diesel said. "There's a game tonight. I need the television."

"Okay," Lula said. "I'll take the bed."

I watched her limp off to the bedroom and heard the door click closed.

"You just gave my bed away!" I said to Diesel.

"She said she didn't mind sharing."

"I'm not sharing a bed with her. She snores. Loud! You share the bed with her, and I'll take the couch."

"Not gonna happen," Diesel said.

I put the leftovers in the fridge and got a half-eaten tub of ice cream from the freezer. I took it into the dining room and positioned myself in front of my laptop before remembering I had no internet.

"Crap," I said.

Diesel sat across from me. "I like it. I can't communicate with anyone. I can't research anything. I have the perfect excuse to go old school and do my job without interference."

"You still have a phone."

"Only if I answer it."

"Do we have a game plan for the Oswald capture?"

"Right now, I'm sitting, waiting for information. There are a lot of people in the field. Some are mine and some are Morelli's."

"Is Morelli communicating with you?"

"Not directly," Diesel said.

I gave him my raised eyebrows look. "You've tapped into his phone?"

"Would you have a problem with that?"

"Maybe."

"Then the answer is *no*," Diesel said. "We didn't tap into his phone."

"Good to know," I said.

I finished the ice cream and stood. "I'm going out. I want to look in on my parents and make sure everything is secure there. And I'm going to check in with Ranger."

"Make sure you're home by ten o'clock," Diesel said.

"Curfew?"

"That's when the match starts. You don't want to miss it."

I gave him a thumbs-up. I had no idea who was playing or what they were playing. Rugby, soccer, tennis, polo, checkers. I suspected this was going to be a long night that required a lot of wine. Maybe I should get some vodka. This might be a martini marathon.

I went to my living room window and looked down into the parking lot. I didn't see anyone lurking in the shadows. No sporty black Porsche in the vicinity of my Ford Focus. No blue sedan. Good deal.

———

Grandma and my dad were watching television when I walked in. Dinner had been cleared from the dining room table, and it looked sadly empty without Melvin and Charlotte. My mom was in the kitchen, knitting.

"How long is it now?" I asked.

"Seventeen feet," my mom said.

"You sound excited about it."

"It's an accomplishment. It's satisfying. It's something I can see and touch, and I know that I made it. It takes me an hour to make a pie and it gets eaten in ten minutes. When I scrub a pot, no one notices that it's clean. People only notice when pots are dirty. My *thing* doesn't disappear in ten minutes like a pie. My thing grows!" She held part of the thing up. "Look at it! I made it. I made something that's seventeen feet long! I did it all by myself. The yarn is soft when I touch it, and I have all different colors of yarn. It's like a painting or a sculpture."

"Wouldn't you rather make a sweater or a hat?"

"That would ruin it. It would have to be perfect. I'd have to think and count stitches. This way if I make a mistake, it's all part of the beauty of it. My thing isn't perfect because it's a reflection of life. Life isn't perfect. Besides, a sweater or a hat would come to an end. It would be done. My *thing* can go on for as long as I want. I could knit this forever."

It was easy to take my mom for granted. She'd accepted the role of being the sane, sensible, adult member of the family. She made sure the bills were paid, the house was clean, food was on the table, and she did damage control as best she could for her crazy daughter and mother. Truth is, it was a convenience for us to convince ourselves that this was all she wanted, that she had no other needs. And then, *bang,* she knocks me over by discovering something as simple as knitting and turns it into her own art form, her own therapy for getting through the day, her own life philosophy. She's making a *thing* because it checks a bunch of her boxes. I was jealous. I didn't have a *thing*.

"Maybe I should try knitting," I said.

"Really? You'd really like to try? I can get you started. I have extra needles and yarn," my mom said. "You can pick out any color you want from my basket."

A half hour later, I was back in the Focus with blue yarn, two knitting needles, and three inches of Thing2. I called Ranger and asked about Melvin and Charlotte.

"They spend most of their time in their rooms," Ranger said. "That's to be expected. We don't have much common area. They come out to eat and they look happy. No attempt to leave. They're quiet. Not engaging with my crew. I'll assign someone to socialize with them a little tomorrow."

"Thanks," I said. "I owe you."

"Babe," Ranger said, and he disconnected.

———

Rex was running on his wheel when I walked into the kitchen at nine o'clock. I said hello and gave him a corn chip. He stuffed it into his cheek, deposited it in his soup can, and returned to the wheel. This was one of the good things about a hamster. They were polite, and you never really knew what they were thinking. He didn't give me attitude because I gave him a crappy corn chip instead of a delicious Cheez Doodle. The other good thing about hamsters was that they had very small poop. The bad part was that they seemed to produce a lot of it.

I poured myself a glass of wine and took it into the living room along with my knitting. Diesel was slouched in a chair, talking on the phone. He nodded at me, flicked a look at my yarn and needles, and continued to listen to the person on the other end. He finally hung up and turned to me.

"What are you doing?" he asked.

"I'm knitting," I said.

"Why?"

"It's something to do," I said. "It's Zen. It's the new yoga. And it's a way to express myself."

"It looks boring."

"That's the wonderful part. You don't have to think. You just *knit*. You become one with the yarn."

"Darlin', it seems a tad repetitive."

"That's because I only know how to do one kind of stitch. I can only knit. I don't remember how to purl."

"Doesn't that bother you?"

"It turns out that purling isn't necessary. I'm making good progress just knitting."

"I imagine the wine helps."

"Wine is essential."

"We'll be sleeping together on the couch, so feel free to get a little drunk."

"Are you suggesting you would take advantage?"

"In a heartbeat, but only if you wanted me to take advantage."

Oh boy.

I went back to my knitting, concentrating on my stitches.

"It's not as easy as you would think," I said. "You have to get the needle into one of the loops on the other needle, and then you have to snag the yarn and pull it through."

Diesel watched me struggle to get the needle into the loop. "My standards aren't always that high for romantic partners, but you're on the borderline of not making the grade," he said.

"You don't understand the nuances of knitting. It can be a reflection of life."

Diesel was slouched back in his chair, grinning. "I take it all back. You're incredibly lovable when you're earnest. What are you knitting?"

"I'm knitting a thing. It's like a scarf but it's longer. I could knit it forever if I wanted."

"So, you aren't knitting anything?"

"I'm knitting something. It just doesn't happen to *be* anything."

"I'm getting turned on," Diesel said. "What would it take to get you to knit naked?"

"Ick!"

"Give me a break," Diesel said. "The soccer match doesn't come on until ten o'clock. I've got an hour to kill."

"You're going to have to kill it by yourself."

"That's not as much fun."

Diesel sat up a little straighter. "What's that sound?"

"It's Lula snoring."

"That sound isn't coming from anything human."

"You could be right, but I'm pretty sure it's Lula."

"It sounds like Chewbacca dying."

CHAPTER TWENTY-ONE

The sun was shining when I dragged myself out of sleep. I was in the living room, and I was lying on top of Diesel, snuggled against him with his arms wrapped around me. I'd be lying if I said I hated it. He was warm and comforting, but I needed to roll off him and start my day. This was easier said than done. His grip on me tightened when I moved.

"Hey!" I said. "Wake up."

Diesel opened his eyes. "What?"

"I need to use the bathroom and you have a death grip on me."

"Sorry," he said, releasing me. "You kept sliding onto the floor. I was afraid you were going to get a concussion."

I stood and stretched, and Diesel sat up.

"Listen," he said. "Silence. You should check to see if she's breathing."

I knocked on the bedroom door, opened it a crack, and peeked in. "Are you okay?" I asked.

"I feel like I've been run over by a truck, but aside from that I'm good."

"The dress I bought you is on the dresser."

"I'll be out in a minute. I need coffee bad."

I closed the door and turned to Diesel. "She's alive. And here's more good news. When you sleep in your clothes it makes the morning so much easier. I don't have to get dressed."

"That would work if it wasn't for the vodka rigatoni stain on your shirt," Diesel said.

I looked down at my shirt. "Damn."

I went to the kitchen and got coffee brewing. Lula limped in a couple of minutes later.

"This dress is real comfy," she said, "but I feel like I'm wearing a tent. Everything's all loose around me. Nothing's squeezing me together. I'm all jiggly. I feel like Jell-O."

I was going to have to inject bleach into my brain to get rid of the mental image of Lula as jiggly Jell-O.

"I'm going to take a fast shower and then I'm going to the office," I said. "Do you feel well enough to go home?"

"Yeah, I'll be slow on the stairs but aside from that I'm okay. And if we stop at the office on the way, I can get my morning doughnut."

I planned out the day while I was in the shower. Stop at the office, take Lula home, pop in at Rangeman to talk to Melvin and Charlotte, check with Diesel on possible O.W. sightings. Ditto Morelli.

My hair was still wet when I collected Lula in the kitchen

and maneuvered her out of the apartment, into the elevator, and across the parking lot.

"I'm going to be more selective who I shoot after this," Lula said, easing herself into the passenger seat. "This is a total bummer. You just don't want to go around shooting indiscriminately. It looks like a little bullet but turns out it's a big deal when they gotta dig it out of you. Who would have thought?"

"Really?"

"I guess I always knew it was a big deal," Lula said, "but it's different when it's you that got shot. It gives you a different perspective. Like I might still shoot someone if I have to, but I'll feel more sorry for them."

"Are you sure you want to stop at the office?"

"Hell yeah. And I deserve the Boston crème on account of I'm wounded."

I parked at the curb and left Lula in the car.

"Lula is on her way home, but she wants a doughnut," I told Connie.

"Take the box," Connie said. "I already had one."

"Anything new come in? Any gossip about Oswald?"

"Nothing. It's been quiet. My mom's going to bingo tonight. She might pick up something there."

I gave Lula the box of doughnuts and pulled into traffic.

"I've gotta make another appointment with my cosmic advisor," Lula said. "I need to know when my moons are going back to where they're supposed to be. I gotta do something to help my juju."

"Maybe it would help if you stopped waving your gun around, yelling that you were going to shoot people."

"That's not it," Lula said. "I was doing my job. I should have gotten good points for that. It's definitely about the moons."

I parked in front of Lula's apartment and helped her up the stairs.

"It's not so bad if I go up one step at a time," Lula said, letting herself into her small apartment. "And it feels good to be home. It was nice at your place, but I kept getting woke up by someone snoring."

"Me, too," I said. "It should be better tonight. Let me know if you need anything."

I left Lula and drove to Rangeman. Ranger's parking spots were all filled so I was pretty sure he was upstairs. I parked in a place reserved for visitors and went directly to the third floor. He was waiting for me when I stepped into his office.

"You saw me on a monitor?" I asked.

"At the gate. When you parked, and in the elevator," he said.

"I thought I should check on Melvin and Charlotte."

"Melvin is in the control room. He's reviewing our system for cybersecurity. Charlotte is downstairs in the gun range. It was her choice of activity. They're an interesting pair. They have a common intellectual bond. They're obsessed with hacking and gaming to the point where they can barely hold a conversation about anything else."

"Charlotte wanted to learn to shoot?"

"Only because she was fascinated with the mechanics of the gun." Ranger leaned back in his chair. "When they think no one is watching they hold hands."

A bubble of emotion caught in my throat. I knew the wonder

of those early steps in a relationship. Holding hands, the first kiss, a shared smile.

"I'm happy for them," I said.

"Do you remember the first time we held hands?"

I took a beat to think about it. "No. Do you?"

"No," Ranger said, "but I remember the first time I had to handcuff you to me to keep you safe."

"You were overbearingly protective."

Ranger grinned. "Good memories."

I nodded agreement. The initial power struggle with Ranger had been frustrating at best, but it was worthy of a smile as a memory.

"You're still overbearingly protective," I said.

"And you're still alive," Ranger said.

I gave him another nod of agreement. "Over time, I've come to appreciate your desire to protect."

"And my other desires?"

I smiled. No answer was necessary on that one.

I moved toward the door. "Let me know if there are problems with Melvin or Charlotte."

I drove through town, keeping watch for Oswald. I didn't see Oswald, but I spotted Andy Smutter panhandling in front of a coffee shop on State Street. I found a parking place a block away and walked back to Andy.

"Hey," I said. "How's it going? Remember me?"

"Stephanie Plum," he said. "Are you here for coffee? They have wonderful cinnamon buns."

"I'm here for *you*," I said. "You skipped out of the hospital."

"I'm not used to sleeping indoors and it was very noisy."

"I'm surprised you're in town. No ducks. No trees."

"I thought I would try an urban experience. It turns out this is a good location. I see the same people every day and they're very generous. Homeless people are currently the *in* thing. I almost have enough saved for a ticket to France. My dream is to live the Hemingway life in Paris."

"He made a living by writing."

"True. And I think I might try that."

"Sounds like a plan," I said. "Unfortunately, you have to re-up on a court date before you can jet off to Paris."

"I can't see Hemingway re-upping."

"You aren't Hemingway."

A woman walked past us and ignored Andy's hat that held some loose change.

"I hate to be rude," Andy said to me, "but you need to leave. You're a financial liability."

"This is ridiculous," I said.

I pulled cuffs out of my back pocket and clapped one on his wrist. I reached around for his other hand, and he shrieked and jumped away from me.

"Police brutality!" he shouted.

"First off, I'm not a cop," I said. "Second, you haven't seen any brutality yet, but I'm seriously considering kicking you in the knee."

He gave me a shove that knocked me back against the coffee shop window, and he took off running. I chased him for two blocks before he ran out of steam and tripped over another homeless person taking a nap in a doorway.

"Freaking vagrants are all over the place," he said, lying on the ground. "I mean, who sleeps in a doorway in the middle of the day?"

My lungs were burning. I bent at the waist to catch my breath. "People on drugs sleep in doorways in the middle of the day," I said.

"Well, it's horrible," Andy said. "Something should be done."

"I agree." I pulled him to his feet and snapped the second bracelet on him.

The guy in the doorway was sitting up.

"Hey, man," he said to Andy. "You got a couple bucks on ya?"

I pulled a five out of my pocket and gave it to him.

"God bless," he said.

I tugged Andy down the street, toward my car.

"You could have given that five dollars to me," Andy said.

I helped him navigate a curb. "I'm giving you something better. I'm giving you a chance to straighten your life out."

"I'd rather have the five dollars," Andy said.

CHAPTER TWENTY-TWO

Lights were off in the office when I walked in. Connie was sitting at her desk, tweezing her chin.

"I have a body receipt for Andy Smutten," I said. "I ran into him in town."

"I'll write you a check for the capture," Connie said. "It's about the only thing I can do. The computers just went down. We have no electric."

A message buzzed on my phone, and I read the message to Connie.

"This power outage is a warning. I'll restore power in ten minutes. If you don't give me the last two Baked Potatoes, I'll cut power for as long as it takes. You have until midnight Friday to turn them over to me."

I called Ranger. "Did your electric just go out?"

"Yes," he said. "We're on a generator."

"Oswald is taking responsibility. He wants Charlotte and Melvin."

I read him the message.

"This is becoming a suicide mission for Oswald," Ranger said. "There are places in Europe and Asia where hackers are protected. It's more difficult for a hacker to hide here, and Oswald's obsession with the Baked Potatoes is making him vulnerable. He's making stupid moves. Attacking the power grid will bring the feds in with resources we wouldn't ordinarily be able to access. From what we've been able to see, this is a local outage, but it's still going to get federal attention."

I ended the call with Ranger, the lights blinked on, and Connie's computer came to life.

"It's amazing that Oswald can do this," Connie said. "I have a hard time managing the apps on my iPad."

Diesel strolled in. "Oswald is brilliant but he's a complete wack job."

"Did you get his message?" I asked.

"Yes. He's being a real jerk. He's making my job impossible. Now I'm going to have to contend with the government. Melvin treated everyone to a porno movie, and by the way he chose a classic. When he was caught, it was brushed off as a prank. Oswald proved he can cut the electricity to half of Trenton. No one's going to laugh it off."

"We have twenty-four hours before he pulls the plug again," I said.

"He's not living in his car like Charlotte was doing. He's holed up somewhere with good internet. He probably has multiple computers and a backpack filled with hacking tools," Diesel said. "I have people watching the train station and hanging out on street corners in town. Oswald is like the invisible lunatic."

"I know someplace in town that has good internet," I said. "And the owner isn't in residence. Suppose Oswald didn't just happen along when Lula and I were getting clothes for Charlotte. Suppose he's been living there?"

"Alongside the cop who took him down?" Diesel asked. "I like it. Let's go for a ride."

Diesel had the fun car, but I had the crappy stealth car, so I drove. I did a drive-around in Charlotte's neighborhood, looking for the Porsche or a blue sedan. We saw four blue sedans. No Porsche. I drove past the front of the townhouse, and I cruised down the back alley. The cop car wasn't parked on the street and there was no activity. No one walking. No dogs barking. No street traffic. It was almost noon and the neighborhood felt deserted. Everyone was at work, I thought.

I parked on the cross street, and we walked down the alley to Charlotte's house. I used her key to let us in and we stood in the kitchen for a couple of beats, listening.

"Wait in the hall where you can see both doors and I'll clear the house," Diesel said.

I watched him go up the stairs and listened while he went room by room. He came down and walked through the downstairs.

"He's not here," he said. "No clothes, no trash, no toilet seat left up."

I went to the kitchen and looked in the fridge. I found the usual condiments plus a takeout box with half a stale sandwich, an expired strawberry yogurt, and two bottles of Russian River Pliny the Elder beer.

Diesel looked over my shoulder. "The beer has Oswald written all over it."

I called Charlotte and asked her if she left half a sandwich, a strawberry yogurt, and two bottles of beer in her fridge. The answer was no.

"He might have been here," I said to Diesel, "but I think he vacated after he was shot. I don't see any Band-Aids in the trash. No half-used first aid cream lying around."

"Did the police search this place?"

"Not while I was there, and I made sure the door was locked before I left. There wasn't any reason for them to search inside the house."

"I can't see him moving into Melvin's loft," Diesel said. "He'd be noticed. He couldn't hide his car and he'd be trapped in there. One door in and one door out."

"I suspect Gerard Gouge's apartment is unoccupied, but it was a major crime scene. His neighbors would notice someone living there."

"Let's look at it anyway."

———

It was easy to find Gouge's apartment. It was the one with the yellow crime scene tape still tacked across the door.

"Do your thing," Diesel said to me. "Knock on some doors and see if anyone's seen Oswald."

I pulled his photo out of my messenger bag. "He looks different without the ponytail," I said. "Are you coming with me?"

"No. This is a garden apartment, and Gouge had a ground floor unit. I want to see what's going on in the back. I'm sure there's a back door."

Gouge had the middle unit. There were three apartments on both sides of him. No one answered in the first two. An older woman answered in the end unit. I introduced myself and told her I was bond enforcement and looking for a man who might have been associated with Gerard Gouge. I showed her the photo; she looked at it and shook her head.

"Sorry, I haven't seen him," she said. "There were a lot of people here in the beginning, though. It would have been easy to miss him in the crowd."

I walked back past Gouge's apartment and rang his next-door neighbors' bell. I heard a dog barking, but no one came to the door. I did an involuntary shudder at the thought that this might be the tongue muncher. I moved on to the next house and a young woman answered with a baby in her arms. I introduced myself and she invited me in.

"I'm Catherine," she said. "Mary Jane Kuleski is my mom. She sees your grandmother at bingo sometimes."

"Grandma said she ran into your mom at the deli, and she said that you knew Gerard Gouge. I'm looking for a man who might have visited Gerard." I showed her Oswald's photo.

"I think I saw him two days ago except he didn't have a ponytail. The police cars and crime scene van left and about an hour later, this man went to Gerard's door. The yellow crime scene tape was across the door and the man stood there for a minute staring at it and then he turned and went back to his car. I was outside, pushing Sara in the stroller, so I noticed him."

"What kind of car did he have?"

"A blue sedan. It looked new. It was clean."

"Thanks," I said. "I appreciate the help." I stepped outside. "This looks like a nice neighborhood."

"It's okay," she said. "It feels kind of creepy knowing what happened to Gerard. It's hard to forget something like that. We're thinking of moving."

I was about to knock for the second time on the last apartment door when I saw Diesel come around the side of the building. I joined him in the parking lot, and we walked to my car.

"Did you break in?" I asked him.

"No, but the crime scene tape had been partially ripped off."

"I met Mary Jane Kuleski's daughter. She thinks she saw Oswald two days ago. She said he went to the door, stared at the yellow tape, and left. He got into a blue car."

"And then maybe he came back at night and let himself in through the porch slider," Diesel said.

"Hard to believe he would try to live here."

"Easier to believe that he came back looking for something."

"Gerard's laptop," I said. "The one I took from the bedroom."

We got into my car and sat for a moment.

"Where do we go from here?" I asked.

"Lunch," Diesel said.

I drove out of the apartment complex, got onto the highway, and five minutes later I pulled into the parking lot to Lumpy's Diner. The name wasn't great, but the menu consisted of seven pages of classic diner food that was absolutely edible.

We were lucky enough to get a booth by the window, giving us a view of the highway. Bucolic waterfalls, cows grazing, and fields of wildflowers are okay if you're on vacation. If you're a working girl eating in a Jersey diner you want the urban energy of traffic.

I ordered a vanilla milk shake, grilled cheese, and fries. Diesel got a burger.

"A lot has happened in a week," Diesel said. "Two grotesque deaths, two geek rescues, you almost got run over by a train, and Lula got shot."

"We haven't made any progress on capturing Oswald."

"We've kept him from killing the last two Baked Potatoes. He was having fun in the beginning, but I imagine he's grinding his teeth down to nubs now. He can't get to Melvin or Charlotte. And while he's preoccupied with this he doesn't seem to be moving forward with his global threat."

"It's global?"

"I don't know. Maybe it's not global. Maybe it's just international."

"Is the system he hacked back to running normally now?"

"My understanding is that the area of weakness still exists but hasn't been exploited. The longer Oswald waits to make his big move, the more time my employer has to fix the issue."

"Okay, that's sufficiently vague but I get the gist of it."

"It's what I know," Diesel said. "The less I know, the less I can give away if I happen to be in a drunken stupor."

I finished my grilled cheese and fries and reached for my messenger bag. "We've hit up all of Oswald's known haunts except his rental."

"The bat house?"

"We assumed it was just being used for a phony address, but

what if he decided to move into it? It's close to town. It probably has good cell service and internet. We never checked back on it."

Forty minutes later we were on Dugan Street. I parked in front of the two-story house, and we looked up and down the street. A couple of junker cars were at the curb but there were no Porsches or newly washed blue sedans. Diesel and I walked to the door and into the house. We climbed the stairs to the second floor, and I knocked on the door to Oswald's apartment. No answer.

Diesel opened the door and I softly announced bail bonds enforcement. Always good to cover my ass and go by the book. We walked through the rooms, and it was clear that someone had recently been there. A couch cushion that was misplaced, the television remote left on an end table, a cardboard Starbucks coffee cup in the trash. The bed looked like Goldilocks had tested it out. The pillow wasn't perfectly plumped, and the quilt was slightly wrinkled.

"There's nothing personal left lying around," Diesel said. "No clothes, no bathroom stuff, no computer, no food in the fridge. But someone has been here."

"I can have Ranger set up a surveillance camera."

"That would be useful," Diesel said.

We went downstairs and took the hallway to the back door. There was a small patch of dirt that served as a yard and a three-car garage that opened to the alley. Two of the garage spaces were filled with junk being stored. The third was occupied by a blue sedan.

"Interesting," Diesel said. "If he isn't in the house and he isn't in this car, where is he?"

There was a loud explosion on the street in front of the house.

"It's just a wild guess," I said, "but I think he's laughing his ass off, hiding in someone's shrubbery."

"I doubt he's laughing his ass off," Diesel said. "I would guess that he's in a blind rage that we caught him in his house."

We walked around the house and stood on the front lawn, watching my car burn. A couple of people had congregated across the street, and I could hear a siren in the distance.

Ranger called. "Babe," he said. "Your GPS just went dead."

"That's because someone blew up my car."

"It was only a matter of time," Ranger said. "Are you okay?"

"Yep."

"Do you need a ride?"

"Eventually, but not immediately. I'm at Oswald's rental house. There are some things I need to take care of here."

I filled Ranger in on some of the details, asked for the camera, and ended the call. I called Connie next, gave her the plate on the blue car, and asked her to check on it.

A cop car parked a safe distance from my inferno, and a fire truck turned onto Dugan several blocks away.

"I'm going to the garage," Diesel said. "I don't want Oswald circling around and escaping in the blue car."

Connie called back. "The plate you gave me belongs to Fred Mechanti. He has an East Brunswick address, and he reported a blue Toyota Camry stolen four days ago."

"Thanks," I said. "I found Fred's car. Oswald has been driving it."

"I'm sure Fred will be grateful," Connie said. "One more thing. Vinnie is flying into Newark with an FTA at eight o'clock, and he needs a ride. I can't pick him up because I'm taking my mother to a baby shower at the firehouse. Can you get him? It's not like we can put someone in shackles in an Uber car."

"No problem. Text me the flight information."

I called Morelli. "Oswald just blew up my car," I said. "I wasn't in it."

Morelli went silent and I imagined him staring down at his shoe, trying to compose himself.

"Okay," he finally said. "Is there more?"

"Yes. Diesel and I decided to check out Oswald's rental house. We did a walk-through and saw signs that he'd recently used the house. We went outside and found the blue car in the garage. I had Connie check the plate. Turns out it's stolen."

"Good to know," Morelli said. "I'll send someone to collect it."

"And that's when we heard an explosion on Dugan Street, and it turned out to be my car," I said. "We're thinking it was Oswald."

"Do you know where he is now?"

"No, but he can't have gone too far. He's probably on foot."

"I hear sirens," Morelli said.

"The second fire truck and an EMT truck just arrived."

"I'm at my desk. Give me ten minutes to get to you."

"Do you have the address?"

"Don't need it. I'll go to Dugan Street and follow the smell of burning rubber."

I disconnected and blew out a sigh. There was a good possibility that my moons were not in alignment.

Diesel joined me. "There's a Rangeman car in the alley, and two men who look like the Hulk in Rangeman clothes. The blue car is secure without me."

"Connie ran the plate. The car's stolen."

"Not much of a surprise," Diesel said.

"Morelli is on his way. I need to stay here to dispose of what's left of my car, but you could wander around and look for Oswald."

CHAPTER TWENTY-THREE

It was late afternoon by the time my car was towed and the last fire truck drove off. Morelli had been called away for a homicide on Stark Street, and Diesel had given up on the Oswald search. I waved at the Rangeman SUV, they drove over to me, and Diesel and I got in.

I gave them my parents' address. Grandma's brother had bequeathed his 1953 Buick to Grandma. It was a nightmare to drive but it was free and available to me when I needed it.

My mother was knitting when I stopped in to tell her I was borrowing the Buick.

"How long is your thing?" I asked.

"As of three o'clock this afternoon it was twenty-three feet long," she said. "Are you staying for dinner?"

"No," I said. "I have to pick Vinnie up at the airport."

"I have leftover meat loaf."

"I'll take it," I said.

My mom stopped knitting and packed a bag filled with leftovers. "Here's something of everything," she said. "There's enough for two if Diesel is still with you."

"Thanks," I said. "He's waiting outside. He had some phone calls to make."

I backed the Buick out of the garage and Diesel hopped in.

"I feel like I'm in a Travolta movie," he said. "We could make babies on this front seat."

"You know nothing," I said. "The backseat is the baby maker."

I chugged home in the bulbous, baby blue and white gas guzzler and parked next to Diesel's Bronco.

"I have to pick Vinnie up at the airport tonight," I said. "Can I borrow your car?"

"Are you sure you want my car? It doesn't have portholes in its hood like your car."

"If I drive the Buick to Newark, I'll have to stop six times for gas."

I let us into my apartment and unpacked the food bag. Meat loaf, mashed potatoes, gravy, green beans, a couple of apples, an orange, a bunch of bananas, homemade chocolate chip cookies, a tub of vanilla ice cream.

"Your family never disappoints," Diesel said. "They always rise to expectations."

We fixed plates and ate in the kitchen.

"Vinnie comes in at eight o'clock, so I'm leaving here at six," I said. "You never know what traffic is going to be like on the turnpike, and Vinnie isn't going to want to sit around in the terminal with a guy in cuffs."

"Do you want company?"

"Don't you have anything better to do?"

"Almost anything is better to do," Diesel said.

True enough.

"I have a videoconference at ten o'clock," Diesel said, "but I can do it on the road."

"I thought you weren't doing any of that anymore."

"It was a pleasure short-lived. Ana got me up and running again."

"It's not necessary for you to tag along," I said. "Just don't drink all the wine. I'm going to need a glass after an hour in the car with Vinnie."

I brushed my hair up into a ponytail, hung my messenger bag on my shoulder, and drove off in the yellow and black Bronco. I hit traffic ten miles before the airport turnoff on the turnpike and slowed to a crawl. This wasn't a disaster. I'd allowed for it. Besides, I was in a cool car, and I had a superior sound system with a seventies station blasting out music. I reached the airport exit, navigated the jumble of signs, and pulled into short-term parking for terminal B. I went into the terminal and saw on the big board that Vinnie's plane had landed, so I showed my paperwork to TSA and went straight to Vinnie's gate.

This wasn't my first felon pickup, so I knew the drill. Vinnie would be the last to leave the plane. They wouldn't have checked luggage. We'd go through the terminal as efficiently as possible, straight to the car.

Vinnie had gone to Miami to escort Larry Lucca back to

Trenton to stand trial for identity theft. Lucca had skipped out on his Jersey court date in favor of partying in South Beach. Vinnie had tracked him down and apprehended him.

People were beginning to straggle out of the jetway. I was standing close to the open door, watching for Vinnie. The flow of deplaning passengers stopped, and a flight attendant stepped out. Vinnie followed with Lucca. Lucca's hands were cuffed in front of him. Not as secure as hands cuffed behind, but it would allow Lucca to use the restroom.

Vinnie looks like the human version of a ferret. Slim, black hair slicked back, beady little black eyes, no apparent bone structure. His shirts are too shiny, his pants are too tight, and his rings can substitute for brass knuckles.

Lucca stood three inches taller than Vinnie and weighed about a hundred pounds more. Lucca looked like he could play defense for the Packers.

Vinnie had his hand on Lucca's right arm, I took the left arm, and we guided Lucca through the crowd of people waiting to board.

"I gotta go to the bathroom," Lucca said.

"You're going to have to hold it," Vinnie said.

"I can't hold it anymore," Lucca said. "I didn't go on the plane and now I have to go."

I wouldn't ordinarily care, but I was about to put this monster guy in Diesel's cool new car. I wasn't sure what all Lucca had to do in the bathroom, but I didn't want him doing it in the Bronco.

"Maybe you should let him go to the bathroom," I said to Vinnie.

Vinnie growled, narrowed his eyes, and yanked Lucca toward the men's room. I stood guard outside. A couple of men came out. No Vinnie or Lucca. A man went in and came out. Still no Vinnie or Lucca. I was about to call Vinnie on his cell phone when Lucca burst out of the men's room and ran past me. No handcuffs. I could hear Vinnie swearing inside the men's room. I figured if he was swearing, he had to be okay, so I took off after Lucca. He was big, but not especially fast. He was plowing through clumps of people, knocking them aside like they were bowling pins. I was running in his wake. I was more agile, but I wasn't exactly Olympics track material.

We were running flat out following exit signs. Lucca stopped for a moment, confused by the signs, and I body-slammed him. He didn't budge. He turned and looked at me like *what the hell?* I slid down his body and wrapped my arms around his leg. He tried to kick me loose, but I held tight. He got his bearings and took off power walking, dragging me along on his leg. People were clearing the way for him, looking on in horror. Okay, truth is, I felt stupid. I mean this was embarrassing, but I wasn't giving up. I didn't care if he dragged me all the way to Carteret, he was going down.

I could hear noise behind me. It was the *weee-ah, wee-ah* siren of a people mover cart. I looked over my shoulder and saw the cart and its flashing red light. It caught up to us and Vinnie jumped out. He had a cop with him. I still held tight to Lucca. Lucca turned and flailed out with his arm, catching a guy carrying a chili dog and a shake. The guy went to the floor and the dog and the shake dumped on me. I was beyond caring.

Lucca got cuffed, and I was pried loose from his leg and helped to my feet. Vinnie looked even worse than I did. He had a bloody gash on his forehead and an eye that was starting to swell and bruise.

"What?" I asked, looking at Vinnie.

"He head-butted me in the crapper," Vinnie said. "Knocked me out and got the key to the cuffs."

"It's one of my specialties," Lucca said. "It's like my head's made of granite."

Vinnie thanked the cop and the cart driver and pressed some money into their hands.

"Do you want some first aid?" I asked Vinnie.

"No," he said. "I want to get this asshole locked up in jail."

We marched Lucca across the road and into short-term parking. Vinnie smiled when we got to the Bronco.

"This is what you're driving?" he asked.

"It belongs to a friend of mine," I said.

"Sweet," Vinnie said. "No wonder you didn't want Lucca taking a leak in it."

———

I chose to take Lucca to the back door of the police station rather than parking in the lot across the street and walking him over. It was late. It was dark. I had chocolate shake down the front of me and chili in my hair.

Vinnie walked Lucca in, and fifteen minutes later Vinnie came out with his body receipt. Mission accomplished.

"Now what?" I asked Vinnie. "Do you want to go to a clinic to get your head stitched together?"

"No," Vinnie said. "Take me home."

Vinnie lived in an upscale neighborhood in Ewing Township. I took Perry Street to West Hanover and got a call from Diesel.

"One of my men on the street spotted Oswald leaving a Starbucks on State Street. Oswald got into a black Porsche and long story short, my man was following in a cab and a couple minutes ago he lost Oswald a couple blocks before Stark Street. I don't know where you are but if you're in the area keep your eyes open."

"I'm stopped at a light on West Hanover. I'm taking Vinnie home and I'm not far from Stark."

I hung up and told Vinnie to look for a black Porsche 911. I gave him the plate number and I turned onto State Street.

"I might see it," Vinnie said. "There's a black car half a block in front of us that could look like a 911. Who are we tailing?"

"I'm hoping it's Oswald Wednesday."

"The black car just turned onto Stark."

I was four cars back and I got stopped by a light. I put my flashers on and jumped the curb and crept along on the sidewalk until I got to Stark. Vinnie was loving it.

"This is what it's all about," he said. "The chase. And I don't care what anyone says, you've got balls the size of Volkswagens."

I got onto Stark and saw the 911 ahead of me. I got close enough to read the plate and knew it was Oswald's car.

"Call the police and tell them we have Oswald Wednesday in pursuit," I said to Vinnie. "Tell them we're on Stark Street."

I called Ranger on my phone and told him we were following Oswald's Porsche. Problem was that it might not be Oswald behind the wheel. No matter, I was committed to the chase.

Stark Street starts out okay but the farther you travel the

worse it gets, until it looks like a war zone with rats the size of dinosaurs. When we got to the fifth block the pill pushers and lady plumbers disappeared from the street corners. The Porsche was still in front of me. Impossible to know who was driving. I didn't see any sign of the police. The Porsche pulled to the curb in the middle of the sixth block, and someone got out from behind the wheel and ran into a dark alley between two bombed-out buildings. Vinnie and I got out and ran into the alley. Vinnie took the lead with gun drawn. We reached the end of the buildings and heard gunfire on Stark Street. We turned and cautiously crept back to Stark, staying in the alley's shadows.

A large black SUV, a Tahoe maybe, was next to the Bronco. It fired one last shot and the undercarriage of the Bronco caught fire. The fire licked up around the car and the black SUV drove away.

"What the what?" I said.

Two minutes later a Rangeman SUV angle-parked behind the flaming Bronco. Ranger's Porsche parked behind the Rangeman SUV. I came out of the alley and stood on the sidewalk, gaping at Diesel's Bronco.

Ranger came over and draped an arm around my shoulders. "Babe," he said, "you destroyed two cars in one day. Way to go."

"I was following the Porsche. It parked and someone got out and ran into the alley. Vinnie and I chased him and all of a sudden there was gunfire back on Stark. When we got to the street a black SUV was shooting up Diesel's car."

"This is the yellow and black Bronco?" Ranger asked.

"Yes."

Tank was standing next to Ranger. Tank's name says it all. He's second in command at Rangeman and he watches Ranger's back.

"Yellow and black's gang colors," Tank said. "This part of Stark belongs to Demon. Yellow and black is Venom colors. You don't drive a yellow and black car in Demon territory. The shooters probably thought someone was in the car."

Another Rangeman SUV and two police cars arrived.

"You're getting special treatment," Ranger said to me. "The police won't ordinarily patrol this block."

"I'll talk to them," Tank said.

I looked around.

"The Porsche is gone," I said.

"Probably just spare parts by now," Ranger said. "No self-respecting Demon would let a Porsche go to waste."

"Do you think a fire truck is on the way?" I asked Ranger.

"Not a chance," Ranger said.

I took a picture of what remained of the Bronco for insurance purposes.

Ranger picked a chunk of chili out of my hair. "Food fight?" he asked.

"A hiccup in an apprehension."

"I'll take you home," Ranger said. "Tank will do cleanup here. Jorge just arrived. He can take Vinnie home."

"Sounds good."

We walked back to Ranger's car and he opened the door for me. "Your place or mine?"

"My place," I said. "I need to break the bad news to Diesel."

———

Diesel was sprawled on the couch, watching television, when I walked in.

"Good thing there's sports," he said. "Everything else on television is worthless."

"I have bad news."

"Worse than my television announcement?"

I showed him the picture of his car.

"What is it?" Diesel asked.

"Your car."

Diesel sat up and looked at the picture again. "You should have used low light mode. All I can see is a bonfire."

"That's your car."

"The bonfire?"

"Yep."

"Has it ever occurred to you that you should be using public transportation?"

"Vinnie spotted Oswald turning onto Stark Street. I was on his bumper when he parked and ran into an alley. Long story short is I left the Bronco temporarily parked in gang territory and somebody fired about fifty rounds into it, and it caught on fire."

"And then you took its picture?"

"I thought you might need it for insurance purposes. There's also a police report."

"What happened to Oswald?"

"Disappeared," I said.

Diesel stood and stretched. His T-shirt rode up, exposing his toned abs, and I might have attacked him if I didn't have chili in my hair. Thank goodness for chili.

"You smell good," Diesel said. "You smell like a chili dog. It's making me hungry." He walked past me, into the kitchen. "Do you want something? Beer? Leftover whatever it is we've got in the fridge?"

"No thanks," I said. "I'm going to take a shower and go to bed."

"Ana came in and did some tidying up while you were gone. She's got fresh sheets on the bed. Just in case you're feeling domestic. That's a chore you can cross off your list."

No wonder he was taking a nap on the couch when I came home, I thought. Ana probably exhausted him. At least she had the courtesy to change the linens.

CHAPTER TWENTY-FOUR

Diesel was already at his computer when I shuffled into the kitchen for morning coffee.

"This isn't normal," I said. "You're supposed to still be asleep. You never wake up before me."

"It occurred to me while you were in the shower last night that Oswald would need a way to get home. He probably conducted whatever business he was doing in the alley, found out he didn't have a car, and walked away from the scene. The logical thing for him to do would be to look for a car to steal but in that part of Trenton that might be a problem. Cars have wheel locks and alarms. So, he might walk a couple blocks into a safer neighborhood where he could get picked up by Uber."

"Smart thinking," I said.

"It gets better. I had Melvin hack into the Uber computer,

and he texted me an hour ago with the information. Uber did a pickup four blocks from Stark Street at the right time and took the customer to an address on East State Street. The customer was Oliver Welk. Oliver Welk is one of Oswald's known aliases."

"So, we're back to State Street."

"Your dad's cab pickups and drop-offs, the sightings, and the Uber drop-off are all within a four-block area and all on State Street. Ground zero is the intersection of East State and South Broad. I have the map up on my screen. It's strange. He keeps coming back to this area, but he seems to camp out in other unoccupied spaces like his rental apartment and his victims' homes."

"Maybe he feels safer moving around."

"In the beginning of the week you saw Oswald leaving an office building on State Street. We never circled back to that building," Diesel said. "We should check it out."

I poured my coffee into a to-go mug, grabbed a frozen waffle, and hung my messenger bag on my shoulder.

"It's fifty degrees and drizzling," Diesel said.

I snagged a sweatshirt from the hooks by the door. "I'm ready."

We got to the parking lot and the only transportation option was the borrowed Buick. Diesel drove so I could enjoy my breakfast.

"I've driven tanks that cornered better than this car," Diesel said.

"Where did you drive tanks?"

"Afghanistan."

"I didn't know you were military."

"I'm not . . . exactly. Don't ask."

"Mercenary?"

"No. That would be a big cut in my pay grade, and I wouldn't have an Ana."

"Do you by any chance know someone named Gabriela Rose?"

"No. Should I?"

"It was just a thought that crossed my mind. There seemed to be similarities in your lifestyles, with the exception of fashion."

Diesel came to the intersection of South Broad and East State Street.

"Turn right on State and take any parking place," I said. "The building is on the first block, across the street."

"Easier said than done," Diesel said, struggling to parallel park. "This car is a beast."

We got out of the car and Diesel looked at me. "If we leave the key in the ignition, someone might steal it."

"No doubt," I said. "It's a classic in primo condition. And no, we aren't going to leave the key in the ignition. Big Blue belongs to Grandma."

"Does she drive it?"

"She doesn't drive anything. She had her license taken away. Permanently."

"Vehicular homicide?"

"She likes to go fast, and she demolished a police car. Fortunately, no one was in it." We crossed the street and I stopped in front of the building. "This is it."

Many of the buildings in this part of town were multiple use. Retail businesses on the ground floor and condos or professional offices on the upper floors. This particular building was all offices. We went into the lobby and looked at the directory on the wall. Four floors. The first floor was dedicated to a dentist and an insurance company. All other floors were occupied by a variety of businesses.

We started canvassing on the second floor. We'd open the door and look inside. If someone was in there we'd step in, show them the photo of Oswald, and ask if they'd seen him. If the door was locked, Diesel would open it. We did the top three floors and got a big zero.

We'd saved the dentist office on the first floor for last because neither of us wanted to go into the dentist office. The receptionist immediately recognized Oswald.

"He was here a couple days ago," she said. "He was a new client. He lost a filling, and we were able to squeeze him in."

"Did he give you an address? A phone number?" I asked.

She checked back through her appointments. "Here he is," she said. "Oliver Welk. He lives on Dugan Street." She wrote the address and phone number on a sticky note and handed it to me. "I'm a big fan of the police," she said. "They rescued my cat from a storm sewer last year."

I gave her a thumbs-up and Diesel and I left the building.

"Does anyone ever question your badge?" Diesel asked.

"Almost never. A lot of people who have no experience with bail bonds assume it's part of the sheriff's office."

Diesel dialed the number on the sticky note. He smiled and hung up. "That was the number for the DMV."

"Oswald came out of the building and turned left before we started to chase him," I said.

We walked left and covered two blocks with no success at spotting Oswald. The drizzle had stopped but the sky was overcast and there was a chill in the air.

"Whose dumb idea was this?" Diesel asked.

"It was your dumb idea. You wanted to circle back to the office building."

"I've circled enough."

"Okay, do you have any other dumb ideas you want to try?" I asked him.

"There's still the *Use Stephanie as Bait* idea."

"I can't get excited about that."

"I'm starting to lean toward letting Oswald pull the plug on the grid at midnight and then he's the feds' problem," Diesel said.

"What about Auntie?"

"Auntie would be unhappy."

"Is she really your aunt?"

"Only in the broadest sense that she might be human," Diesel said.

"And she's your boss?"

"She's everyone's boss."

We'd been walking while we were talking and now were back at the Buick.

"We need a car," Diesel said. "I always thought it would be fun to own a muscle car, until I drove this."

"I imagine Ana is working on it."

I needed an Ana. More than that, I needed a fast infusion of cash so I could buy another crappy car.

Lula called. "You gotta come rescue me," she said. "I can't take another day being locked away up here. I'm getting claustrophobic. And I'm getting left out of stuff. I don't know what's going on, and somebody probably ate my doughnut."

"It's only been one day."

"Yeah, but I'm a people person. I'm gregarious. Where are you? What are you doing?"

"I'm in town with Diesel and we're not doing anything."

"I heard your car got exploded. Are you driving around in Diesel's cool Bronco?"

"No. That got exploded, too. I've got the Buick."

"Well, I can't be driven around in the Buick all day. It's got no sound system. You need to get another car. Come and get me, and we can go shopping."

"Lula is ready to solve the world's problems," I said to Diesel.

"I'll hang out here," he said. "I'm not doing any more door-to-door, but surveillance sounds manageable."

Lula was waiting at the curb when I pulled up in front of her house. She was wearing black tights that bulged slightly where she was bandaged, black biker boots, and a bright yellow sequined tank top under a black leather jacket. Her hair was hidden under a pink Marilyn Monroe–style wig.

"Ow," she said, getting into the Buick. "Ow, ow."

"Are you sure you want to do this?"

"Hell, yeah. I'll be fine. I just need a doughnut. Maybe a bucket of chicken."

"I thought we could check in with Connie and then pick up your car."

"Perfect. I'm ready to kick some butt. I want a piece of that Oswald creep."

"We're working on it."

"Are you making any progress?"

"Diesel thinks we are, but I'm not convinced."

Lula's red Firebird was parked in front of the office. I pulled in behind it and Lula got out.

"Ow, ow, ow, ow," she said, limping up to the office door.

I opened the door for her, and she limped in. "Ow, ow, ow, ow."

Connie looked over her computer at Lula's leg. "I guess that hurts," Connie said.

"Only when I walk or move or breathe," Lula said. "Where's the doughnuts?"

"I skipped the doughnuts this morning. I didn't think you'd be coming in," Connie said.

"This office is going to heck," Lula said. "One day we gotta eat bagels instead of doughnuts and then next thing you know there's nothing. Not even a stale bagel."

"We can get a box of doughnuts on the way to get a bucket of chicken," I said.

"I guess that would be okay," Lula said. "It's not like we're on the same schedule, anyway. This would be more like lunch doughnuts."

"Anything new going on here?" I asked Connie. "Has anyone seen Oswald?"

"No word on Oswald. Vinnie called in and said he had a headache."

"Lucca head-butted him in the men's room."

"Vinnie said you saved the day. He's giving you credit for the capture. Do you want a check, or do you want me to deposit it in your account?"

"Deposit it. I need a car."

"That could be first thing on our agenda," Lula said. "We should go car shopping. There's a new place where the farmer's market used to be in North Trenton. I got a special relationship with the owner, Slick Eddie. He used to negotiate levels of enjoyment when customers wanted to spend time with my friend Nicole. Nicole and me worked the same corner on Stark sometimes during the rush hour."

"I guess it wouldn't hurt to look," I said.

"He'll give you a good price," Lula said. "He owes me some favors. And now that I've been shot, I can play the pity card. The way I see it, if you got cards you gotta play them."

I helped Lula make her way back to the Buick and I drove to the bakery.

"I'll wait here," Lula said. "I want a dozen Boston crèmes."

I came back with the Boston crèmes and drove to Cluck-in-a-Bucket.

"I want a big bucket of extra crispy," Lula said. "And then I want curly fries and some Clucky Biscuits with gravy. No, wait. Skip the gravy. I don't want to get gravy on my tank top. Gravy's hard to get out of sequins."

I returned with the food and drove to North Trenton. The car lot was next to an auto body repair shop. I thought this arrangement was very convenient for spiffing up beaters so they looked nice, and also for creating new VIN tags to stick on the car if one was needed. Not that I was judgmental. Every car deserved an owner, right? It wasn't the car's fault if it had an unfortunate history.

Lula got out of the Buick and approached the extra-large guy who was standing in the doorway of the cargo container office.

"Ow, ow, ow, ow," Lula said.

The guy recognized Lula and was all smiles. "Lula! Good to see you. Been a long time. What's with the ow, ow, ow?"

"Some lunatic shot me. Can you imagine?"

"Anybody I know?"

"He's an out-of-town lunatic," Lula said.

"I see you're driving a classic," he said. "Are you looking to trade it?"

"No," Lula said. "Stephanie needs a car. Gotta be four doors and in good shape. She's on a limited budget but I know you'll give her a good deal."

He spread his arms wide. "Take a look at what's here. Let me know if you see something you like."

"None of these cars have prices on them," I said to Lula.

"Don't worry about it," she said. "He's a businessman."

I thought that might be code for fence, but best not to ask.

"How about this white Honda CR-V?" I asked.

"Good choice if you're on a budget," Slick Eddie said. "It's a 2002 and in great shape. Low mileage."

"How much is it?" I asked.

"How much money do you have?"

I did some fast calculations. I just got some decent recovery money for Lucca. The mooner, the bakery smasher, and the duck roaster were all small change, but they added up.

"Four thousand and thirty-five dollars," I said.

"You're in luck," he said. "That's what this car cost. Congratulations."

"You've got a nice variety of cars here," Lula said to Eddie. "You've even got some luxury cars."

"There's a market for the high end," Eddie said. "I sold a Porsche this morning already."

That caught my attention. I knew someone who might be

in the market for a new car that could be purchased under the radar.

"I know someone who was looking to buy a Porsche," I said. "His name is Oswald Wednesday."

"That's the dude," Eddie said. "Is he a friend?"

Lula stepped forward. "Not exactly," she said. "We've been looking for him. He owes us some money, if you know what I mean."

Eddie gave his head a shake. "That's what happens when you don't have a negotiator working on your behalf. That would never have happened if you were on my team."

"Are you still actively negotiating?" Lula asked him.

"No. I gave that up. It's a young man's game. I'm all about the car lot now. And I have part interest in the auto body."

"I wouldn't mind having some information on Oswald Wednesday," Lula said.

"I'll give you what I have," Eddie said.

CHAPTER TWENTY-FIVE

I drove the Buick back to my parents' house and Lula followed me in my new CR-V. I ran in to tell Grandma I brought her car back and Lula hobbled after me.

Grandma and my mother were at the kitchen table. Grandma was playing a game on her laptop and my mother was knitting.

"Look at you up and around," Grandma said to Lula. "I heard you got shot."

"Twice," Lula said. "In the leg."

"Is that the bulge in your tights?" Grandma asked. "Is it all bandaged?"

"Yeah," Lula said. "Do you want to see?"

Grandma leaned forward and Lula pulled her tights down so Grandma could see the bandage and the stitches on the lesser wound.

"That's a beauty," Grandma said. "It looks like they did a good job with the stitches, too. That's important so they don't leave a scar. And I see you're wearing one of them thongs. I tried wearing a thong a while back, but I got hemorrhoids from it."

"My booty was made for a thong," Lula said. "They fit just right on me on account of I got a lot of cheek. That's the secret to being a successful thong wearer."

"I brought the Buick back," I said. "I was able to get another car."

My mother's thing was in a massive heap on the floor at her feet.

"How long is your thing?" I asked.

"Twenty-seven feet," my mother said.

"It's nice you got a hobby," Grandma said to my mother, "but it's taking up half the kitchen. You're gonna have to find a new place to knit."

"It's not a hobby," my mother said. "It's my destiny."

"You made more sense when you were hitting the hootch," Grandma said.

"Are you and Joseph going to be here for dinner?" my mom asked.

I did a mental head slap. It was Friday. Date night. And I had Diesel sleeping in my bed. Plus, I was looking at a countdown to Trenton going dark at midnight.

"Maybe," I said. "I have a lot going on. Probably you shouldn't count on me."

"Good thinking," Grandma said. "It could be a skimpy dinner unless we figure out how to eat the thing."

Lula and I got back to my Honda and I called Diesel.

"I'm texting information to you on Oswald's new car," I said. "It's a three-year-old black Porsche Panamera with tinted windows. I've also got the plate number for you. He got the plate when he bought the car."

"Do you suppose the plate was made in someone's basement?"

"It's possible it was taken off someone else's car."

"How do you know all this?"

"I bought a car from the same guy who sold the Porsche to Oswald."

"That's my girl," Diesel said. "I bet you got a bargain."

"The car salesperson used to arrange business meetings for one of Lula's friends from a previous life."

"I'll keep my eyes open. I'm staking out State and South Broad."

I called Morelli and gave him the same information. "I might not be able to do date night tonight," I said. "I need to keep searching for Oswald. Let's reschedule date night for tomorrow."

Lula had polished off two doughnuts while I was gone and she'd focused her attention on the chicken and biscuits.

"I'm in a mood to sniff out that loser Oswald," she said. "I'm pretty sure my moons are lined up again and I got my juju back from you, being that you destroyed two cars in one day. That's like old times."

"Do you have any ideas about where you want to sniff?" I asked Lula.

"I've been thinking about it. We know that he spends time in the downtown area. So where does he eat? He doesn't seem like a fast-food person. And the way he moves around doesn't make it easy for him to do gourmet cooking. He could be eating in nice restaurants but that would make him easy to see. And anyway, I'm guessing by now he's running out of clean clothes. So that leaves takeout food and stores with fancy prepared food. We can go to the fancy food stores and flash Oswald's picture. I got an app on my phone that tells me where they are. And then you could ask Melvin to hack into some of the food delivery people."

"That's brilliant."

"Yeah, and I wasn't even high when I thought about it. Okay, so I might have been double dosing on the pain meds but I'm a big girl. You gotta take that into consideration when you prescribe for me."

"Are you on meds now?"

"No. I used them all up and they won't give me anymore. I could get some from the hair salon but I'm afraid Amy is still there, and I'd have to make an appointment."

I called Melvin and asked if he could hack into delivery services in the downtown area.

"Easy peasy," he said. "Are we looking for deliveries to O.W.?"

"Yes. How's life at Rangeman?"

"It's amazing. Ranger lets me hang in the control center and the internet speed is unbelievable here."

"How about Charlotte?"

"I think she misses the freedom of being able to move around outside, but she's able to keep her business going here. And she likes the egg salad and fresh fruit at the dining area. We always eat together."

"Let me know if you get a hit on the deliveries," I said. "I'm in the field."

"Roger," Melvin said.

"He's a nice person," Lula said. "I'm glad he didn't get his tongue cut out."

By the time I was rolling down South Broad, Lula had a list of stores to visit.

"There aren't a whole lot of specialty shops in our targeted area," Lula said. "I've got seven possibilities. If we don't score in any of them, I can search a larger area."

I turned onto State Street and Diesel called. "I'm hanging out on State Street, and I think you just drove by. Is that your new SUV?"

"Yep. Lula had a genius idea. Oswald has to be getting food somewhere. We're checking it out."

"He's a food snob," Diesel said. "Ditto wine."

"We figured. I'll let you know how it goes."

I parked on a side street a couple blocks and around the corner from Diesel's surveillance spot and pulled Lula's list of eateries up on my phone. Four out of the seven possibilities were on East State Street. I hit all four while Lula stayed in the car. None of the four had an employee who recognized Oswald's photo. When I returned there were three doughnuts left in the box, and two pieces of fried chicken left in the bucket. Lula was asleep, snoring. I heard her half a block away. It sounded like someone was working with a chain saw.

I decided it was easier to walk to the remaining three stores than to try to wake Lula.

Newman's Specialty was one block off State. It was a high-end deli that had cases of packaged entrees, salads, and sandwiches. It also had delicacies like caviar, smoked salmon, foie gras, and Swiss chocolates.

I showed Oswald's picture to the woman at the register and got an immediate response.

"He's become a regular customer," she said. "I hope he isn't in any trouble. He's so charming. Very discerning. Has preferences in caviar and salmon."

"It's a small matter," I said. "I believe he might have some useful information. Do you know where he lives?"

"No. Sorry. He pays cash and he's never asked for delivery."

"Is he here every day?"

"No. It's random. Frequently he'll stop in after work. Once he mentioned that he took the train to New York."

"Thanks," I said. "This has been helpful."

The last two stores were Korean groceries and couldn't identify Oswald as a customer.

I left Lula sleeping in the car and walked down State Street to where Diesel was lounging in a doorway.

"You look like a street person," I said.

"Mission accomplished."

If I was being honest, he looked like a sexy street person, if such a thing existed.

"A woman working in a gourmet deli a block away said Oswald is a regular customer," I said. "She told me that he frequently came in after work, but not on any set day of the week."

I saw Diesel's focus move from me to something in the near distance, across the street. I followed his line of sight and saw Wulf. He was in front of a coffee shop, watching us.

"What's this about?" I asked Diesel.

"No clue," Diesel said. "Maybe he's shadowing me."

"Is that normal? Does he always follow you around?"

"Only when hell gets boring."

"He isn't the spawn of Satan, is he?"

Diesel smiled. "He's always evasive when I ask him that question."

"So, what is it about him that you dislike?"

"I went to grade school and to summer camp with him. He lied and cheated his way through. He didn't have to. He has a genius-level IQ. He found it amusing to game the system. I did, too, but I wasn't as good as Wulf."

"That's why you dislike him? Because he's better at lying and cheating than you are?"

Diesel grinned. "No. I was good enough at lying and cheating to get by. Wulf was the sneaky loner who put snakes in sleeping bags at camp and never got caught."

"Did he put a snake in your sleeping bag?"

"Only once."

Wulf wasn't wearing his cape. He'd replaced it with a black leather jacket that I'd kill to have. He gave a curt nod to us, turned, and walked away.

"No attention span," Diesel said.

"I'm going back to my car. Let me know if something exciting happens."

CHAPTER TWENTY-SIX

Lula was awake and sitting up when I returned. I approached the car and Oswald stepped out from behind a van. My attention immediately went to the remote controller he held in his hand.

"Guess what I've got," he said, waving the controller. "This is real-life gaming. I've got your friend wearing enough explosives to take down this whole block. Yes, but then you'll kill yourself, you're thinking." He shook his head. "You would be thinking wrong. I can explode one charge at a time with this device. For instance, I could just take off one gigantic breast. Or I could turn half of her into bloody mush. The technological advances that have been made in detonation are amazing.

"Fortunately for me, fate stepped in, and some misguided thugs blew up your car last night, allowing me to complete my transaction. Ordinarily I would have had plenty of explosives, but

I've had so many good opportunities to use my stash lately that I had to purchase more."

"My understanding is that you lost your car as well."

"Yes. That was a shame. I liked that car."

I think I was putting up a pretty good show of staying calm, but inside I was a mess. My heart was pounding and my stomach was sick.

"Get behind the wheel," Oswald said, pulling a gun out of his pocket. "We're going for a short ride."

He took me to the end of the block, across South Broad, and down two more blocks. I pulled into an unsecured underground garage and parked next to Oswald's recently purchased Porsche. The garage was mostly empty. Some junker cars and several pickups were scattered around. Light was dim.

"What is this?" I asked.

"It's a condo building that's just been bought and is due for a full building renovation. It's empty except for me and a couple vagrants. Both of you get out and go straight to the stairs."

"I can't do stairs on account of you shot me," Lula said. "And you got my hands in twisty-tie handcuffs so I can't even pull myself along."

"You will do stairs, or I will blow you up in the garage," Oswald said.

"What about the elevator?" Lula asked.

"The elevators don't work," Oswald said. "This building is scheduled to be gutted in two weeks."

"Ow," Lula said, getting out of the car. "Ow, ow, ow."

"Here's the deal," Oswald said to Lula. "I'd rather not leave you here where someone might find you. And I'm not carrying you up four flights of stairs. So, either you stop saying *ow* and walk up the stairs or else I'll encourage you to cooperate by shooting off your fingers one at a time."

"That would be a mean thing to do," Lula said.

"I like doing mean things," Oswald said. "I get off on it." He looked at me. "I know you carry a pair of cuffs on you. Get them out and put them on."

I took the cuffs out of my back jeans pocket, cuffed myself, and held my hands out so he could see. Lula hobbled to the stairs and took them one at a time. She got to the first floor and stopped.

"You got any drugs on you?" she asked Oswald. "I could use some drugs. I took all my pain meds ahead of time."

"Keep climbing," Oswald said.

Lula got to the second floor and stopped again.

"I got to catch my breath," she said. "I'm worn out from you shooting me. I barely made it out of the hospital."

"I shot you in the leg," Oswald said. "You probably didn't even bleed with all that fat. I meant to shoot you in something vital, but I was in a hurry."

"What do you mean *all that fat*? I happen to be solid muscle except for my titties. I was toned perfection before you shot me."

I couldn't tell if Lula was serious or stalling. Either way it was working to my advantage. Ranger would be able to trace my car. And then it hit me. I bought the car this morning. Ranger wouldn't have had time to put a tracker on it.

"Move!" Oswald said to Lula.

"I can't go any further," Lula said. "My leg is burning like fire."

Oswald drew his sidearm. "I'm not going to bother with you," he said to Lula. "I'm going to start removing fingers from your friend here."

Lula limped up the stairs, grunting and saying the occasional *ow*.

We got to the top floor and Oswald motioned for us to go to the end unit. He unlocked the door and we stepped into a large condo with windows that looked out over the city. It would be beautiful when it was renovated. At the moment it was a wreck. Dingy wallpaper, half peeling off. Wood floors that were scarred from carpet removal. A bare bulb where a chandelier once hung. The kitchen was mostly intact. There was a pump bottle of dishwashing liquid by the sink and a small dish drain with clean dishes and cutlery in it. The counter held a roll of paper towels, a salt and pepper shaker, and a charging station. A small fry pan was on the electric stove top. Everything was very neat and relatively clean. The dining area held a card table and four chairs.

"Is this home?" I asked Oswald.

"Such as it is," he said. "What it lacks in luxury it makes up for in safety and convenience. The building hasn't been condemned, so it's remained accessible. My car is hidden. It's not in a neighborhood where people pay attention to their neighbors. The building next door is due for demolition."

"I'm curious," I said. "Why were you going back to the empty Baked Potatoes' houses?"

"I collected equipment as best I could on my redemption visit. When I brought it all back here and I started downloading and looking at files, I realized I didn't have what I needed. So, I went back to do a more thorough search. In the case of Charley Q, I stayed a while because it was comfortable and it had fast internet speed. You ruined that for me. Just as you ruined my use of the rental property."

Lula had settled herself on a folding chair in the dining area. She was sitting straight, careful not to squash the explosives that were taped to the vest she was wearing.

"Now what?" I asked Oswald.

Oswald shrugged out of a backpack. "Now I get in touch with Diesel, since he's inserted himself into the middle of this operation."

Oswald took cell phone photos of Lula and me and sent them to Diesel.

"I'm sorry I won't get to see his reaction," Oswald said. "Our paths have crossed several times but never at this level. The stakes were never especially high before this. This time the stakes are significant, and you're frosting on the cake. I really hadn't counted on capturing you, but I couldn't resist when I saw you park your car. Especially since your friend was an easy mark. I had the cuffs on her before she even woke up."

"You better not have taken liberties with me while I was sleeping," Lula said to Oswald.

"Women remember my liberties," Oswald said. "If you aren't in pain and you don't have scars, I didn't take liberties."

"That's sick," Lula said. "You should go get help. There are programs for sick people like you."

"I like being sick," Oswald said. "I get pleasure from it."

"I thought you got pleasure from hacking," I said.

"I get satisfaction from hacking. And I get money and respect. Pleasure is in a separate category. Before we're through I hope to get some pleasure from you."

A lightning flash of revulsion mixed with terror shot through me. I felt cold sweat beading on my upper lip and my palms were sweaty. I bore down on the fear and ordered myself to get it together.

Oswald's phone rang and I knew from his face that it was Diesel.

"Yes?" Oswald said, answering the ring. He listened for a beat and his expression changed from one of enjoying the moment to one of hard contempt. "Here are my terms," Oswald said. "I want Charley Q and HotWiz. I will exchange them for Stephanie Plum and her large, loud friend. Right now, she's intact, but that will change if you don't deliver. If you don't know where the last two Potatoes are you need to use every resource to find them. If I don't hear good news from you by midnight, Ms. Plum will lose a finger. And she will continue to lose fingers every hour after that until I have the hackers."

Oswald disconnected. His face was pale with red splotches on his cheeks. "I will not be denied," he said.

"I don't think he knows where they are," I said. "I tracked them down and briefly spoke to them, and then they went into hiding."

"Not my problem," Oswald said. "If I don't get satisfaction from eliminating the last of the Potatoes, I'll get satisfaction from you, so you'd better hope your boyfriend finds them."

I wasn't sure if he was talking about Morelli or Diesel, so I ignored the boyfriend remark.

"I don't understand this redemption vendetta," I said, speaking slowly, making an effort to maintain control over my voice. "Why is it so important that you eliminate the Baked Potatoes?"

"They had the audacity to hack me."

"My understanding is that they thought it was a challenge. They didn't realize you'd be upset."

"They knew exactly what they were doing. They were unseating the king. If it became known what they accomplished, it would be a crushing defeat for me."

"They're just some B-level hackers that got lucky," I said.

"Those lucky hackers managed to infiltrate my servers. And one of them managed to install ransomware that locked down an entire system."

"I find that hard to believe."

"Believe it."

"Okay, so even if they did install some ransomware, I don't see where it's such a big deal. You're the genius hacker. Can't you just fix it?"

"They locked me out of a year's worth of work precisely when I was about to execute the most spectacular hack and ransom demand of my career. I was about to become the most famous hacker of all time."

"Hunh," Lula said. "You don't look like all that to me. Melvin might be a better hacker. He replaced the evening news with a classic porno. What were you going to do that could beat out Melvin?"

"I hacked into the Russian sector of the International Space Station," Oswald said. "In case you don't know, the ISS consists of various modules owned by Japan, the U.S., the EU, and the Russians. I was able to install software that enabled me to gain control of the ISS propulsion systems. I was about to ransom one hundred million dollars from each of the participants. If they didn't pay up, I had the ability to crash the station into Moscow, Tokyo, Paris, or New York City."

"Is that really possible?" I asked.

"Of course it's possible," Oswald said. "I was preparing to give a demonstration of my capabilities when the Baked Potatoes bumbled in and hijacked what had up to that point been a perfectly executed hack."

"Would you really crash the space station into one of those cities if they don't pay?"

"Without hesitation." He grinned and his smiling face was even more frightening than his angry face. "Truth is, even if they pay up, I'll crash the ISS regardless. NASA fired me from my consulting job and blacklisted me a decade ago. My ultimate revenge would be to take out Goddard Space Flight Center in Maryland." More scary smiling. "Sweet, right?"

"Yeah," I said. "Sweet."

Omigod, I thought, this guy is completely insane. He's like Dr. Evil in an Austin Powers movie. All he needs is a Mini Oswald.

"Can't you just retrace your steps and sort of start over?" I asked him.

"It's not something I can do overnight. However, what I *can* do in a relatively short amount of time is find the Baked Potato who's keeping me from accessing the encrypted program I was using to control the ISS."

"What happens when you find the Potato?"

"I'll persuade him or her to remove the ransomware and the world will be good again."

I suspected the world wouldn't be good for the Potato.

"There are only two Potatoes left," Oswald said. "I find it hard to believe Diesel won't give them up to save your life."

"How do you know it wasn't one of the other Potatoes?"

"I know because I tortured them, and they had nothing to tell me."

"And then after you tortured them, you killed them?"

"My fans would expect nothing less."

I nodded. "Of course. I get that."

I looked over at Lula and her eyes were rolling around in their sockets. I glanced down at my watch. Our little chat had used up forty-five minutes of my finger countdown.

"Are you still going to shut the grid down at midnight?" I asked Oswald.

"Probably. It depends on timing. Pulling the plug on the area's electric will help me make my exit. Darkness and confusion are always helpful."

Oswald took his laptop out of his backpack and set it on the card table.

"I have work to do now. I'm going to have to move you out of here," he said. "We're going down the hall to the bedroom on the left."

"Ow," Lula said, standing. "Ow, ow, ow."

"You're going to be the first one to lose a tongue," Oswald said to Lula. "I'd cut it out now, but it leaves a mess."

"That wouldn't be good," Lula said, "because I notice you keep your hidey-hole nice and neat. Even your dishes are clean in your dish rack. I bet your refrigerator has its jars all lined up and spotless. No ketchup smudges or anything. I'm surprised that you could tolerate all the blood involved in the throat slitting and tongue circumcision."

"It was necessary," he said. "I had to make a statement. I thought the tongue amputation was a nice touch. And while the blood is messy, the sight and feel of it is pleasant."

"I would never have thought of that," Lula said. "I bet you would have made a good butcher."

I looked over at Oswald to see if he was going to kill Lula on the spot.

"I think you're right," he said, smiling. "I would have made a very good butcher."

Lula walked into the middle of the bedroom and looked around. "There's no furniture in here. How are we supposed to sit?"

"Not my problem," Oswald said, stepping out of the room, closing and locking the door.

Lula went to the door and tried the handle. "Yep, it's locked, all right." She crossed the room and looked out the window. "There's an alleyway down there and the building next to us looks worse than this one. The windows are dirty and some of them are broken. It looks abandoned."

I looked out at the building. "Oswald said it was going to be torn down."

Lula shimmied down a wall and sat against it. "Do you think Diesel will give up Melvin and Charlotte?"

"No. I think he'll go to Ranger for help, and they'll come in here like commandos."

"That might get me blown up," Lula said.

"Oswald plans to blow us up anyway. He wouldn't have told

us about the space station if he intended to trade us for Melvin and Charlotte. He wanted to vent and to brag and we were a safe audience."

"It's that damn freaking moon that did this to me," Lula said. She looked down at the vest. "Do you think you can get me out of this?"

"I'd be afraid to try," I said. "It looks complicated, and I don't know anything about explosives."

"This is depressing. I never got to do a hair correction. What are people going to think when they see me dead with bad hair?"

If Oswald detonated Lula's vest there wasn't going to be enough of her left to fill a jelly jar. I didn't think she had to worry about her hair.

"I don't suppose you have your cell phone on you," I said to Lula.

"He took it," Lula said. "How about you?"

"He took mine, too."

A small bright spot in the whole ugly situation was that if Oswald didn't disable my phone, Ranger could track it.

From time to time Oswald would check on us. He'd open the door a crack and peek in. This would last maybe ten seconds before he'd slam the door shut and lock it.

"What the heck is he doing out there?" Lula asked. "I don't hear any sounds. We've been locked in this stupid room for hours."

"I imagine he's working. Finding the shortest route to crash the space station into something."

———

It was beginning to get dark in our bedroom. The sky was overcast and the sun was setting. Not a lot of light was filtering in between the buildings. My peripheral vision caught a flash of motion at the window. I turned to see what had caught my attention and saw Melvin in a homemade harness, dangling on a rope, looking in at us. He was wearing a bike helmet with a GoPro camera attached and he looked terrified.

"Holy crap," I whispered, and I made a motion to Lula not to say anything.

A second rope dropped down. It had a harness attached and Melvin pantomimed that it was for us.

Lula and I rushed to the window and tried to open it. I got the latch turned, but the window wouldn't budge.

"It's old and stuck," Lula whispered. "It needs a good shove. On the count of three . . . one, two, three."

We jammed our hands against the window frame, but it didn't move.

Melvin had his feet and his hands against the window like Spider-Man. His eyes were wide, staring at Lula and the vest with the explosives attached.

"I can't see any way of doing this except to break the window," Lula said.

"It'll make too much noise. It'll bring Oswald in here."

"Yeah, but what if we break the window and you don't waste any time getting your ass up the rope to the roof."

"What about you?"

"I'll stop Oswald."

"You're going to sacrifice yourself for me."

"What the hell. My moons are for shit anyway."

"Not gonna happen. If Melvin is here, I'm sure Ranger isn't far behind. We'll hunker in and wait."

The door to the bedroom crashed open and Oswald walked into the room. "What's going on?"

"Nothing," Lula said. "We were just talking."

Oswald spotted Melvin and went for the gun that was stuck under the waistband of his jeans. Melvin pushed off the widow, swung out on his tether, swung back, and broke through the window glass feetfirst. He lost momentum and slammed back against the wall and the smashed window.

"Nice of you to drop in," Oswald said to Melvin, holding him at gunpoint. "I've been looking forward to this."

I heard a scrambling sound on the outside wall of the building and turned in time to see Charlotte slide down the second rope like it was a fire pole. She had her arms and legs wrapped around the rope and she had a gun in her hand.

Oswald swung around, pointed his gun at Charlotte, and she shot him. There was a look of astonishment on Oswald's face, blood spurted out of his chest, and he fell over and crashed to the floor.

No one moved or spoke. We all just stood there breathing hard. Charlotte was the first to say something. She was holding tight to the rope and her eyes were huge and glassy.

"Help," Charlotte said.

We all rushed to the broken window and pulled Charlotte inside. She sat down hard on the floor and made a sound that was something between a giggle and a sob.

"I'm okay," she said, stifling another sob. "I'm okay." She looked at Melvin. "Are you okay?"

"Yeah," he said. "I'm okay."

"I'm okay, too," Lula said.

I joined in. "Me, too."

We all looked at Oswald, lying on the floor. He wasn't okay.

Lula walked over and looked down at him. "He has a hole in his chest the size of a grapefruit."

"I was on the roof, watching the relay from Melvin's GoPro, and I was afraid Oswald was going to shoot Melvin," Charlotte said.

"Are you alone?" I asked. "How did you do this?"

"You asked me to hack into food delivery services, and I found several recent deliveries to this building," Melvin said. "I tried to access the building's security cameras, but it turned out there weren't any, so I did some investigating and found out the building was vacant and due to be renovated."

"We went to tell Ranger," Charlotte said, "but he wasn't at Rangeman. He was at a break-in somewhere. We were in the control room, wondering what we should do, when a call came in from Diesel, saying that Oswald had Stephanie and was going to start torturing her unless we were turned over to him. Hal was in charge of the control room, and he asked us to return to our rooms."

"You've got cuts on you from the window glass," Lula said to Melvin. "I'll go to the kitchen to see if there's Band-Aids."

"This was all our fault," Melvin said to me. "We were the ones whose hacking started all the killing, so we decided we were the ones who should end it. We didn't want anyone else getting hurt."

"It was my fault," Charlotte said. "When the Potatoes hacked into Oswald's system, we knew we'd accomplished our goal, and everyone instantly signed out. Except me. In the very short time we were all in, I noticed something odd. So I stayed and prowled around and didn't like what I found. I was the one who started the killing because I was the one who installed malware in Oswald's system. I knew he had the ability to do something terrible and I took it upon myself to stop him. I didn't think it would come to any of this."

"You look like a hero to me," Lula said from the kitchen. "How'd you get out of Rangeman is what I want to know."

"We went back to our rooms and I hacked into the control room and put a ten-minute block on Ranger's security system. It shut down the cameras and unlocked all the doors. We ran downstairs to the shooting range and got a gun, and then we left Rangeman and walked to this building. We weren't sure what we would do if we found Oswald, or even if Oswald was in the building. We went into the garage and saw that there was a car parked by the stairs. When I looked inside, I spotted your messenger bag."

Lula was opening and closing cupboard doors and slamming drawers shut in the kitchen. Every time she slammed a drawer, we would all jump, for fear of her setting off her explosives.

"We decided we would go through the building and look for Oswald," Charlotte said. "I had the gun and we thought maybe we could get the drop on him. If I had him at gunpoint, we could call Rangeman, and they'd come take over. So, we went floor by floor and we were really quiet, and when we got the top floor one of the doors was locked. We listened at the door, and we thought we heard someone moving around."

"The thing is, there weren't any voices," Melvin said. "We

didn't want to do something stupid and make things worse, so we went back downstairs to regroup. That's when we thought about going next door. The building was boarded up with a condemned sign on it, but it looked like it was still sound, so we broke in and went up to the floor across from Oswald. There was a light on in one of the rooms and it looked like Oswald was working at his computer."

"The other window was dark, and we were wondering what to do next when we saw you," Charlotte said to me. "You were standing with your back to the window. We tried to get your attention, but you wouldn't turn around. And then you disappeared. I think you must have sat down on the floor."

Lula came back into the room. "I couldn't find any first aid stuff, but I got a couple kitchen towels."

"It's just this one cut on my arm," Melvin said, holding the towel against it.

"I almost wet myself when I saw you hanging outside the window," Lula said. "You must have some rock-climbing experience."

"I watch the Travel Channel sometimes," Melvin said.

"We could see that the roof of your building was flat," Charlotte said, "and it looked like air-conditioning units up there, and that's when we got the idea to try to rescue you. We got a couple lengths of rope from the hardware store on the next block and tied them to one of the air conditioners. The plan was that Melvin would go down with the second harness. We thought we could do it because the distance between the roof and window looked manageable.

"We didn't plan on the window being painted shut," Melvin said.

"Well, it all worked out perfect in the end," Lula said.

Not completely perfect, I thought. Lula was locked into a vest loaded with explosives and we had a dead Oswald on the floor.

"Does anyone have a cell phone?" I asked.

Charlotte gave me hers and I called Ranger.

"We're okay," I said when I connected to Ranger, "but Lula needs someone to defuse some explosives."

"I'm on it," Ranger said. "Diesel called me when Oswald got in touch with him. I saw the photos of you and Lula. Is Lula still wired?"

"Yes."

"We're about to enter the garage to the building you're in. What's the status of Oswald?"

"Very dead. How did you get here so fast?"

"When we got power back, the control room located your phone in a dumpster on State Street. We sent a drone up and it took several hours of searching but we finally got a visual of Charlotte and Melvin on the roof, tying ropes to the air units. Even before the drone gave us the address, we were all staged in the target area."

"We're on the top floor," I said. "Don't yell at Melvin and Charlotte. They tried to do the right thing."

"I'll have words with them and then I'll offer them jobs," Ranger said.

Minutes later Ranger, Tank, Ranger's explosive expert Eugene, and Diesel walked into the bedroom and stopped just short of Oswald. They stood hands on hips, looking down at him.

"He looks like he's been shot with a cannon," Diesel said.

"Smith and Wesson .44 Magnum," Charlotte said, still holding the gun.

Diesel nodded. "Yep. That'll do it."

"I borrowed it from the gun range in the basement of Rangeman," Charlotte said. "I didn't expect to use it."

Eugene crossed the room to Lula and examined the vest. "Someone knew what they were doing with this," he said. "State of the art. Do you have the remote?"

"It might be on Oswald," I said.

Ranger bent over Oswald, found the remote, and handed it to Eugene. Eugene pressed a button and a small green diode blinked out on Lula's vest. Eugene took a pair of scissors from his backpack and cut away Lula's cuffs and the duct tape that was securing the vest.

"I'll take care of the vest," Eugene said to Ranger. "I'll set it off at our outdoor range."

Ranger nodded. "Hal should be in the garage. He was following us. He'll give you a ride."

"I wouldn't mind getting a ride, either," Lula said. "I need tequila. I need a cheeseburger. I'm done. Stick a fork in me."

"Get someone to take Lula home," Ranger said to Tank.

"It would be best if everyone keeps everything that happened here to him or herself," Diesel said.

"I already forgot it," Lula said.

Ranger unlocked my cuffs. "Did you call Morelli?" he asked me.

"No. Should I?"

Ranger looked at Diesel. "Your call."

"It would put him in a bad position," Diesel said. "I'm sure he could handle it, but let's leave him out."

Wulf walked into the room from the kitchen. He looked at Oswald and smiled. "Nice," he said.

"No cape," I said to Wulf.

"A cape is evening wear," Wulf said. "It would be tacky to wear one before midnight." He took a photo of Oswald and sent it to someone. An answer immediately came back.

"What's the word?" Diesel asked.

"Auntie is pleased," Wulf said. "She wants the body. There's a chopper on the way. It will help to avoid paperwork." He looked at Melvin. "Can we land a helicopter on the roof?"

"I don't think there's room," Melvin said. "It's mostly air-conditioning units."

"Then we'll have to hoist the body," Wulf said.

Twenty minutes later, Oswald was wrapped in black plastic garbage bags, and we were all on the roof, watching the chopper get closer and closer. It hovered above us and dropped a basket. Diesel and Ranger secured Oswald in the basket, the basket got hoisted up and pulled inside, and the chopper flew off.

"I have a plane waiting for us. The usual location," Wulf said to Diesel. "See you, cuz."

There was a flash of light and a lot of green smoke, and Wulf was gone.

"Holy cow," Melvin said.

Diesel was smiling. "Elvis has left the building."

We returned to the apartment. Diesel packed Oswald's belongings into his backpack. He gave me a kiss on the cheek and whispered "next time," in my ear. "Ana has already collected my things from your apartment." He nodded at Ranger and left the apartment.

"Jeez," I said to Ranger.

"Babe," Ranger said, wrapping an arm around me, steering me toward the door.

We all trooped down the stairs and got into cars. Melvin and Charlotte went with Tank. I went with Ranger in my car. Two Rangeman SUVs were parked in the garage and four Rangemen were standing, waiting by the cars. They would sweep the apartment and make sure everything was tidy.

We drove the short distance to Rangeman, and Ranger, Melvin, Charlotte, and I gathered in Ranger's office.

"You need to stay here for one more day," Ranger said to Melvin and Charlotte. "There's a possibility that Diesel's organization will want to debrief you. After that you're free to go. Make sure you come see me before you leave."

Melvin and Charlotte went to the dining area, and I went upstairs with Ranger to his apartment. He closed the door behind us and I stood for a moment feeling the calm wash over me. The lighting was subdued and the air was slightly cool. The space was mildly masculine with everything in order thanks to his housekeeper, Ella. We went into the kitchen and Ranger gave me a glass of wine.

"Hungry?" he asked.

I nodded. "Yes."

Ella had left a fruit and cheese tray in the fridge. She'd also left a tray with assorted finger sandwiches that included smoked salmon and caviar with crème fraîche. Ranger lived well. We took the wine and food to the small dining area.

"This is nice," I said. "Thanks for helping me."

"It's been interesting."

"How much do you know?" I asked him.

"Enough not to want to repeat any of it. Diesel was forced to confide in me. How much do you know?"

"Oswald was talkative. He had to vent and brag to someone, and since he never intended to release Lula and me, we were a safe audience."

"So, you know about the International Space Station?"

"Yes. I finally understand why Diesel was dispatched to get Oswald." I took another sip of wine. "Morelli isn't going to be happy that Oswald suddenly disappeared."

"He's smart. He'll put most of it together and let it go. If it ended any other way, it might have turned into a media circus and that wouldn't be in anyone's best interest."

"Agreed."

It was almost ten o'clock by the time I returned home. Diesel's things were gone and Ana had left a vase of fresh flowers on my kitchen counter. I'd never gotten to meet her, but I liked her style and I was in awe of her competence. I gave a corn chip to Rex and told him how the Baked Potatoes had saved the space station. And saved me.

———

Morelli and Bob showed up at my apartment for the delayed date night at six o'clock on Saturday.

Morelli took me in his arms and kissed me. "Date night is better late than never," he said.

"It's going to be *lots* better," I told him.

"It's been brought to my attention that Oswald has left the country."

"Really? Who brought it to your attention?"

"It was a brief notice from intel, mixed in with many other brief notices."

"Case closed?"

"You tell me," Morelli said.

"The case is closed," I said. "Of course, that's just my opinion."

"Yeah, mine, too."

I brought him into the kitchen. "I have a surprise for dinner."

"Chinese? Italian? Burger night?"

"None of the above," I said. "I actually made dinner all by myself. Okay, so I made it at my mom's house, but I still made it all by myself."

"I'm ready," Morelli said.

I took the lid off the cake plate and held the cake out for Morelli to see.

"Chocolate cake," I said. "Just like my mom's, only *I* made it."

Morelli swiped some frosting off with his finger and tasted it. "I'm in love," he said.

This is nothing, I thought. Wait until he sees the giant television in my living room.

Get ready for the launch of a blockbuster new series by Janet Evanovich. *The Recovery Agent* is coming in March 2022! Here's a sneak peek.

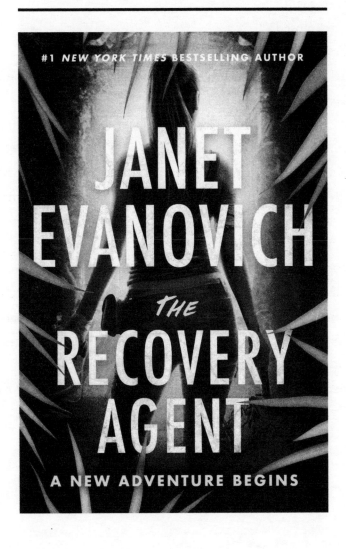

Gabriela Rose was standing in a small clearing that led to a rope and board footbridge, which was swaying in the wind. The narrow bridge spanned a gorge that was a hundred feet deep and almost as wide. Rapids rushed over enormous boulders at the bottom of the gorge, but Gabriela couldn't see the water, because it was raining buckets and she could barely make out the far side.

She was celebrating her thirtieth birthday deep in the Ecuadorian rainforest. The birthday wasn't important to her. She was all about the job. Her long dark brown hair was hidden under her Australian safari hat, its brim shading her exotic almond-shaped brown eyes. She was 5'6" and slim. She kept in shape for the job but also because she liked pretty clothes. And pretty clothes didn't always come in size fourteen.

She was with two local guides, Jorge and Cuckoo. She guessed they were somewhere between forty and sixty years old, and she was pretty sure that they thought she was an idiot.

"Is this bridge safe?" Gabriela asked.

"Yes, sometimes safe," Jorge said.

"And it's the only way?"

Jorge shrugged.

She looked at Cuckoo.

Cuckoo shrugged.

"You first," she said to Jorge.

Jorge did another shrug and murmured something in Spanish that Gabriela was pretty sure translated to "chickenshit woman." *Let it slide,* Gabriela thought. Sometimes it gave you an advantage to be underestimated. If things turned ugly, she was almost certain she could kick his ass. And if that didn't work out, she could shoot him. Nothing fatal. Maybe take off a toe.

It had been raining when she landed in Quito two days ago. It was still raining when she took the twenty-five-minute flight to Caco and boarded a Napo River ferry to Nuevo Rocfuerte. And it was raining when she met her guides at daybreak and settled into their motorized canoe for the six-hour trip down a narrow, winding river with no name. Just before noon, they'd pulled up at a crude campground hacked out of the jungle. Four hours on foot after that, following a trail that barely existed. All in the pouring rain.

She'd been hired to find Henry Dodge and retrieve a ring he was carrying. Not a lot of information on the ring or Dodge. Just that he couldn't leave his job site, and he'd requested that someone come to get the ring. Seemed reasonable, since Dodge was an archeologist doing research on a lost civilization in a previously unexplored part of the Amazon rainforest. The payoff for Gabriela was a big bag of money, but that wasn't what convinced her to take the job. She was a treasure hunter. For profit and for pleasure. She was an amateur anthropologist, a descendant of Blackbeard, a history buff, and a collector of pirate plunder. The opportunity to visit a lost-cities site was irresistible.

"How much further?" she asked Jorge.

"Not far," he said. "Just on the other side of the bridge."

Ten minutes later, Gabriela set foot on the dig site. She'd been on other digs, and this wasn't what she'd expected. There was some partially exposed rubble that might have been a wall at one time. A couple of tables with benches under a tarp. A kitchen area that was also under a tarp. A stack of wooden crates. A trampled area that suggested several tents had been recently used and recently abandoned. Only one small tent was left standing.

There were no people to see except for one waterlogged and slightly bloated dead man lying on the ground by the rubble, and a weary-looking man sitting nearby on a camp chair.

"This is not good," Jorge said. "One of these men is very dead, and something has eaten his leg."

"Panther," the man in the chair said. "You can hear them prowling past your tent at night. This site is a hellhole. Were you folks just out for a stroll in the rain?"

"I was sent to get a ring from Henry Dodge," Gabriela said. "I believe I was expected."

The man nodded to the corpse. "That's Henry. Had some bad luck."

"What happened?"

"He was checking on an excavation in the rain first thing this morning, fell off the wall and smashed his head on the rocks. Then a panther came and ate his leg before we could scare it away. Everyone packed up and left after that. Too many bad things happening here."

"But you stayed," Gabriela said.

"They couldn't carry everything out in one trip. I stayed with some of the remaining crates and the body. Cameron said he would be back with help before it got dark."

"Do you know where Henry kept the ring?" Gabriela asked.

"It's on his finger," the man said. "He felt it was the safest place."

Gabriela looked at the dead man's hand. It was grotesquely swollen and clenched in a fist. The ring was barely visible.

"Someone needs to get the ring off his finger," Gabriela said.

No one volunteered.

Gabriela flicked a centipede off her sleeve. Could the day get any worse? She was wet clear through to her La Perla panties, her boots and camo cargo pants were covered with mud, and she had bug bites everywhere. *All part of the jungle experience,* she told herself. The dead man with the swollen hand was not. The question now was, how bad did she want the ring? The lost-cities site had turned out to be a bust, but there was still a payday attached to the ring. So, the answer to the question was that she wanted the ring pretty damn bad. Without the ring, there would be no big bag of money. And she needed the money to finance her own treasure hunt.

"I've come this far," she said. "I'm not going back without the ring." She looked at the man in the chair. "I need to pry Dodge's hand open and work the ring off his finger. I need gloves and a baggie. I know all archaeological sites have them."

The man shrugged his shoulders as an apology. "They were all packed out. Truth is, we were shutting down before Henry happened. Henry was the holdout. He found the ring, and he thought there was more here. The rest of us didn't care."

"We need to leave now," Jorge said. "It will be bad to be in this jungle after sunset. Hard to find the way, and panthers will be hunting at night. We have maybe five hours of daylight left."

"I'm not leaving without the ring," Gabriela said.

Cuckoo took his machete out of its sheath and *whack!* He chopped Henry Dodge's hand off at the wrist.

"I suppose that's one way to go," Gabriela said. "I would have preferred to try my way first."

"He's dead," Cuckoo said. "He doesn't need the hand."

He picked the hand up by the thumb, grabbed Gabriela's daypack and dropped the hand in.

"Problem is solved," Jorge said.